TROUBLED BY THE HIGHLANDER

A Scottish Time Travel Romance-Highlander Forever
Book 6

REBECCA PRESTON

Illustrated by
NATASHA SNOW

Edited by
ELIZABETH A LANCE

CONTENTS

PREVIEW OF HIGHLANDER
FOUND

CHAPTER 1

They always said doctors made the worst patients.

Karen Frakes turned over restlessly in her bed, grimacing a little as even that slight movement made the room lurch and spin. She'd spent her whole career working hard, pushing herself to her limits and beyond every single day, determined to be better, sharper, stronger every minute that passed... and now here she was, stuck in bed and barely able to sit up. It was hard not to feel frustrated. Easy enough to tell a patient they needed rest if they wanted to recover... much, much harder to take that advice from yourself. Or from another doctor. Even if they were her colleagues, there was just something so grating about the way they looked at her, tucked up in bed like this… feeling utterly useless and more than a little frustrated to have fallen sick.

That was meant to be rule number one, for an epidemiologist and medical doctor like Karen and the rest of her team. She'd been meticulous with her infection prevention — checking and double-checking her protective gear whenever she visited a patient, sanitizing herself thoroughly wherever she went, obeying regulations to the letter. She'd always been a stickler for that stuff — almost to the point of annoying everyone around her (and that was saying something, in their line of work.) But somehow, she'd still managed to fall sick.

And it sucked being sick far from home. That was what she felt most keenly as she languished in her bed, impatiently waiting for the illness to lift so she could get some work done. Tunisia was a beautiful place, and while she'd been well, she'd enjoyed what she'd seen of the capital city Tunis, where she and her colleagues had been sent as part of a delegation from the National Institute of Health. And it was a good hospital to be sick in, that was for sure. But overall, feeling as wretched and miserable as she did, she'd have preferred to be home in her own bed.

But that wasn't an option. Hadn't been for a couple of weeks now. She and her group had been sent over when a strange new respiratory condition had been observed in the city. From what they'd gathered, it was an airborne virus, with symptoms similar to a common cold or flu… but in a considerable percentage of cases, the fever got quite serious indeed. There had been enough deaths — and the spread had been fast enough — to alarm the World Health Organization and cause a spike in media coverage around the world. So, the NIH had sent them over to investigate, to work in the hospital that was taking in the more serious cases.

When Karen had gotten sick, the disease had just been granted epidemic status. Now, she didn't quite know what was happening. Ever since her fever had started spiking, her colleagues had refused to discuss work with her, insisting that she focus on getting well before she tried to keep working through a pretty serious illness. It was aggravating. Ninety percent of cases didn't require hospitalization at all — the fatigue, fever and respiratory symptoms made them pretty uncomfortable, of course, not to mention contagious, but they were generally safe to stay home and recover there in quarantine.

Karen had hoped that she'd be one of those ninety percent — after all, she was young, she was in good shape, she was hardly a member of a more at-risk group when it came to the disease. When she'd started noticing symptoms and the test had come back positive, they'd put her in a hospital bed just for convenience — there were plenty to spare, after all, and it saved her a trip back to her accommodations. But as the days had gone on and her symptoms had gotten worse and worse, it became clear that hospitalization had been the best thing for her.

Frustrating! Incredibly frustrating, she thought, the spike of annoyance followed by a familiar wave of dizziness as her fever and malaise made it clear that strong emotion could wait until she was better. There were so many better things she could be doing with her time than languishing here in a hospital bed like some kind of… invalid. Ever since she'd been a little girl, she'd been a terrible patient when it came to getting sick. Her mother had had to almost tie her to the bed to get her to stay home from school when she was unwell… she'd lie in bed, gripped with anxiety that she was falling behind at school, wasting time just lying around in bed. That had been when her interest in medicine had started, actually. She'd always loved school and missing it because of a cold or stomach bug made her furious… so she'd started, at age ten, doing her research. She'd learned about the importance of hand washing, how diseases were transmitted — then she'd stumbled upon research about the immune system. It had fascinated her utterly… and, she remembered with a smile, it had been a little flame that her parents had enthusiastically fanned.

And here she was, twenty years later, working for the NIH. It was her dream job — had been ever since she was a little girl. And though the chances of getting sick had always been slim, and she'd always laughed her mother's concerns away, now she felt a little guilty. She sat up slowly, reached for her phone as she gritted her teeth through the nausea. She'd told her parents she'd fallen ill, though she'd understated the severity of the condition a little… her mother fretted too much at the best of times. It was just a nasty flu. It'd be gone soon…. and she could get back to work dealing with it.

The worry, of course, was that it would spread to other countries. So far, the spread seemed to be contained locally… but they had their concerns about the disease's incubation period. So far, it was looking like symptoms took between a week and ten days to show themselves — and some evidence also suggested that patients were contagious during almost that full period. That spelled disaster. When Karen had gotten sick, they'd been in talks with the local government about instigating some quarantine procedures for the more vulnerable members of the public — the elderly, people with chronic lung conditions or who were immunocompromised, or very young children. She wondered how all that was going now. Nobody would speak to her. This illness, she knew, had the potential to be of worldwide interest… every move they made right now was critical. It was frustrating as hell that nobody was keeping her abreast of what was going on… but she knew that it would be infinitely worse for them to risk getting infected by her. That was why they weren't visiting as much. She understood. She'd have done the exact same thing if it had been one of her team mates, and not her, in this bed.

But it was her. And it was awful, as much as she was trying not to think about it. The fever was all-encompassing, a dull, sick presence that made her head swim. She felt inches from unconsciousness all the time — it was an active effort to stay awake, to stay focused on the here and now. Her body felt like a complete stranger to her... weak and exhausted, she could barely raise a hand without feeling like it weighed a thousand pounds. And in the back of her mind, a lingering fear — one that had hung around since she was a child, one she'd never quite managed to banish entirely — a fear that this was worse than she thought, a fear that the disease's fatality rate just might be about to get another number...

But that was ridiculous. She was a thirty-four-year-old non-smoker in excellent health. She wasn't going to die — she was just going to feel like crap for a few days, and then she was going to recover, and with any luck she'd get some immunity from the disease out of it. That was, unless it mutated again... early days, still. Sighing, Karen expended the last of her energy and rolled over, her eyes drifting shut as she settled into a deep, deep sleep.

CHAPTER 2

Wet and cold, that was the first thing she became aware of. Her clothing was soaked through with what felt like cold water… and the air around her, bracing and sharp. She shivered, still deeply asleep, feeling her limbs stir and shift as she struggled out of what felt like the deepest sleep of her life… where was she? What was going on? Flashes of her whole life danced in a confusing tangle around her face — her apartment back home in Georgia, her parents' house, the hotel in Tunis, the hospital room… none of it seemed to fit. Confusion warred with her exhaustion. Had she been moved? What was going on?

Fighting hard, she opened her eyes, grimacing a

little at how sleep-encrusted they were. She reached up with one hand to wipe some of the grit from her eyelids and realized that her white-blonde hair had come down — she usually kept it pinned up, but she must have disturbed it during her sleep. But that quickly became the last thing on her mind as she felt an unmistakable shove in her shoulder and looked up to see a sheep peering curiously down at her.

A sheep. Patiently, Karen waited for the dream to clear up… then frowned as the world came into sharper and sharper focus. It was sunny, that was the first thing she noticed — her hospital room had been all interior walls, without so much as a window to look through. But that wasn't all. Rather than lying in a hospital bed, she was sprawled out among wet grass, with a blue sky above her and the gentle sounds of water not far from where she lay. But that was impossible.

"What the hell are you doing here?" she croaked at the sheep. Seemingly offended, it turned and trotted away from her, bleating indignantly — she saw it join a small group of other sheep and they shambled off together across what was unmistakably a grassy field. Blinking hard, she looked around her. To her left, a grassy field, rolling away toward thick trees. To her right… an enormous body of water, ringed by a rocky beach. A lake, she assumed — though she had no idea what lake it could be. What was the nearest body of water in Tunis? And how the hell was it so cold? It had been the height of summer when they'd arrived, and northern Africa wasn't exactly chilly during its long summer days.

Was this some kind of vivid hallucination? She looked down, frowning a little. She was still in her hospital pajamas, and she was shivering in the cold of the morning. It was morning, wasn't it? The sun was still low in the sky, but there was a freshness to the air that told her it was early. Where the hell was she? How the hell had she gotten here? And more to the point — what the hell had happened to her fever? She felt good as new — aside from the lingering drowsiness of having been awoken from such a deep sleep. Had she dreamed herself well? Dreams were never this vivid.

The sound of shouts on the air disturbed her from her confusion and she sat up straight, surprised to see a couple of horses approaching. There was an old man on one, wearing strange clothes — they struck her as profoundly medieval, for some reason, though she couldn't put her finger on why. He was in his fifties maybe, a skinny older man with a worried look on his face, and it was clear from his body language that he was deferring to the man on the other horse.

This guy made her sit up and take notice. He was younger than the first man, and the first thing she noticed about him was his grey eyes and the soft brown hair he wore tied back from his face. He was also, she realized with a start, enormous. As he slid down from the back of his horse, she stared at him dazedly. Was that a kilt he was wearing? She'd never seen someone wearing a kilt in real life before — except for a guy who'd come through town to play the bagpipes at a school assembly when she was a kid. Was he some kind of musician, maybe? No — he wasn't carrying a set of bagpipes, but she did see what looked like a sling on his belt, with a bag of what must have been stones for it on the other hip. She frowned. Her little brother had had a slingshot when they'd been kids — what the hell was this guy doing with one?

"You weren't joking," the kilted man said to the older man, who had stayed on his horse. Why did he look so worried? He kept shooting sidelong glances toward Karen, as though he was uneasy about even acknowledging that she was there. "Good morning, missy!"

Missy, was it? She'd have been annoyed by that if this guy weren't so easy on the eye — and if his expression hadn't been full of such unmistakable kindness. "Hi," she offered back, feeling herself clam up. Ridiculous. Even in the middle of what had to be some kind of very vivid fever dream, she couldn't talk to handsome men to save her life.

What was it about her that made her shut down like this? In the rest of her life, she was perfectly socially capable. She was charming, even — charismatic, a good leader, a people person. This hopeless shyness had come on when she had been thirteen and had experienced her first ever crush on a boy in her class — he'd thought she'd hated him because she never spoke to him, but the truth had been a lot more pathetic. It was a big part of why romance hadn't played a big role in her life — that, and her busy job. Now she was in her mid-thirties, without a significant relationship to speak of under her belt — all because men who looked like this one sent her into a tailspin.

"I'm Connor Grant," the man was saying to her, easy and friendly as anything. "Do you remember anything about how you got here?"

"Nothing," she managed, not sure exactly what was happening. Was she actually — here? It felt real enough, but it was impossible, wasn't it? Unless she was missing a significant chunk of her memory... a few weeks' worth at least, given that the illness seemed to have completely cleared up. That was a worrying thought.

"Aye, that's to be expected," Connor said with a smile that was oddly reassuring, even though she had no idea what he meant.

She trusted this man, she realized with a start. Was it because he was attractive? she wondered. Or was it because she was mostly convinced that this was a dream, and therefore it didn't matter what was happening? A bit of both, she decided.

"What's your name, lass?"

"Karen Frakes," she said automatically. "What's your accent?" She'd been trying to place it. Working for an organization like the NIH meant she ran into a lot of people from around the world, but she'd never been much good with accents.

Connor grinned at her. "Good to meet you, Karen. My accent's from the same place I'm from. The same place we are right now." He gestured around them, from the water of the lake to the tree-line a few hundred yards behind them. "Scotland."

She nodded to herself. That was an odd one… but not entirely unexpected. Her dreams tended to take her all around the world, just as her job did. She'd never been to Scotland before, but it made about as much sense as anywhere else. *It is a beautiful place,* she thought unexpectedly. She wouldn't mind it if she were actually here… but of course that was utterly impossible. Wasn't it?

Connor was offering her his hand, and she took it, smiling gratefully as he hauled her off the damp ground with one motion. *I must look a mess,* she thought with a stab of alarm, looking down at her muddy pajamas and reaching up to touch her tangled bird's nest of hair.

"Let's get you a change of clothes and a hot meal," he said firmly.

All she could do was nod.

CHAPTER 3

Connor helped her up onto the back of his horse. The older man made some excuse and rode off not long after — from what he'd mumbled in his thick accent to Connor, it seemed he was a shepherd of some sort. That explained the sheep, she guessed, impressed with her delirium's logical consistency. Usually her dreams made no sense at all. This one was very rational indeed. There was something a little troubling about that.

But it was pleasant enough, sitting on the back of the horse... especially once Connor had jumped up as well. Gently he prompted her to put her arms around his broad, strong back — she obeyed happily enough, feeling her heart flutter in her chest. He was warm, a pleasant change from the chill of the air on her wet clothes, and the feeling of the horse moving under them was very pleasant, too. He turned the creature around and urged it up the slight slope away from the shore of the lake, where she saw a dirt road that traveled along the treeline.

"So, you don't remember anything about getting here?" Connor called to her over the sound of the horse's hooves on the dirt road.

She shook her head, then realized he couldn't see her. "No," she called back, feeling a bit ridiculous. "I was in bed at the hospital in Tunis, and now I'm here, I guess." She laughed. "Here. Whatever that means."

"You think it's a dream, then?" he asked pleasantly, as though he'd been expecting this.

That was a strange thing for a hallucination to say. There was more internal consistency to all of this than she was comfortable with. If she hadn't known any better, she'd have sworn that this might actually be real…

"I mean, I don't know what else explains it." She shrugged. "Any ideas?"

"Quite a few," he said, and there was something

knowing in his tone that sent a shiver down her spine. "You won't believe me, though."

"Try me," she said. "I'm a doctor and a scientist. We're all about evidence. If you have evidence, I'll accept even the most outlandish theory you've got."

"Well, keep that in mind." Connor chuckled. "Keep it in mind when I tell you that you're in Scotland and it's the sixteenth century."

She took that in for a moment. "Right. Why not add some time travel, right?"

"I told you that you wouldn't believe me."

"Can you blame me?"

He laughed. "I suppose not. But you'll come around to the truth, sooner or later. Just like the rest."

She frowned. "The rest?"

"Aye, the rest. There's a whole army of you, or thereabouts. Women from the future, brought back here to us at the Sept of Clan Grant."

She felt strange, having this utterly bizarre conversation with the back of Connor's head. She wanted to see his face, to figure out if he was messing with her from the expression that he was no doubt wearing. This was a joke… right? It had to be. She glanced over her shoulder, watched the trees moving by as the horse slowly plodding along the road toward… where? Where was he taking her? To this Sept, whatever that meant? Suddenly, the complacency she'd been feeling earlier was beginning to fade. The more time passed, the harder it was to write all of this off as some kind of delirium…

"Brought back?" she asked, trying to keep her focus. Good thing her fever had cleared up… otherwise she'd be utterly incapable of taking any of this in. "By what? Magic?"

"Got it in one." The man chuckled. "You weren't wrong — you *are* clever."

"Seriously?"

"I did say you wouldn't believe me —"

"Just tell me," she said with a sigh, shaking her head. "Get all of this madness out in one go, then we can go from there, okay?"

"Fine. I'm not exactly an expert, though. I'm a member of the Guard and I've seen my fair share of strange things, but it's the scholars of the Sept who'd really be able to give you a thorough explanation. That, or Old Maggie, but the last time I disturbed her this early I got quite an earful for my trouble."

"Magic?" she prompted him, feeling amusement war with impatience.

"Right. Magic. So, if it's been the same for you as it has been for the other women, you would've come to us through what's called the Burgh. That's a — a kind of magical gateway between our world and the world of the Fae."

"The what?"

"Faeries. Goblins and ghouls and spooks — think of any old wives' tale you've ever heard, and the source of it's probably the Fae. Again, I'm no expert — I've run into my share of Unseelie monsters, and I know what I need to for my work, but… well, anyway. The other women were brought back by the Sidhe. We call them the Lords and Ladies, sometimes. Seelie Fae — that means they're friendly, more or less, and that they mean well."

"And they brought me through this magical gate."

"Aye, that's about the size of it."

"Can I go back?"

"Well," he said, and for the first time a note of discomfort seemed to creep into his voice. "The thing is — the Burgh's at the bottom of Loch Ness. So, it's a bit of a swim, even if you were to know how to open it… then you'd need the Sidhe to help guide you home, and they're not exactly known for giving out favors for free." Something about his voice suggested he was hiding something — but that was the furthest thing from her mind right now.

"Did you say Loch Ness?"

"Aye, that's where we are." He nodded to the water besides them, and she felt a laugh break out of her chest.

"Seriously. Is the monster home?" she joked.

But Connor didn't laugh with her. "We don't see much of the Monster these days, I'm afraid. She was wounded with iron recently, and it's made her shy."

"You're messing with me."

"I assure you I'm not," Connor said gently. "I wouldn't do that. Not with something this important, at any rate."

She mulled over what he'd told her, feeling deeply strange. What was it about him that made her trust him so completely — despite the utter ridiculousness of what he was saying? Medieval Scotland — time travel — magic and faeries and monsters? "How do you know all of this?"

"I'm of Clan Grant. We're sworn to — well, to sort of protect humankind from the Fae, and vice versa. We watch over the Burgh. Act as go-betweens between the Fae and the human world. And we deal with the Unseelie when they come through."

She took a deep breath. "Right."

"It's a lot to deal with all at once," he said softly, glancing back over his shoulder at her.

She felt her heart skip a beat. Up close, he was even better looking than she'd thought, and she was acutely aware that her arms were around him, keeping her steady on the horse's back.

"For now, I suggest we focus on one thing at a time. First stop, getting you a warm change of clothes. Second stop, a good hot breakfast."

"I'm not really —" she said automatically, but to her surprise her growling stomach cut her off. She raised an eyebrow. "I guess breakfast couldn't hurt."

Connor was right. One thing at a time. That way, she might be able to figure out what was going on here without absolutely losing her mind.

CHAPTER 4

They rode into town about ten minutes later, and Karen had to take a few deep breaths. Sure enough, what she saw backed up the utterly insane claim that she'd traveled back in time. It was a quaint medieval village, built on a sloping piece of land descending toward the shore of the Loch, where a number of docks were set up with fishing boats moored at them. There was a main road that rose up the hill toward a rather large church at its peak, and clusters of little cottages lined the road. Smaller streets branched off from it, too, but Connor drew her attention back to a large building on the corner of the road out of town and the street that led away toward the church. It had three stories — she could tell from the windows — and the sign out the front marked it as an inn.

"This place has the best ale in town," Connor explained with a wink. "And I know the publican well. He'll put you up for as long as you need… and I reckon his daughter'd be about your size."

They headed through the door together, and she peered about, fascinated by the place. A fireplace sat in one wall, surrounded by chairs and tables that were empty at present. The bar was rough wood, as was the majority of the furniture — it all had a distinctly handmade look to it. And, she noticed with some pleasure, it was warm in here. On the ride, her hospital pajamas had dried a little, but they were still pretty thin when it came to keeping the cold weather at bay.

"Connor Grant, you rascal." A broad man emerged from a back room, a rag tucked into the pocket of the pants he was wearing and a smile on his face. "Drinking already? Who's this?" he added, blinking a little as he took in Karen.

"Thomas, this is Karen Frakes. She's new in town," he said, and Karen saw a meaningful glance pass between the two men. "She'll need a room, if you've got one to spare."

"Plenty," Thomas said, turning his bright blue

eyes to Karen. "You're welcome here, Karen. Will you be wanting something to eat, too?"

"Aye, and she'll need a change of clothes, too," Connor added, business-like. "Did that girl of yours leave anything behind when she went off with her fellow?"

"There's a few pairs of old riding clothes, I think," Thomas said. "I'll see what I can track down. You warm yourselves by the fire. It's a cold summer's morning and no mistake," he added with a chuckle. "At this rate we'll all freeze by autumn."

They settled into a pair of chairs by the fireplace, and Karen was grateful to warm her hands by the little fire that crackled in its hearth. "So — you work in town?" she asked Connor, feeling a little awkward in the silence. Despite all the utterly mad things that were being thrown at her, she still couldn't quite shake the shyness that she felt as a result of being around a guy she was attracted to. Utterly ridiculous, she knew. "What does being a guard entail, exactly?"

"Well, in any other town it'd mostly be about keeping an eye on the rowdy local lads and mediating disputes between farmers all day long," Connor said with a shrug. "But around here things are a little different. We keep an eye on the mundane stuff, sure, but we're also keeping watch for supernatural happenings. Fore-warned is forearmed — and more dangerous things than pretty women come through that Burgh."

She felt herself blush a deep scarlet at the compliment. Terrified she was going to clam up entirely, she spoke, grabbing the first subject that came to mind. "I'm a doctor."

"Is that so?" He could tell she was blushing — his eyes were twinkling, and she was deeply, deeply grateful he didn't press the subject. As exhilarating as it was to be flirted with, even slightly, by a guy like this, she was very interested in keeping her cool right now.

"Yeah. A doctor and an epidemiologist."

"Now that's a new word to me."

"A specialist in the spread of diseases," she explained. "We study how diseases affect popula-tions, how they spread and how they can be contained. I was working on an outbreak of a new flu in Tunisia when…" She frowned a little. "Well, when I got sick. But I don't know how I got from there to here."

"We've had disease go through the village and castle before," Connor said, his face solemn. "It's an awful thing. And you say you've made it your life's work?"

"Well — it's useful," she said, shrugging her shoulders.

"And dangerous."

"Yeah, I guess so." She shivered a little, thinking of the nasty flu she'd come down with. What had happened there? Why was she well again? Would Connor have any insight? "We were looking into a new respiratory condition when I … well, when I came here, I guess," she said with a frown, glancing around the walls of the inn. "I caught it. I was in hospital before I was here, actually. Hence the pajamas," she added, plucking at the fabric. "But I seem to be completely well again now."

"That'd be the Sidhe," Connor said with a smile. "The Seelie Fae have healing magic beyond what we mortals understand. They'd have taken care of whatever was ailing you before sending you on through the Burgh."

"Why?" she asked, blankly. "I mean — why me? Why bring me here? Why pull me out of bed like that?"

Connor hesitated, a worried look in his eye that made her curious — but before she could pry any further, the publican Thomas was back, a bundle of clothing in his arms and a broad smile on his face. "I knew that girl wouldn't have been able to pack all her things. Here you go, Miss Karen. Not exactly the most ladylike fare, but better than what you're wearing," he said as he presented the pile of clothing to her. "She always was a bit of a tomboy."

Did women only wear skirts around here, or something? The clothing looked perfectly reasonable to Karen… then again, she'd worn nothing but scrubs and protective gear for the last few weeks, so she wasn't exactly a fashion expert. She thanked Thomas warmly for the clothing and he led her up the winding stairs of the inn to a little room with a wooden bed decorated with a warm and cozy quilt. There was also a table — on top of which was a steaming bowl of soup that made her mouth water.

"I'll leave you to eat and get changed," Thomas said, heading for the door.

She reached automatically for her pockets — then frowned. "Thomas, I have no way of paying you," she said, alarmed.

He just waved a hand at her. "The Watch has it taken care of, don't you worry," he said with a smile. "You focus on settling in for now and let me know if there's anything you need. One of the girls will bring you some hot water for a bath later tonight."

And with that, he was gone, leaving her to peer curiously around the room she was in. By herself, it was a little harder to distract herself from the mounting weirdness of the situation she was in… but the hot soup was calling to her, and she set about quieting the growling of her stomach before she sat back in her chair, the bowl empty and her hunger sated.

This wasn't a hallucination, she had to admit that to herself. It had gone on far too long, been far too vivid and consistent. Like it or not… she was actually here.

Which meant she had a whole lot of funda-mental assumptions about science to interrogate.

CHAPTER 5

After her meal, she changed into the
clothes that Thomas had brought for her.
He'd been right about his daughter being
the same size as her — the pants were as comfortable as any of her own back home, and by the time
she'd layered a tunic and a warm woolen sweater
onto her top half, she was feeling warm and
comfortable. There was even a pair of boots that
was maybe a size too large — they fit for now,
though, and she made a mental note to get a few
extra pairs of socks to pad the too-large boots out
before she did any serious walking.

She headed back downstairs, wanting to talk
more with Connor about the strange situation she'd
found herself in — but to her dismay, he'd headed

off, Thomas explaining that he was on duty. It seemed the Watch patrolled the village regularly, keeping an eye out for any kind of trouble that might be stirring... she remembered what he'd said about goblins and monsters and shivered a little, peeking out the door where she caught a glimpse of the long road out of town. Thomas explained that at the other end of that road stood the Sept of Clan Grant — a great castle built on a little island close to the shore of the Loch, with a land bridge that connected it to the mainland. *A real life castle,* she thought with a shiver of anticipation. Would she see it one day?

The morning passed pleasantly enough — she sat by the fire and half-dozed, half-meditated, trying to give herself the mental space and time to process what was going on. A big part of her kept expecting to wake up from the dream... but that didn't seem especially likely. The more time passed, the more consistent this delirium felt. And as much as it was utterly irrational... what was she supposed to do, just deny the evidence of her eyes? She was here. Fever dreams were never like this — and besides, her fever was long gone.

Around lunchtime, people began drifting into the pub for lunch. She watched from her vantage point by the fire, fascinated by the odd parade of townsfolk who came through — farmers and shepherds, a handful of guards wearing kilts like Connor had worn — none as handsome as him, though, she noticed with a secret little thrill running down her spine — and a pair of young women who giggled and laughed as they sat together at the bar. She gathered from what she heard of their conversation that they were milkmaids, and smiled to herself, thinking of the historical fantasy novels that her little brother was so interested in. There were always milkmaids in those — it hadn't occurred to her that that was actually a real job.

Thomas was quickly run off his feet fetching and carrying drinks for the patrons of the bar, but before long a young woman arrived, jumping behind the bar and joining him with a practiced ease. She moved back and forth between the patrons, chatting and laughing, and Thomas soon disappeared into a back room. Before long she saw him emerging again with plates of food, and so lunch service swung into action.

A group of young men at a table by the window seemed to be getting louder and louder as the late morning gave way to afternoon. They were drinking flagon after flagon of ale at a pace that put even the medical students Karen knew to shame. There were half a dozen of them total, all looking to be in their early twenties or so, and Karen was grateful that her vantage point wasn't visible from where they were sitting — given the unpleasant things they kept saying to the barmaid every time she went over to take their next order, they didn't seem like particularly pleasant company. Still, their voices were loud, and it was their conversation she heard the most of. Two of them were in some kind of argument about who was responsible for an illness they'd both seemingly come down with.

"Robert, you're dumb as a cow's rear end and twice as ugly," one of the young men slurred, slamming a fist on the table. The floppy-haired, blue-eyed young man seemed to be their leader, or something like it — the others seemed to defer to him, listening closely when he spoke. "It's your stupid fault —"

"It's got nothing to do with me, Danny." The one he'd called Robert looked taller than his friend, with a lanky frame and dark hair. "You poxy git —"

"I'm not the poxy one. It's those poxy damn milkmaids —"

"And whose idea was it to follow 'em?"

In that unpleasant way that young men had of

escalating situations, the two of them were suddenly on their feet, squaring off in the bar. Karen found herself rising to her feet and moving toward the scene, sensing a fight about to break out — sure enough, Danny shoved Robert hard in the chest, sending the taller young man staggering back with a surprised yelp. As he raised his hands, Karen's eyes narrowed. There was something wrong — red lesions covered his hands, maybe four or five of them, red and weeping. She wrinkled her nose at the sight of them but was quickly distracted by the scuffle that broke out. Thomas was there immediately, shouting over the jeers of the other young men that the pack of them could behave themselves or get out.

"Careful," Karen said quickly, grabbing him by the shoulder as he went to intervene physically in the scrap. "Those lesions on their hands look unpleasant."

But the young men had broken apart, their attention caught by something else — and as the leader's piggy little eyes fell on her, Karen realized with a sinking feeling in her chest that she was the next distraction. Great. She'd been in town for all of two hours and she was already getting unwelcome attention from the town's local drunks.

"And who's this uppity bitch, then?"

"You should leave," Karen said levelly. "Those sores on your hands need cleaning."

The group of young men tittered, and Danny's eyes narrowed — but he shoved his hands into the pockets of the trousers he was wearing, clearly a little self-conscious about them. "Mind your own business, slag," he snarled, "or I'll tear a piece off you."

She opened her mouth to respond, stunned and angry — but before she could, the slam of the door pulled her attention that way. There stood Connor, a look of radiant anger on his face and his hand on the weapon at his hip. From the looks on the young men's faces, this was more than they were willing to deal with just now — they slid out of their seats and melted away toward the exit of the pub, though Danny shot a lingering, ugly look at her over his shoulder as he left.

"Those bloody troublemakers again?" Connor asked Thomas, heading over to join them once he'd seen the group of young men out of the pub. Karen couldn't help but notice the way the two young women at the bar watched them leave — a mixture of apprehension and keen interest on their faces. She resisted the urge to roll her eyes. There was no accounting for taste, it seemed. Still… it had been rather pleasing to see Connor in action. The way the young lads had melted before his stern countenance… she fought the blush that was threatening to rise to her cheeks.

"Who are they?" she wanted to know, looking up at Thomas and Connor, who were exchanging identical looks of vexation.

"Danny's little band of idiots," Connor said with a roll of his eyes. "They've been causing trouble since they were kids."

"They're all herdsmen," Thomas explained with a roll of his eyes. "Usually they limit themselves to bullying the milkmaids, who are at least used to their nonsense by now, but they've taken to causing trouble here, too."

But Karen wasn't worried about the young men getting drunk at lunch time. She was worried about the sores on their hands. She had an awful feeling she knew what they were.

CHAPTER 6

Once it was clear that the young men had been well and truly banished, Thomas showed Connor and Karen over to a table by the window, clearly grateful that the watchman had sent away the troublesome clientele. Where had they gone? Karen wondered. She wouldn't have minded getting a closer look at the lesions on their hands... but she tried to shift her mind away from that when Thomas returned with two steaming bowls of stew for her and Connor. It wouldn't do losing her appetite — not when she was about to have lunch with one of the most gorgeous men that she'd ever met…

"Sorry you had to run into those louts so early," Connor said with a grimace, clearly still thinking about the young men. "Most of the village folk aren't quite such bad company, I promise."

"I'm mostly worried about those wounds on their hands," she said, frowning a little. "Do you know if there's an illness going about?"

He looked surprised... and a little worried. "Aye, now you mention it — the herds have been struck with an illness lately, and it's made the leap to a few of the milkmaids. I heard them grumbling about the sores on their hands last week."

"Interesting," she said softly. She could remember reading about cowpox when she was just a little girl, well before any of her medical training — she'd been fascinated by how the disease, related to the much deadlier smallpox as it was, actually brought about immunity to smallpox as a side effect of having had it. Vaccinations owed their origins to the simple disease — the word itself was related to the Latin for 'of the cow'. But it wasn't exactly a pleasant illness... and from the looks of those lesions, poorly cared for as they had been, it would be quite likely to spread. "Do they know how to stop it spreading?"

"I'm not sure they'd care if they did." Connor shrugged his shoulders. "You met them. They're not exactly considerate young men."

"It's not a pleasant disease. Still, they should be grateful to get it," she shrugged.

"Why's that?"

"The immunity to smallpox, for a start."

His eyes widened, and she bit her lip, remembering at the last second what time period they were in and feeling an odd little wave of dizziness at how mundane that realization had felt — was she really accepting that she'd traveled through time to get here? What if she did some kind of damage to history by sharing medical knowledge that was too advanced? Wasn't that what a time paradox was?

"What do you mean?"

"The diseases are closely related," she explained. She'd never been able to resist talking about diseases with anyone — they were fascinating, and besides, she was rather enjoying the thrill of having Connor's close, fascinated attention. "So, once you've had cowpox, your immune system is equipped to deal with smallpox as well." She hesitated at the blank expression on his face. "Your immune system is… well, your body's got ways of fighting off diseases. We call those ways the immune system."

He still looked nonplussed.

"Think of it like… training. If you've never

fought someone with a sword before, that person is likely to hurt you. But if you practice against someone with a sword…"

"Then you'll do better against someone with a dagger," Connor said, his eyes widening. "You're saying the human body works like that?"

"Something like that," she said, not wanting to mislead him. "I mean, that's a big oversimplification, but…"

"You'd better meet Kay, I think," Connor said thoughtfully as he finished his stew, gazing at her over the table.

She nibbled at her own bread roll — it was difficult to eat when her stomach was already so full of butterflies. Those gray eyes were so breathtaking… "Who's Kay?"

"You'll like her. She speaks like you do," he said with a grin. "Like she's constantly translating something complex into language we peasants of the past will understand."

"I'm not —"

"It's alright," he said warmly, and she blushed, embarrassed that he'd found her lecture condescending. "I don't doubt you know a great deal that's a mystery to the folk around here. And I'm looking forward to hearing more of it."

She shook herself a little, only just catching up with what he was trying to tell her. "Wait — so you're saying this Kay is from the — from my time? From the future?"

"That's right," he said with a smile. "She arrived, oh, a year or so back, through the Burgh, same as you. My cousin fell head over heels for her and that was the end of it. They're wed, now."

Her eyes widened. The idea of traveling back in time to this strange place… and then not only settling in, but even marrying one of the locals? It was ridiculous… unthinkable… and yet, she couldn't help but let a small part of her imagination steal away to a little cottage where she'd bake things and Connor would come home to her at the end of the day… she shook her head, a little annoyed with how ridiculous the fantasy was. There was no way she was even entertaining the possibility. She had no idea what it was like to live with a man from her own time — let alone this medieval place she'd found herself in. Hell, she wasn't even fully convinced it wasn't a dream. Still… some part of her still wondered what it might be like. She loved her career and was incredibly proud of everything she'd worked to achieve, but romance… that was something she'd never quite excelled at, was it?

"Anyway, I think you'd like her." Connor shrugged, and she realized with a start she'd been ignoring him. "She'll be coming down tomorrow afternoon to check on the herds — she's something of an animal expert, from what I understand. Some kind of specialist in your time."

"Is she — was she a vet?"

"Aye, I think that's what she calls it."

She found herself looking forward to meeting this woman more than she'd expected. It wasn't long before Connor had to excuse himself and return to his patrols — she watched him go with a smile, then headed upstairs to her room. The bread and stew had been warm and delicious, and though her body felt healthy and fever-free, she was oddly tired. *Probably all the stress of waking up in a brand new country and era,* she thought with an odd little laugh that ripped itself free of her before she could silence it. Was she really just going to … believe this? She peered out of her window, where the placid waters of the Loch were glinting in the afternoon sunlight. That sure was a lake, alright. But Loch Ness? The sixteenth century?

What other explanation was there, though? She'd always been a rational woman who believe in the evidence of her own eyes… and the evidence overwhelmingly supported Connor's claims about when and where she was, no matter how absurd it may seem. There was more investigation to be done, that was for sure… but for the time being, what was the point of refusing to believe what she was seeing?

This was medieval Scotland. And she was just going to have to make the best of that.

CHAPTER 7

She spent the afternoon by herself in her room, gazing out the window and watching the afternoon go by. It felt nice, just sitting by a window and letting the time go by… especially compared to her usually hectic schedule. But the fatigue got stronger and stronger, and it wasn't long before Karen decided to treat herself to something that she hadn't had time for since well before med school… an afternoon nap.

Feeling oddly like a criminal, she crept over to the little bed and pulled back the covers, tucked herself in, and shivered a little as her body heat began to warm the cozy bed. It wasn't long before her eyelids were sliding shut and she drifted into a deep, restless sleep. She woke up an hour or two later, feeling a little disoriented. She'd been half expecting to wake up in the hospital again, surrounded by quietly beeping machines, feverish and horribly unwell again… but no, the only thing wrong with her was a bit of sleep in her eyes and a slight crick in her neck from the way she'd settled her head against the pillow.

She dozed on for a little while, pleasantly warm in the little bed, letting her mind wander. After a long period of being unwell, it felt unbelievably good to be feeling whole and hearty again. But it wasn't long before darkness crept into the room, and she sat up with a frown, realizing she could hardly see. And it wasn't like there was going to be a light switch to flip, was there?

Frowning, she got up and pulled her woolen sweater back on over her head before padding down the hallway in her too-big boots and making her way down the stairs. It was early evening and the bar was already beginning to fill up with various townspeople, some of whom she remembered from earlier in the day, some of whom it seemed had only just arrived. To her great dismay, she saw the group of young men from earlier sitting at the table they'd been sitting at when she'd met them, and she gritted her teeth, hoping they hadn't seen her. They were deep in conversation amongst each other — and she noticed to her satisfaction that Danny, the leader, had wrapped his hands in bandages. Good. At least she'd achieved something with that little conflict. She only hoped it wasn't too late to stop him from spreading it to his friends… but she had an unfortunate suspicion that wherever he'd caught the disease, they had been, too…

The barmaid who'd been there earlier was still working, and Karen gave her a smile as she bustled past. To her surprise, the woman returned presently with a flagon of ale for her — she bit her lip, about to explain that she hadn't meant to order it, but the barmaid's eyes had flicked over to the men in the corner and there was a look of worry on her face that stilled Karen's objections immediately.

"Those lads," she said softly, in that thick accent that Karen still wasn't quite used to, as charming as she found it. "They were talking earlier about you."

"They were?" She was surprised to have made such an impression.

"Aye. They've figured out you must be new in town, and that you're staying here at the inn. They've been trying to figure out ways of getting upstairs. Getting into your room tonight."

A chill ran down her spine as she stared across

the busy bar at the young men, all of whom now seemed distinctly more menacing. Telling them off the way she had earlier, had felt fine in the light of day… but the idea of confronting them in her room, late at night, with nobody else around to protect her… that, she didn't like.

"Do the rooms lock?" she asked, trying to think back to the room. It seemed an odd thing to have forgotten… but she had a lot on her mind. The barmaid shook her head, wiping diligently at the table that Karen was sitting at as a cover for her continued presence.

"No. But I'd not go to bed alone if I were you."

Karen's eyes widened. "What do you mean?"

The barmaid's eyes twinkled as she looked up at her. "Saw you getting cozy with our Connor Grant earlier. Caught the looks you two were exchanging. I daresay he'd help you…"

"What! No — we just — we're not — that's not —"

The barmaid giggled, a pleasant sound. "It's alright, lass," she said with a grin. "Though I'll warn you he's somewhat popular among the ladies around here. Don't go giving him your heart right away, or he's liable to break it. Not out of malice, though. He's a good soul — and Lord knows his family's been trying to get him to settle down for years now." She smiled, her eyes still dancing. "But you didn't hear it from me. I've said too much," she added, scooping up her cloth. "You enjoy your ale."

"I don't have any money," she said plaintively. "I'll have to pay you back —"

"On the house," the woman said, waving a hand dismissively. "The drink and the warning. We women have to look out for each other in this world, hmm?"

Karen nodded. With that, the barmaid was gone, and she smiled to herself as she sipped at the ale, which was thick and rich and utterly delicious — even though she'd never been much of a beer person, she felt she could definitely come around to it.

But what was she going to do about the young men who intended to come up to her room in the night? She couldn't just let them, that was for sure. Should she alert Thomas to their schemes? What could he do about it? And hadn't he been kind enough to her already, putting her up free of charge, feeding her, and clothing her, and refusing to consider payment from her? She bit her lip… and just as she was losing herself in worry, she heard the door thunk open and in came Connor in

that familiar kilt, his gray eyes scanning the room…
and lighting up when they fell on her. He started
heading over, and the thought that he'd actually
been looking for her made her blush.

"How are you settling in?" he asked with a smile
once he'd taken the seat opposite her. She sipped
her ale to hide the butterflies fluttering in her
stomach.

"Better than I'd expected, honestly. It's… it's
such a bizarre thing to think about, but… I mean,
it's pretty obviously true, right? And if — time
travel is possible, then I guess magic is possible, so I
guess… I was wrong about a bunch of stuff." She
shrugged her shoulders. "Science is all about
knowing when you're wrong. But —" She hesitated,
her eyes flicking over to the young men by the door,
who were getting steadily more drunk as the
evening wore on. "The barmaid told me… Danny
and his friends were trying to get up to the rooms
upstairs. Thinking about —"

"They wouldn't dare," Connor growled, his eyes
narrowing with vexation. "I'm not surprised they
were making daft threats, though. Pack of utter lay-
abouts. I've been asking around," he added with a
shrug. "Talking to the herdsmen they're supposed to
be working for. It seems that since the sickness has

swept through the herds, they've been using the illness as an excuse to slack off work. And you know what they say about idle hands."

"I just wish there was a lock on my room," Karen said with a shudder. "Or, failing that, a knife under my pillow."

Connor chuckled… but his eyes were thoughtful. "Well, I can arrange a knife for you," he said thoughtfully. "And a lock. But as for tonight… why don't I do you one better?"

A flash of what the barmaid had said came back to her and she froze, hardly daring to believe what she'd heard. Could he mean — surely not. Surely not.

Unless…?

CHAPTER 8

But in the end, to her secret dismay, Connor didn't end up sharing her bed that evening — and probably for the best, she thought. What would he think of her, sleeping with someone she'd just met? What would the villagers say about her? No — when they'd finished their meal, Connor took her upstairs and informed her that he'd be sleeping outside her room that night. She'd tried to argue with him, but he'd insisted — said it was part of his duty as a man of the Watch. And so, feeling equal parts grateful and embarrassed, Karen had bid her new friend good-night, then closed herself away in her room to get some sleep.

Maybe it was the long afternoon nap she'd taken — or maybe it was the knowledge that

Connor was sleeping just outside the door to her room — but Karen took a long time to get to sleep that night. She couldn't stop thinking about him lying out there… or about the drunk young men downstairs. What if they did come up to bother her? What if they hurt him? She found herself listening intently, trying to make out the sounds of footsteps on the stairs, bracing herself for the sounds of a fight out there on the landing… and at some point, the effort of listening put her straight to sleep. She woke just after dawn, feeling bleary but reasonably well-rested.

She dressed quickly, eager to see Connor, to find out if anything had happened — sure enough, when she pulled the door open, there he was, lying right in the doorway with his head pillowed on his rolled-up cloak. He stirred at the sound of the door opening, and blinked those gray eyes up at her, making her heart skip a beat.

"Any trouble?" she asked gently, and he shook his head, sitting up and rubbing his face with one big hand.

"Cowards, all six of 'em. Though I did see one or two of them creeping up the stairs. Think they spotted me and changed their minds about it."

"Thank you so much," she said honestly,

wanting to reach out and hug him but a little worried about being too forward… even if part of her didn't give a damn about what anyone thought of them, just wanted him close to her… "I wouldn't have slept a wink without you out here."

"Of course," he said gently.

"I owe you one, Connor."

"I tell you what," he said, his eyes dancing mischievously. "I'll call that favor in right now. Why don't you have breakfast with me?"

She rolled her eyes. "I can't pay for breakfast. You buying me a meal is hardly me paying you back, Connor." He got to his feet, wincing a little and stretching his stiff muscles. She made a sound of dismay in her throat. "And now you're sore from sleeping on the freezing ground —"

"Well, if you're offering to rub my aching body down for me," he said, his eyes twinkling — and she was so shocked by the open flirtation that she almost tripped and fell down the stairs.

Chuckling, he let it go, and they walked down the stairs together, Karen's face still burning furiously. She remembered what the barmaid had said about Connor — about how he was a flirt, a man about town, a playboy… but somehow, knowing that he was this way with all the girls didn't do much to still her beating heart.

Thomas brought them breakfast — the innkeeper seemed to be everywhere all at once, and he gave them a broad, knowing smile when he brought two steaming bowls of oatmeal out of the kitchen in the back. Too late, she realized what it must have looked like — the two of them coming downstairs together — but Thomas was already gone, and she blushed furiously, hardly daring to meet Connor's eyes for fear of what she might find there. But Connor only laughed.

"It's alright, lass. I'll explain to him that nothing happened. A strictly honorable night all around. You needn't worry about word spreading."

"I mean, not that I mind, or anything, I just…" She took a deep breath, trying to get control of herself. Focusing on work had usually helped her get over awkward interactions with attractive men… but she was loath to bring up cowpox over breakfast. It was a pretty unpleasant disease, and while med school had thoroughly drummed any leftover squeamishness out of her, she didn't want to spoil his breakfast. So, she asked him how the disease had been spreading.

"We first noticed it a few weeks back. It's gone

through herds before, but I don't recall it being shared with the milkmaids before." He tilted his head, looking curious. "Your work, in the future — it concerns diseases like this one, doesn't it? Do you know much about it?"

She smiled, swallowing her mouthful of porridge hastily. "I do. It's one I've studied, for… for a few reasons, actually. It has some historical significance."

"You were speaking yesterday about ways of stopping it from spreading. Why don't you fill me in? I can start spreading the word to the villagers, letting them know how to avoid the thing."

"That's a great idea," she said, smiling at him. Getting the word out to the villagers early — before the disease had started spreading in earnest — would be the best course of action. That was what they hadn't quite managed to pull off in Tunisia… the disease had spread quickly before many quarantine measures could be put in place. "From what I remember, it spreads mostly through contact with infected bodily fluid. The main symptom is those lesions on the hands and forearms — the sores we saw on those unpleasant young men yesterday. Touching those lesions is what spreads the infection. They start on the udders of cows, you see — that's why milkmaids are so often the first to fall sick. They're the ones touching the udders all the time, so the sores spread to their hands."

"Then they touch other people," Connor agreed thoughtfully — then chuckled to himself. "It's no wonder those lads are falling sick. Can't keep their hands off a pretty young woman to save their lives."

"It's not a nice disease," she said with a frown. "Nothing fatal, but it does knock a person out of action for a few months. The sores are painful and weepy, and usually accompanied by fever, fatigue, body aches…"

"Aye, I've heard that at least one of the maids is too unwell to work," Connor said, shaking his head. "It doesn't seem to be affecting those young men just yet, though — and only two of them had the sores."

"It takes a week or so for the lesions to show up." She shrugged. "At any rate — tell the villagers to avoid any contact with anyone with sores. No touching at all — not the sores, and not any other part of their bodies, either. You never know when the disease could have been transferred from a sore to the rest of someone's skin. Think of it like… ink," she said, remembering a useful video that had done the rounds online. "It hangs around on what-ever it touches."

"I'll spread the word," Connor said, nodding firmly. "And I'll keep my gauntlets on when I'm dealing with livestock for the time being, I think."

"Good idea," she said, smiling. Armored gloves weren't exactly equivalent to PPE — but anything was better than nothing.

They finished their breakfast, then Connor escorted her out of the inn. She was looking forward to the day, she realized with surprise. Looking forward to meeting Kay... and maybe getting some answers about just what the hell was going on here.

CHAPTER 9

It was a beautiful day. Was it warmer than yesterday, or had she just acclimatized to the chill in the air? Connor had brought two horses today, but he hesitated as he led her toward them, glancing back at her anxiously.

"Now, I wasn't sure if you knew how to ride. Some of the ladies hadn't been near a horse when they first got here. But I didn't want you to feel like you had to ride behind me again."

"No," she said quickly, then shook herself. "No, I mean — I didn't mind that, but — I know how to ride. I took lessons when I was a kid," she added with a smile. "Me and my brother."

"Good," he said with a smile. "The gray's yours, then. She's a sweet old thing — not much of a turn of speed on her, but she's steady as a rock and will go all day and night if you let her. Nice smooth stride, too. One of Liam's favorites," he said with a grin. "Liam's my cousin. Kay's husband."

Sure enough, the mare he'd brought for her to ride was sweet and placid, with a step so smooth that she almost felt like she wasn't on horseback at all. It had been a few years since she'd been on a horse, but there was something about it that was hard to forget, and she felt a broad grin break out over her face as they set off up the road that ran through the middle of the town up toward the church standing on the hill. The village was busy at this time of morning, and Karen was aware of more than a few curious stares from passersby — all of whom also offered Connor cheerful waves and called greetings to him. He was well-liked, it seemed.

"That's my cottage," he pointed out cheerfully as they rode past a little cottage on the main street of town, a few doors down from the church. "I used to live at the Keep, but I moved down here as a permanent village guard a few years ago."

"Keeping an eye out for strange women crawling out of the lake?" she called back with a smile.

"Aye, that's most of the job."

They rode past the huge, foreboding church. It was oddly familiar. Karen's mother was Catholic — her father an easy-going agnostic who'd gone along with whatever her mother wanted — so she had a passing familiarity with the rituals, and a handful of churchgoing memories from her childhood, most of which were steeped in deep unease. She'd never felt especially at home in a church… the concept of God, while theoretically comforting, was so touched with fear and dread of having done something wrong that it had always been a relief to talk to her father, who didn't much care one way or another whether God was watching. Just be good for the sake of being good, he'd told her, and any God worth his or her salt will respect that.

She was about to ask Connor what the church folk thought of all the supernatural stuff — but they'd already ridden past the church, heading down a path that wove its way through the woods, and she decided to leave the subject of religion for another day. After all, she'd only just met this man. Religion was a topic that could wait until they were better acquainted.

The dairy farm they were headed for was about a half hour's leisurely ride, and by the time they had reached the farm she'd remembered her riding lessons enough to be itching to go faster. They hitched their horses to the farm's gate and headed through the front gate, past the beautiful old farmhouse to a sturdy barn that stood beyond it. There was a paddock behind the barn, full of maybe a hundred cows, all milling about together, making soft sounds that carried on the warm summer air.

Leaning on the fencepost were three people, who turned as Connor called a greeting. The first was a man in maybe his seventies, wizened and ancient with a pair of keen blue eyes that seemed to size Karen up the moment he saw her. Somehow, she just knew this was the farmer — especially as the other two seemed oddly familiar. One, a tall man with blond hair braided behind his ears and a dancing smile on his face — the other, a slender, tall woman with wavy dark hair pushed back by a rather incongruous looking modern headband. This had to be Kay — and her husband, Liam, whose resemblance to his cousin Connor couldn't be denied.

"You must be the famous Karen. Good to meet you," Kay said warmly, stepping forward to shake her hand. "I'm Kay." God, it was good to hear another American accent. "This is my husband Liam. And this is Neil, who owns this farm."

"You're some kind of expert on all this, I'm told?" the old man said, narrowing his eyes at Karen. It was clear from his disgruntled expression that they wouldn't get much of a chance to chat — he had one topic on his mind, and one topic only. "My herds've been sick for weeks."

"Cowpox," Kay confirmed, shaking her head a little. "Thankfully, it won't do any lasting harm to your herds, Neil." She was raising her voice a little — the old man must have been a little hard of hearing.

Liam cleared his throat. "It would be best for us to separate the sick animals from the healthy ones, to slow the spread of the illness. Is that something you can do, Neil?"

"Not with my lay-about farmhands," the old man said, disgruntled. "Useless as anything, the lot of them. Say they don't want to work with sick animals. Say they're worried about catching it. Is there anything else I can do?" he added, sounding hopeful. "Old Maggie might know of a salve or something to cure them…?"

"Nothing we can do, unfortunately. No vaccines," Kay added in an undertone to Karen, who nodded. "The best hope is to quarantine the sick ones."

"And hope it doesn't spread to any other herds," Liam added, frowning. "Do you still graze the herds together down by the river?"

"Aye, we do," Neil said with a grimace. "Put a stop to it once we noticed the pox on a few of them, though."

"It may already be too late," Kay said with a heavy sigh. "The disease has an incubation period of a week or so. We'd better check with the other farmers in the area."

"Guess I've got some herding to do," Neil said with a grimace.

But Karen frowned, glancing up at Connor — who was way ahead of her, volunteering to help with the work. Kay and Liam were quick to volunteer as well, and it wasn't long before the four of them were riding out into the paddock, setting about the work of dividing the sick cows — which Neil pointed out from his vantage point on the fence — from the healthy.

Overall, not exactly what Karen had been expecting to put her medical degree toward.

CHAPTER 10

All told, there were about fifteen sick cows among the herd — not that many, but it was nevertheless tricky, fiddly work to split them off from their friends and herd them into the smaller paddock adjacent. The sun rose to its zenith then began to sink toward the horizon — by the time noon had come and gone, Neil had disappeared inside to bring them a meal of pies they ate on horseback, and it wasn't until mid-afternoon that the herd had been successfully split into two, healthy and well animals, and a thorough final check conducted of the well animals to ensure no signs of disease were on them.

They said their farewells to Neil, who thanked them gruffly for their help, and rode back toward town, exhausted and aching. Still, Karen couldn't help but feel a tingle of pride. There was something about the physical nature of the work that made her feel oddly accomplished. Her muscles were warm, and the horse felt good beneath her… and more to the point, she was looking forward to having a good chat with Kay. They'd tried their hardest to talk on horseback, but a paddock full of recalcitrant cows wasn't exactly a good atmosphere for getting to know somebody.

It was reasonably quiet when they reached the inn. Liam and Connor headed for the bar, arms around each other's shoulders, and Kay and Karen found themselves together at a table by the fire. They'd washed their hands and faces clean, and it felt very pleasant to sit by the fire together.

"So," Kay said, her eyes twinkling. "How absolutely mad are you finding it so far?"

"Oh, solid eight out of ten," Karen said thoughtfully, winning a laugh from the veterinarian.

"How long have you been here? Connor said it's been a couple of days?"

"Yeah, around that. Feels like — well, feels simultaneously like much longer and much shorter."

"You're doing well." Kay shrugged. "My first few days here I felt like I was on the edge of a nervous breakdown. I didn't believe any of it was real, thought I was going insane, thought I was having some kind of fever dream, or a stress-induced hallucination…"

"Yeah, I considered all of those," Karen said thoughtfully. "But I mean… if I got through med school without hallucinating about Scotland, I figure nothing else is gonna be able to cut it. I'm here."

Kay laughed. "That's one way of looking at it. I'm glad you're settling in okay," she smiled. "It's a pretty — wild experience."

"How many of us are there?" Karen wanted to know, leaning forward with interest. "Connor said — five?"

"Anna, Nancy, Elena, me, Helen — yeah, five. And you make six. All of us from the twenty-first century… right?" she added.

Karen nodded.

"And all of us American. I'm from Wisconsin," she said with a smile. "You?"

"Colorado, originally. But I live in Georgia now. I work for the NIH," she added, grateful for the look of recognition that flicked across Kay's face.

"Brilliant. I've been thinking about what we'd do if a proper epidemic came through — bubonic plague, all that stuff. I've been the closest thing to a doctor we've got. Well, me and Maggie — though she's less of a medical professional and more ... ah, well, you'll see when you meet her."

Karen tilted her head, fiercely curious about this Maggie everyone kept mentioning so mysteriously. But it was clear that Kay had other things on her mind.

"A doctor," she mused, smiling broadly. "Well, I'm glad I'll be able to focus on animal patients."

"Seems like we'll need both of us to sort out this cowpox situation," Karen said with a smile. "You know it's one of the first diseases I learned about? The origin of the word 'vaccination'." She leaned forward, interested to finally talk about this topic with someone who knew where she was coming from. "So — what's the deal with our knowledge, and everything? What happens if we give too much information away? Do we cause a — a time paradox, or something? Obviously, I know a lot more than anyone else here — so do you, and so does Connor, for that matter, now that I've told him a few things... does that do damage to history, somehow?"

Kay shook her head, looking thoughtful. "We've talked about it, but it's hard to say for sure. My theory is that the Sidhe protect us from any negative consequences — both of traveling here, and of the incongruity of what we know with history. It's just a theory, though. Nobody really understands how the Sidhe work… least of all some lousy scientist like me," she added with a grin.

"The Sidhe… they're the faeries that are supposed to have brought us here, right?"

"Right," Kay affirmed. "They're kind of … royalty, from what I can tell. There are two courts on the other side of the Burgh — Seelie and Unseelie. The Seelie are friends and allies — they can be mischievous, or hard to understand, but they've usually got our best interests at heart. The Unseelie are — decidedly not so." She shivered. "When I first got here, there were these creatures that had come through the Burgh… these creepy water horse things. They caused a lot of death and destruction before we managed to defeat them." She sighed. "You get used to it."

"I can't imagine," Karen said, a little chilled by the bleak look on Kay's face. "How long have you been here?"

"A few months," Kay explained. "Nearly a year, actually, now I think about it. Wow. Time flies when you're having fun," she said with a smile on her face. "I love it here, truly. For all its quirks… it's where I was meant to be, you know?"

"You don't miss home?" Karen asked, feeling strange about the idea of this woman simply leaving her whole life behind. "You don't miss… the future?"

"I miss my family," Kay said straight away, shaking her head. "It's awful not knowing what happened with me — knowing that they probably think I died. That's the worst part… but I'm working on it. We all are. Trying to figure out a way of leaving a message for our families, somehow… preserving letters to them that can tell them what happened. It's a long shot," she shrugged, "but given that our parents won't be born for hundreds of years, we've got time." She smiled, the expression lifting the somber atmosphere. "And I miss the hell out of the Internet. What I wouldn't give to Google song lyrics I've forgotten, sometimes…"

Karen couldn't help but laugh at that. "I've got a pretty good memory. Give me a call if I can ever help out with anything."

"Thank God you're here," Kay said, and the two of them laughed. But there was an odd tension to Kay's body — the way she kept shooting glances at her, as though trying to figure out how to tell her something. "You… you know, right?"

"Know what?"

"The Burgh. The Sidhe, bringing you here… you know the deal with all that, don't you?"

"Not even slightly," Karen said blankly. "All I know is that I'm here, and that magic was involved, and that it's definitely not a dream. Unless I've gotten really good at dreaming," she added, hoping to win another smile from Kay — but the woman's face had grown solemn. A little worried, Karen glanced over toward the bar, where Connor and Liam were deep in conversation. It seemed Kay was about to get to the meat of what she wanted to tell her. That was sending a shiver running down her spine… but she didn't know why.

What grim news was Kay about to break to her?

CHAPTER 11

"So how did you get here? How much do you remember?" Kay was leaning forward, a serious look on her bright face.

"Not a lot." Karen shrugged. "I mean — the last I remember I was in the hospital." Kay's eyes widened and she leaned forward even further clearly interested in this particular detail. Why did she look so serious? "Nothing that bad." Karen laughed, waving a hand. "We were in Tunisia — me and my team, I mean, a deployment from the NIH to investigate a new disease that was spreading pretty quickly over there. Quickly enough to be of concern, at any rate."

"Tunisia," Kay murmured, her eyes wide. "I

wish I'd been there. I hate that I never traveled outside of America."

"It was a beautiful place. I didn't spend much time actually seeing it, though. Busy working… and then I caught the damn disease."

"You caught it. That explains it," Kay said heavily, reaching out to squeeze her hand. "Sorry. That must have been… horrible."

"It wasn't so bad." Karen shrugged, a little taken aback by the depth of Kay's sympathy. Was she missing something? What was going on? "I mean, it had similar symptoms to cow pox, actually. Fatigue and a fever… plus some upper respiratory symptoms that were pretty unpleasant. About ten percent of cases were serious enough to warrant hospitalization, but the majority were comparable to a nasty cold."

"And you were one of the hospitalized ones."

"Well, yeah, but only because there were spare beds. I probably would've been fine to recover at the hotel if they hadn't decided it was a good idea not to risk infecting the staff there."

Karen was looking at her closely. "What is the last thing you remember?"

She thought back, trying to work through those

bleary, feverish days to dig up some information that would satisfy Kay, who seemed determined to extract this information from her. Why was she so interested in her last few hours back in the future? Was she trying to figure out how the time travel worked, maybe? "Well, I was pretty sick," she said with a shrug. "Couldn't sit up without feeling dizzy, kept falling asleep… pretty wretched stage of the disease. I must've been close to a turning point, though, because when I woke up here, I was completely better."

"About that," Kay said softly, and her face was full of dismay. "You don't remember anything between falling asleep in the hospital and waking up by the Loch?"

"Nothing," she said blankly. "I figured I just … fell asleep and the Sidhe took me through their… interdimensional portal, or whatever." God, it was handy to have had a little brother who was obsessed with science fiction. All of this felt slightly less utterly mad than it could have.

"It's not quite like that, I'm afraid," Kay said with a sigh. "Look… when I came here, the last thing I remembered was getting run off the road by a truck driving home from a job. I lost control when

I swerved to avoid the truck, plunged through a paddock and straight into a lake. I remembered the car filling up with water… then I was here."

"That's awful," Karen said blankly. "I guess it was good timing from the Sidhe."

"Yeah, it was," she said softly. "But it was more than that. When Anna came here, she was being attacked by a stalker ex with a gun. Elena had fallen down some stairs in a flooded building… Nancy was trapped in an underwater cave-in… Helen had had the brake lines on her car cut —"

"What are you saying?" Karen said blankly. "Everyone was in danger when they came here? I was just lying in a hospital bed —"

"Not just danger," Kay said. "Fatal danger. Between the five of us, we've worked out that… well, the Sidhe brought us here for a reason, that's one thing. We've all been able to make a happy, comfortable life here — none of us would go back to the future, given the choice. But it's more than that. By bringing us here… the Sidhe were saving us from certain death."

Karen let that sink in, staring at the woman across the table from her, who was biting her lip, clearly worried about how she was going to react to all this. "Death," she said blankly. "So… I was going to die of that illness?"

"I'd assume so," Kay said softly. "From what I understand, the Sidhe don't intervene unless there's no other choice. It was death… or coming here."

"I didn't even feel that sick," Karen said faintly, trying to process this. It seemed impossible. She'd always been in such good health… and the disease hadn't felt all that bad. Like a nasty cold, maybe a little worse… but she was being taken care of, she was resting… was it possible? Could she have been at death's door and not even realized it? Surely someone would have told her… but then she bit her lip, thinking of how she'd always treated patients who were at high risk of losing their battle with their illness. Telling them they were in danger was never a good idea — she'd always stay cheerful, encouraging them to keep fighting… she could feel the color draining from her face as the realization set in. Kay, seeming to see this, reached across the table to take her hand and squeeze it, a comforting gesture that drew a half-smile from her even as her mind raced to catch up.

"I know it's a lot to take in," Kay said softly.

"I don't understand. If I was so ill… how am I

better now? It's only been a day and I don't even have a cough," she said faintly, one hand going to rest on her clavicles as if to detect any problems in her lungs. "I was completely well when I woke up in the grass by the lake."

"Same reason I wasn't half-drowned or bleeding when I got here," Kay said with a shrug. "The Sidhe have considerable healing powers, from what I can gather. You'll understand if you ever see Old Maggie at work. And time passes differently in their world to ours. It may have felt like you woke up straight away, but it's possible they kept you for… well, much longer than that."

"I don't remember anything." She frowned, biting her lip.

Kay sighed. "I know it's confusing."

"But — if I was about to die there and they snatched me up to heal me… why didn't they just put me back once I was better?"

"I don't think it quite works like that," Kay explained, a heavy look on her face. "In this time and place… you can be well; you can live a new life. But in our time… in our time, you and I are both dead. And if we go back there…"

"If we go back there, then we'll die?" Karen said

softly, hardly daring to believe what she was hearing. Kay nodded.

"That's what Maggie says, at any rate. And she knows more about it than anyone."

Karen stared down at her hands on the table, finding it difficult to take this in. "I can't go home."

"No," Kay said softly. "But you can make a home here. We'll help you."

She reached deep for the reserves of strength she called on when she was stressed, biting her lip as she hoisted a smile into place on her face. "Thank you," she said softly, meaning it. "Thanks for — being here, for helping me understand."

Kay smiled, but Karen could tell she was worried.

"I think — I might need a bit of time to process," she admitted, feeling a little crowded in the noisy inn.

Kay nodded, getting to her feet. "Liam and I ought to be heading home, anyway. You do what you need to do. But I'll be in town plenty over these next few weeks, dealing with this outbreak — we can talk whenever you want to, okay? And I'll introduce you to the others when I can, too."

Before she left, she pulled Karen into a tight hug — she'd never been much of a hugger, but the physical contact felt good. It seemed to help ground her, at least for a minute.

But as Kay and Liam left the inn, she knew she needed to be alone with her thoughts for a little while.

CHAPTER 12

Karen climbed the stairs slowly, lost in her thoughts, which were spiraling wildly. Suddenly, this whole strange adventure felt a lot more real. In a way, she'd been hanging onto the prospect of getting back home… as though all of this, real as it was, was just a momentary diversion, an odd little journey back in time that would eventually be over. A big part of her, she realized, had been nursing the quiet hope that all of this was imaginary, still, somehow. But what Kay had told her about how she'd gotten here — and why, had dashed that hope.

The more she thought about how she'd felt lying in that hospital bed, the more worried she'd gotten. They'd been giving her a slight sedative, she remembered, thinking back to the drip in her arm — it had been best practice to give patients something to calm them down a little, as it suppressed the coughing, which at a certain point began to do more damage than good as the lungs were affected. Had that sedative disguised how serious the illness actually was? She'd certainly felt a lot stronger than she actually was… it had always shocked her when she'd reach for a glass of water and feel her hand trembling, for example.

She'd nearly died, she realized with a shock as she sat down heavily on her bed. The reality of that set in, making her heart pound and her mind spiral dizzily with shock. She'd always known her job was a little dangerous — being a health-care professional always carried some risk, more in the times of disease outbreak. But the idea of actually dying at her post… of never returning home, never seeing her parents or brother again…

But wasn't that the situation she was in here, now, regardless? There was no way to go home… the Karen Frakes of the twenty-first century had died in that hospital bed, presumably. She looked down at her hands, biting her lips. Was there a body there, lying in that bed? Had she been… cloned, somehow? Or had she just gone missing? That would be a mystery that would plague the department for years, she thought, shaking her head. Impossible to know. Impossible to ever go back there.

This was her life now, she realized, staring around at the little room as though seeing it for the first time with proper clarity. This wasn't a fun little daydream, or a holiday, or a visit… this was where she lived. These were the materials she had from which to build a new life… from which to start over completely. What was she going to do here? How could she practice medicine in the sixteenth century? She'd have to utterly rebuild her practice to be more in keeping with whatever was available to her here… it would take years. That was if she could even practice medicine at all. Didn't women with too much knowledge tend to get burned at the stake around these times? God, she wished she'd taken a few medieval history electives in college…

She was panicking now — she took a few deep breaths, trying to still her racing heart, and reached for a sip of water from the pitcher that sat by her bed. There was a candle burning, a tall, slender taper that had presumably been lit by the innkeeper, or someone who worked for him… she was never going to be able to turn on a light switch again.

Never have a hot shower… never browse the Internet to kill time… never watch TV again…

Her spiral was interrupted abruptly by a gentle tapping at her door. She called for whoever it was to come in, almost on autopilot, and looked up to see Connor's face in the doorway, looking slightly worried. He had a tray in his hands with two plates on it — meat and vegetables, a hearty-looking meal, and Karen realized with a start that she hadn't had dinner yet and her stomach was growling protest after a long day of physical exertion.

"Thought you might want something to eat," Connor said softly. "But I can leave you to yourself if you'd prefer to be alone."

"Don't be silly," she said automatically. "Please, sit down." There were two chairs at the little table in her room — she got up to join him, thanking him for thinking of her as they sat down to eat. Her mind was still reeling at the new revelations Kay had brought to her, but it quieted a little in the interests of getting her meal down. It was amazing, how quickly the body overrode the mind when it came to basic needs like food. And it was nice to have Connor there. Another person's presence could do wonders for halting the relentless creep of overthinking.

"I walked with Kay and Liam back to the horses," he told her. "They're both quite impressed with you. They're glad to have you here."

"Good," she said with a smile. "I'm glad I could make myself a little useful, at least. Can't imagine what kind of debt I'm going to be in to Thomas by the time this is all over."

"There's no need to think like that," Connor said firmly. "Thomas knows full well what you've been through. You were brought to us by the Sidhe — anyone with any sense knows that means you're important. We're more than willing to look after you, Karen." He hesitated, nibbling at his food, clearly trying to find the right words to bring something up. "Kay mentioned… she talked to you about — why the Sidhe brought you here."

"Because I was about to die?" She couldn't help but smile, though it felt like a bitter, broken thing on her face, and Connor didn't smile back. "Yeah, she told me. It's… it's a lot to process. I mean, I'd been thinking of explanations for what's happening to me nonstop, but… well, being rescued from certain death by faeries didn't really come up, for some reason."

"I can't imagine what you must be going through," Connor said softly. "I was born and raised here — I can't imagine traveling to another country, let alone another time. The shock you must be feeling…"

"It's a lot," she agreed, shaking her head. "I think a lot of it's still sinking in."

"I admire you," he said abruptly.

She looked up, blinking in surprise at the force in his voice.

"I admire your courage, Karen. To be dropped in such a strange place to you… and not only to be so kind and friendly to everyone you meet, but to offer to help with the problems in a town that's unfamiliar to you?" He smiled. "You're a formidable woman, Karen. I'm looking forward to knowing you better."

She blushed to the roots of her hair. Usually, she was completely fine with taking compliments — she'd had her share, especially professionally speaking. But when they were coming from one of the most handsome men that she'd ever seen… well, it was harder to keep her cool. But she managed it — thanked him for his kind words. They spent the rest of the evening talking about where she'd come from, about what Tunisia had been like, and by the time he bid her goodnight and headed back downstairs, she was feeling a lot more settled… and the exhaustion of the day was well and truly settled on her shoulders. She put herself to bed, yawning hugely as she settled into the warm embrace of the bed.

She had a lot to process… a lot to work through. But as her mother had always said, all of that could wait until she had a good night's sleep under her belt.

CHAPTER 13

B ut it seemed the night had more in store for her than just a night of sleep. She was out like a light within minutes, but her sleep was troubled by dreams that seemed to stalk her through the night, waking her up every few minutes with a start — just brief images at first, snatches of impressions, memories of her hospital room, of the early days after her diagnosis, when her only symptoms had been a lingering fatigue and an elevated temperature she wouldn't have even noticed if it wasn't for the regular temperature scans that were being carried out on the healthcare staff at the hospital.

In her dream, she found herself in that hospital bed again… but this time, she was as healthy as she'd ever been, frustrated by the blankets that seemed to hold her down against her will. She stirred and thrashed against the restraints, staring up around her as her friends and colleagues bustled in and out of the room, writing notes in files, fussing with the medical equipment, straightening her straitjacket blankets again and again and never making eye contact with her. She found herself begging them to talk to her, to look at her — her voice went from a cry to a scream as she desperately tried to get some acknowledgement, any at all, that she was still here, that she was still alive, that they could see her here…

The dream wore on and grew nightmarish. Her hands and feet were tethered to the bed with thick straps, stopping her from moving. She thrashed and writhed, screaming for help until her head was tied down, too… then they forced a ventilator into her mouth… what was happening here? Why were they doing all this to a healthy patient, a patient who was breathing fine on her own? The shock drove her out of her sleep entirely and she sat up in bed in the inn, shivering in the cold of the night, her heart pounding with the horror of the dream. Grim realization set in. What she was dreaming about wasn't real… but in a way, it was. The treatment that she was experiencing in the dream… that would have been what they'd have done to her body as her health declined… a respirator to breathe for her, a series of tubes and drips to keep her hydrated and alive as her body began to fail… was that how she'd died? Trapped in a bed, desperate for air that she could no longer breathe herself?

It was hard to get back to sleep after that — she lay awake for a long time, gazing miserably at the ceiling as her mind raced. The fact that she couldn't remember her own death… that was what was getting at her. It was as though something was being withheld from her… as though a secret was being kept that she had every right to know. Gritting her teeth, she turned over, settling down into th bed, irritated by how much the dream had frightened her. She counted her breaths, trying to settle her mind with meditation techniques she'd learned as a stress-buster back at med school… and slowly but surely, she felt herself settling, felt her body sinking into sleep again.

This time, the dreams were different. She was still in a hospital bed, but how she knew that wasn't clear — around her, the scene had changed dramatically. Instead of a hospital, all she could see was void, dotted with distant stars… an unimaginably vast space, yet somehow, she knew it was a room of sorts in a much bigger structure. And while she was as still as she had been in the hospital, this time it had nothing to do with being restrained. Her limbs were free to move if she wanted them to… she simply chose not to move. Chose to lie utterly still as a group of shining figures gathered around her, gazing down at her prone body… though how she knew they were looking at her, she wasn't quite sure. All she could see when she looked at them was light, a bright, searing light that somehow didn't make her want to shut her eyes against it, even though it was much brighter than the dark room that surrounded her. They were vaguely humanoid, though the lines that defined them were hard to make out — long, slender shapes, maybe six or seven of them, and as she gazed up at them, she felt a tremendous sense of peace.

Whatever they were — whoever they were — Karen knew, on a level deeper than any instinct she'd ever obeyed, that they were friends. They were on her side. They wanted her to be well… and more than that, they were going to see to it that she was. She could feel them touching her, feather-light though somehow not tickling her… but it didn't feel like the touch of a doctor. It felt like warm sunlight through an open window on her skin, moving this way and that, warming her skin and sinking deep, deep into her body. The warmth began to move through her, through her veins, through the cores of her bones... she felt it gathering in her chest like warm honey, pooling and sinking through her, and she couldn't shake the feeling that it was repairing damage she didn't even know was there. When she took a breath, she realized with surprise it was the first breath she'd taken in quite some time... and it eased into her lungs as smoothly and easily as anything.

The glowing figures seemed to withdraw a little at that, and she got the strangest sense that their work was done, here. They were retreating from her quickly, seeming to get further away even though she couldn't see their legs moving — she sat up, opening her mouth to thank them for what they'd done, for saving her from that dreadful room, for healing her... but before her voice could free itself from her throat, they were gone, and all she could feel was the brush of wet grass and the weak sunlight on her face....

And then she was sitting up in bed, shocked and a little amazed by how vivid the dream had been. Dawn had come — there was light filtering in through her little window and she was feeling surprisingly well-rested given how many dreams she'd had. She sat for a while, trying to process what she'd seen. Karen had always believed dreams didn't mean anything, but given the developments of the last few days, she was willing to revise that belief… especially given how unique and strange that dream had been. Those shining figures gathered around her… it had almost felt like an alien abduction, except for how utterly at peace she had felt with it all. As though she knew, deep in her heart, that they were friends… that they meant only the best for her….

"Sidhe," she breathed aloud, her voice oddly loud in the quiet of the room. Had that been them? Had that dream been a dormant memory of her rescue from her hospital bed? It was an amazing contrast. She wished, feeling oddly sad, that she'd been able to thank them for what they'd done… for the awful death they'd spared her from. Thinking back to the patients she'd treated for the mysterious condition she knew full well how awful it could be in its later stages. Given the choice between that awful death… or a new life in this strange place…. well, she knew what she'd have chosen.

But she had no way of thanking them, she

thought, biting her lip. Or did she? What had Kay said — the Sidhe always brought people here for a reason. Could she have some role to play in this town — some purpose to serve, utterly different from the purpose she'd served back home... but perhaps even more important, if beings like the Sidhe had seen fit to arrange things this way?

She'd do what she could, she decided, filled with a new sense of calm and purpose. She'd do her best to do as much good as she could. That had always been her goal in life — and why should that change, just because her time and place had?

CHAPTER 14

Karen felt much better than she had the night before as she headed down the stairs. Her body was a little achy from the ride the day before — muscles in her legs she hadn't used for a long time protesting at their overwork — but her mind felt clear and calm. It was resignation, in a way… but a positive kind of resignation, a determination to do the best she could with the cards she'd been dealt. And it was gratitude, too. Things could have been so much worse… she could have been dead. Could have been languishing in a hospital bed, dying an agonizing death. Instead, she was eating a hearty breakfast in a charming medieval inn… and there was a gorgeous man coming to have breakfast with her, too.

"How are you, Karen?"

"Better this morning," she said with a smile.

He nodded, searching her face for confirmation that she was telling the truth.

He actually cares, she thought, and that sent a warmth blossoming in her chest that threatened to make her blush again. "Thanks for talking with me last night. It helped a lot." She sighed, taking another mouthful of porridge. "I mean, it's a lot to deal with, but I think… if I can keep busy, find ways of making myself useful here, that'll help."

"Well, funny you should say that," Connor said, raising an eyebrow. "I was going to go visit the sick milkmaids today. Would you like to come with me?"

"The girls who came down with the cowpox first?" She leaned forward, interested. "It'd be good to talk with them about any contact they might have had with other people in the village if we're going to stop it spreading too much between people. We can make a list of who might have been exposed, start working on a quarantine plan — " She hesitated. "I can also have a look at their lesions, too, see if I can help them get better quicker." Sometimes being an epidemiologist made her forget her first job — taking care of patients.

Connor seemed pleased to have her along with

him — he kept grinning over at her from the back of his horse as they rode up the hill toward the house where two of the infected milkmaids lived. He was merely glad to have some help with the problem. *That's all,* she told herself... but she couldn't help but enjoy having Connor's company all to herself.

"There are three of them that we know of," Connor explained as they rode. "Neil told me yesterday that the three of them have been home from work for a week or so, now. Two are sisters — Anne and Rhianne — and Mary's the third. She's a little worse off than the others, from what her brother was telling me. She had a fall about a week ago."

Karen shook her head. "Fever can do that — throws your balance off. Poor girl."

They visited Anne and Rhianne first. The little cottage they lived in with their parents was rustic and charming. Their mother led Connor and Karen through the kitchen, apologizing for the mess — Karen could see soiled bandages soaking in a tub and smiled approval. It seemed the lesions were being cared for well. Sure enough, there were two teenaged girls tucked up in two beds in the room they clearly shared, both of them with bandages wrapped around their forearms.

Connor made introductions — the girls seemed weary and feverish, but they smiled brightly enough as they were introduced, curious about the newcomer. Rhianne was the elder by a few years, but both sisters had the same blonde hair braided neatly behind their ears.

Working carefully — there were no rubber gloves in medieval Scotland, after all, but she made do by covering her hands with a piece of clean bandage — Karen checked both girls' hands, nodding as her investigation revealed the characteristic round lesions that indicated cowpox. They were unpleasant to look at, and both Rhianne and Anne made sounds of disgust when they saw each other's injuries, but they were otherwise well tended.

"Your mother's doing just what she should be," Karen said with a smile. "These will heal in a few weeks so long as you keep them clean — and they won't spread if you don't touch them. Are you feeling okay?"

"I feel dreadful," Anne said plaintively. "I can't stop sleeping. I feel awful about poor Neil having nobody to help him with the cattle."

"Don't worry about that," Connor said firmly.

"We're helping him out, don't you worry. You just focus on getting well."

"Are you going to visit Mary, too?" Rhianne wanted to know, a worried look on her face. "We're worried about her. She's a lot worse than us two — she's got sores all over her."

Connor and Karen exchanged glances. It was unusual for the lesions to spread beyond the hands and forearms — how had Mary managed to spread them elsewhere? They said their goodbyes to Rhianne and Anne and headed for the third milk-maid's cottage, promising to send the girls' best wishes to their sick friend.

A young boy met them at the door, his blue eyes shining brightly under a mop of red hair.

"Good morning, Cameron. How's your sister doing?"

The little boy bit his lip. He couldn't have been more than nine or ten years old, but the look of worry on his face belonged to a much older person. "She sleeps a lot," he said with a shrug. "And she won't eat much, even though Ma always tells her she has to get her strength up… I've been helping look after her sores, too, putting bandages on and everything," he said brightly, puffing out his chest.

Karen couldn't help but smile — though she felt

a twinge of worry and resolved to take the boy aside later to make sure he knew how to avoid getting infected by the cowpox when he was helping his sister.

Mary had her own room up the cottage's little staircase. The window was shut fast and the curtains were drawn — it was stuffy in the room, with the sick, unpleasant smell that gathered in small spaces where sick people spent a lot of time. Mary wasn't much more than a bundle of blankets, and Cameron shrugged his little shoulders when Connor looked at him inquisitively.

"Mary? Are you sleeping?" Connor said cautiously, moving closer.

The bundle of blankets stirred, and a face peered out at them — the same blue eyes as Cameron, a mop of tangled red hair, and a listless expression that made Karen bite her lip. The poor girl looked miserable.

"How are you feeling?"

She shrugged her shoulders, not responding.

Karen moved a little closer, reaching out to tug at the sheets, murmuring to Mary in an attempt to soothe her a little. "Mary, I'm Karen. I'm a doctor," she said softly. "Is it alright if I have a look at your sores?"

The girl tensed, but she offered no protest as Mary eased the sheets back. Sure enough, the tell-tale cowpox lesions were all over her — on her hands and forearms, as well as right up her arms, and on her neck and chest. She was wearing a loose cotton shift that covered much of her small, busty frame, but Karen could see that her legs, too, were covered with sores.

"You poor thing," she said softly, but Mary didn't seem to be listening — her eyes were far away. Feverish, maybe — some people found it hard to focus. "Connor was telling me you fell down?"

"I fainted," Mary said unexpectedly, her voice raspy and ragged. "Fell down the stairs. Got blood and pus from the sores all over me." There was something automatic about her voice, robotic, as though she'd made this explanation dozens of times.

Karen frowned, something about it troubling her… but she pulled the sheet back over the patient, aware that she was shivering a little with the exposure.

"That can happen," she said softly. "The sores are spread by contact… that's why they come up on your hands first. You'd have touched the cow's udders, which had sores, then they spread to your hands… and I'm guessing when you fell you broke your fall with your hands, right?"

Mary didn't respond, but Cameron was listening intently, so she kept talking.

"That might have burst the sores and spread fluid from them across your body. They'll heal soon, though. All you need to do is keep resting, and make sure you don't touch the sores any more. That goes for you too, Cameron," she said firmly to the boy.

But there was something about Mary's expression that was bothering her.

CHAPTER 15

T hey left Mary to her rest — the girl was so withdrawn and quiet that they felt like they were intruding just for being there. Compared to her friends, who were poorly and feverish but cheerful, Mary seemed a great deal worse… though as far as Karen could surmise, they were at about the same stage in the disease. Had the fall shaken her up? That was possible… Karen had worked with patients who were in shock from injuries. But she'd looked her over for any signs of lasting injury from the fall, and aside from a few scrapes and scratches on her hands, she hadn't seen anything…

Cameron was positively vibrating with interest,

clearly worried about his sister and wanting to know more about what he could do for her. He was a good kid, Karen thought with a smile — he reminded her a little of her own younger brother, Stephen. They were a little closer in age than Mary and Cameron — the girl was sixteen, seven years older than Cameron, where Karen's little brother was only a couple of years younger. But still… he'd always wanted to take care of her.

"What can I do to make her get better?" Cameron asked; his bright little face creased with concern. "I bring her soup whenever Ma makes it, and I try to keep her company and tell her stories to keep her spirits up…"

"That's good, Cameron," Karen said with a smile. "Keeping her spirits up is very important. She seemed a little sad."

"She is," he said with a frown. "She used to talk lots more. She must be really sick."

"Just make sure you're careful, okay? You won't be able to help Mary get better if you get sick too. Make sure you don't touch any of her sores, even if you're helping to bandage them, okay? Keep your hands nice and clean, wash them as often as you can, and if you see anyone else with sores, make sure not to touch them either. Can you do that for us?"

The little boy nodded furiously, clearly delighted to have this great purpose. Connor chuckled.

"Seems you've got yourself an apprentice," he said with a smile.

"Is it okay if we come back to check on Mary in a few days?" Karen asked softly. "I'd like to talk to her about anyone she might have accidentally touched, just so we can make sure the disease doesn't spread… but she seems a bit too unwell at the moment, so I'm happy to wait until she's feeling better."

"I'll tell her," Cameron promised. "I'll make sure she's feeling better in a couple of days, I promise."

"You're a good brother, Cameron," Karen said with a smile. It was a little frustrating, not being able to talk to Mary about anyone she might have touched… the girls back at the other house had said they hadn't touched anyone since they'd been sick, but that didn't explain the spread of the disease to the rather unpleasant young men at the inn. Karen had wanted to ask Mary about those boys… but she'd decided against pressing the issue, given how quiet and miserable the girl had seemed. It could wait for a few days… or they could find other ways of investigating how the cowherders might have gotten those lesions.

After they'd finished talking Cameron through the best way to help with his sister's lesions, they headed off into the early afternoon. Karen's stomach was grumbling, but she had plenty of experience in ignoring her own hunger in favor of her work — but Connor clearly had other ideas. They rode their horses into the woods, and he dismounted by a stream, where some wide, flat rocks caught the midday sun. Then he surprised her by withdrawing a wrapped bundle from his pack — several crusty bread rolls, and what looked like a pot of home-made jam.

"I thought you might be hungry by now," he said with a smile, and they sat together on the flat rocks in the warmth of the sun. The bread was absolutely delicious, as was the preserved fruit they spread liberally onto the rolls, and for a while they were content to eat in silence, with only the gentle sound of the water rushing by to keep them company.

"I'm a little worried about the cowherders," Karen said finally after she'd swallowed her last mouthful of bread.

Connor was leaning back on the rock — he'd

taken his hair out of its tie and it was tumbling down across his shoulders as the sun glowed from his skin... the sight of him was utterly breathtaking and more than a little distracting, and she cleared her throat hard, trying to force herself to focus on the task at hand as her heart fluttered in her chest.

"What about them?" he said with a frown. "You haven't had any more trouble with them, have you? Thomas was saying he'd banned them from the inn —"

"Not me personally," she said with a shrug — though she was glad to hear the boys weren't allowed anywhere near where she was staying anymore. "I mean the ones we saw with cowpox lesions. It's strange that they'd have contracted the disease."

"How so? They work closely with the cows."

"Neil said they didn't help with milking them, though," Karen explained. She'd chatted with the old farmer the day before, idly wondering how it was that the young men had contracted the pox, but he'd dismissed her theory that they'd been helping out with milking in the absence of the maids. "They'd have had no contact at all with the lesions, which is what spread the disease."

Connor frowned, looking thoughtful. "I suppose

it's possible they've had contact with a different set of sores," he said, an amused look creeping across his face. "It's not unusual for milkmaids and cowherders to end up in bed together, after all…"

Karen wrinkled her nose at the thought of that… but she had to admit, that was a likely explanation for what had happened. After all, the girls had been sick for a week — that was plenty of time to have spread the infection to the cowherders. "Can't imagine anyone being interested in those young men," she said, and Connor laughed.

"We all made our fair share of mistakes in our youth, didn't we?" he teased her gently, his eyes sparkling. "Are you telling me you never had a flirtation with some rough young man?"

"Not like those men," she said, wrinkling her nose. "But you're right. I might check with the girls, see if they've got lovers among the cowherders — it's better to catch the disease early, especially if it's already spreading so deeply into the human population."

They rode back to the inn together after that, chatting idly about her work back home, and the similarities it bore to what they were doing now. But Karen couldn't help feeling a little distracted, preoccupied by the investigation. There was something here that didn't quite add up… some information she was missing. Information she needed to get her job done.

And she was determined to get to the bottom of it.

CHAPTER 16

The rest of the day passed pleasantly enough. Connor had told her that Old Maggie was coming out to check up on the herds the next day, and she jumped at the chance to be invited along to help — she'd heard so much of this mysterious figure that she was determined to meet her as soon as she had the chance. It seemed Maggie was something of a local expert on livestock as well as on illnesses. Karen was hoping she could shed some light on the Sidhe, and on what strange forces had brought her here. Her decision to make the best of her strange situation was making her feel a lot better, but she still had some lingering questions — and a fair bit of apprehension about the strange new life she was entering.

Knowledge was power, and it seemed Maggie was the one who knew the most about the supernatural goings-on around here. She just hoped the old woman would be willing to share some of her information.

Her night's sleep was restful, and thankfully untroubled by strange dreams, and when she woke at dawn, she felt rested and ready. Her body, it seemed, was already getting used to spending time on horseback, with her legs much less sore and stiff than they had been the day before, and she found herself humming happily as she headed down the stairs for breakfast, looking forward to what the day ahead held. She, Kay, and Connor had volunteered to help the villagers begin to sort through the herds, looking for infected animals and quarantining them separately to help slow or ideally stop the spread of the disease. Cowpox was unpleasant in humans, and problematic in cattle — sick animals had a direct impact on the village's food supplies, after all. It felt strange, to live so close to the actual source of one's breakfast, lunch and dinner… she was so used to being alienated from the source of her meals. One more thing to get used to, she supposed.

After breakfast, she went to collect her horse from the stable. Connor had insisted she keep the mare for the time being — she'd already grown attached to the horse, and she stroked her nose affectionately as she got her tacked up and ready for the day. Having a car was fine... but cars didn't shove their noses into your hands and close their eyes happily when you rubbed their necks. She much preferred this particular way of getting around.

By the time she reached the paddock that had been designated for quarantined animals, she realized with a shock that she'd been running late. The paddock was a flurry of activity — she could see Liam and Connor in the midst of the cows, working hard to separate one animal from its fellows. As she watched, they wrestled one young cow over to the fence, where she saw Kay standing next to a pile of rags... but she got a shock when the rags shifted and she realized that it wasn't a pile, but a person. Shockingly short — well under five feet tall — and wearing what seemed to be at least a dozen layers of mismatched clothing, the figure peered at the cow that was presented to it, then waved an imperious hand and the two men began wrestling the cow away to a paddock where several cows were already waiting.

She urged her horse toward the fence where

Kay was standing next to the woman — then blinked in shock as she almost ran down a slight young woman with bright red hair, who was standing in her path with an imperious look on her face. A girl of maybe sixteen, with a pair of enormous blue eye that held a great deal of authority — she waved Karen down from her horse, curiosity vibrant on her face.

"You're the new one the Sidhe brought, right?" she said breathlessly, taking the horse's reins from Karen's unprotesting hands. "Karen, right?"

"Yeah, that's me," Karen said blankly, a little taken aback by the plucky girl.

"I knew it! You talk just like Kay and the others," the girl said with a grin. "Brilliant to meet you. I'm Kaitlyn. I'm Maggie's apprentice," she added, sticking her chest out with pride evident in her posture.

"I'm looking forward to meeting her," Karen said. "I've heard a lot about her."

"Don't believe a word the villagers say," Kaitlyn said, rolling her eyes. "She's not a witch. Well, I mean... most of what she does isn't witchcraft, anyway. It's not her fault half the people round here are too dumb to know the difference between magic and medicine. Anyway, come on," she said firmly.

"I'll go put your horse with the others. You go meet Maggie."

From Kaitlyn's gestures, Karen surmised that Maggie was in fact the short-statured person she'd mistaken for a pile of rags. She felt an odd thrill of apprehension, though, as she approached Kay and the small figure. For all that she was barely the height of a child, there was something about Maggie that suggested a much more powerful presence. And that apprehension wasn't alleviated by the beady-eyed stare she received when she approached the two of them.

"There you are!" Kay said brightly.

Was she really that late? It was barely past dawn… it seemed she had something to learn about how early people got up around here.

"Karen, this is Maggie. Maggie — this is Karen Frakes, our newest arrival."

"Aye, I can see that," Maggie said thoughtfully.

Her voice was — fascinating. Something odd about it, some kind of resonance that made it more powerful than an old woman's voice had any right to be. There was something about Maggie that suggested her appearance belied her true nature, and Karen made a quiet note not to underestimate this little old woman any time soon.

"Good to meet you, Karen. You're settling in well?"

"Pretty well," she said with a smile. "It's all… pretty overwhelming, but I'm coping."

"I can see that, too. Good," the woman said with a sudden cackle. "A bit of mettle is a valuable thing. I understand you're investigating the spread of the pox?"

"That's right," she said. Had her friends been telling Maggie about all her movements — or did the woman just know things? Somehow, she suspected it could be either. "I'm a doctor — well, I was a doctor. And an infectious disease specialist, back in my own time."

Maggie looked very thoughtful at that. "The Sidhe choose to send us a medicine woman just as an outbreak of pox hits the village. Very interesting. No question as to the role you're destined to play here, hmm?"

She hesitated, not sure how to respond to that. Was she destined to play a role? What role? Was Maggie suggesting that the Sidhe had put her here with some knowledge of what was going on — that it wasn't just a coincidence that an epidemiologist had arrived just as an epidemic seemed about to tear through town? "I'll do my best," she said with a shrug. "I'm used to having a lot more equipment, though…"

"Nonsense," Maggie said briskly. "All you need is a good mind. That one's sick," she added, barely looking away from Karen as Connor and Liam wrestled another cow toward her.

"How'd you know?" Karen said, frowning as she looked after the animal — it didn't have any visible sores on its udders, not that she could make out from this distance at any rate.

"Just a hunch," Maggie said solemnly… though the way Kay covered her mouth with one hand to hide a smile made Karen suspect something else was at play.

CHAPTER 17

S o, the day wore on. It wasn't long before Karen and Kay had gotten involved with the work, heading into the herd to drag animal after animal before Maggie's watchful eye. Some of them were obviously sick, with lesions clear as day on their udders — these they took straight to the quarantine paddock. The ones that seemed fine they took to Maggie, whose practiced eye seemed to be able to tell sick from well… even when there were no visible signs of illness. Karen was a little worried they were putting healthy animals in with the sick ones — but as everyone else seemed to trust Maggie's judgment absolutely, she made the decision to do so as well. After all, she was hardly going to argue with the most respected witch in the village, now was she?

"What are you grinning about?" Kay glanced over to her. They were on the other side of the paddock, taking a quick breather. The villagers had heard that Maggie was in town, checking on the cattle — it seemed every farmer in town was driving his herd down to be inspected, and the paddock was filling up just as fast as they could empty it. The sick herd in the quarantine paddock was growing, too.

"Just thinking about Maggie. She's quite a character."

"Oh, you don't know the half of it," Kay said with a laugh. "She acts all tough, but she's as soft as anything on the inside. Loves shortbread, too. That's her secret weakness." Kay chuckled with her eyes twinkling. "Don't tell her I told you, but if you ever need a favor from her, shortbread's the path to her heart. Especially the kind that Blair makes, up at the Keep."

"How does she know whether the cows are sick?" Karen wanted to know, keeping her voice low. Maggie was far away, but something about the woman suggested that she might have better hearing than a regular person.

"It's either magic or experience," Kay said with a shrug. "Doesn't really matter which, does it? I think she likes people to assume magic, though."

"Is she actually…" Karen hesitated, unsure of how to phrase this. "Can she actually do magic?"

"Oh, yes. She's a half-fae," Kay explained. "She doesn't talk about her parents much, but we know one of her parents were Fae and we think she grew up beyond the Burgh, in the world of the Fae. So did Maeve, up at the Keep. She's actually a Changeling, and has bright silver eyes, which were a gift from the Fae," she explained. "She knows a few tricks, too — mostly uses them to entertain children. Maggie's powers are a lot more … significant, I suppose, seeing as she is actually half-fae. I'm certain she saved my life when I first got here. Most of us got sick when we first arrived here," she explained. "Something about the germs… it might happen to you, too."

That hadn't even occurred to her. "Of course. Our immune systems wouldn't have been ready for the bacteria and pathogens they encountered here…" She frowned to herself. Was she about to fall sick again with some kind of horrible flu she hadn't had a chance to develop an immunity to? What if it killed her? Again?

"Maybe you won't," Kay said with a shrug. "If you were sick when the Sidhe took you, they might've just cured you of all illness. Anyway, if you do get sick, talk to Maggie. She'll set you straight."

The two of them gazed out over the paddocks, taking a moment to enjoy the peace. It was midmorning now — the work had been going on for hours, and Karen was already looking forward to a hearty lunch at the inn once they'd finished quarantining the sick animals. She'd been a little worried about mixing up the herds so thoroughly, but it seemed all the farmers could recognize their own cows, so it would be easy enough to return them to their homes once they were well again and unlikely to infect their fellows. Liam and Connor were working together to separate a cow from the herd, and Connor looked up to meet her eyes as she looked at him, for all the world as though he'd sensed her gaze. He gave her a broad grin and a wave, and she waved back, trying to fight the flush that rose to her cheeks at having been spotted.

But it seemed Connor wasn't the one she needed to have been worried about seeing her blush. Kay had whipped her head around faster than Karen had believed possible, and there was a keen look on her face when she looked back over to her that took her aback.

"What?"

"You've been spending a bit of time with our Connor, haven't you?" she said thoughtfully, her eyes twinkling.

Karen could see where this was going from a mile off. "I know, I know. One of the barmaids at Thomas's inn already warned me. He's a woman-izer, he's a playboy, all of that stuff. It's fine. We're just friends." Not that she would have necessarily minded being more than that, her treacherous mind whispered… but she suppressed that thought as firmly as she could. But Kay was looking thoughtful.

"I actually disagree," she said, raising an eyebrow. "Maybe he was that way a few years ago… but I honestly think our Connor has been growing out of that particular phase. Men always do, even-tually. He's been seen with far fewer women around town of late. I have a suspicion he's interested in settling down."

"That's nice," Karen managed with a shrug, trying to stop her face from burning the way it was. What did it matter to her whether Connor wanted to settle down with some girl? No business of hers whatsoever… but Kay's eyes were gleaming knowingly.

"He seems rather taken with you," she said innocently. "The way he looked up when he saw you riding up this morning… the way he hangs on your every word…"

"He does not," Karen murmured, embarrassed — and, to her dismay, more than a little thrilled — at what Kay was saying.

The woman chuckled, turning her gaze back to the paddock now that she'd clearly satisfied herself that Karen was a little more interested in Connor than she was willing to admit.

"We're just friends, that's all. He helped me when I first got here, so I'm helping him with the epidemic. That's the only reason we're spending so much time together."

"I wouldn't be so sure." Kay shrugged, her eyes dancing. "But whatever you say. I think he's inter-ested. Do with that what you will."

"I'd have no idea," Karen said, rolling her eyes. "I never have any idea if anyone's interested in me. Absolutely useless with men, me."

"That sounds familiar," Kay admitted with a broad smile. "But if it's any consolation… well, if I ended up with the love of my life, you can too." She tilted her head. "But how are you doing, really? With everything we talked about the other night…"

"Honestly, I'm doing okay," she said with a smile. "Thanks for — for filling me in. And for being honest about all of it. It's a lot to handle, but… I think I'll be okay. It helps to have something to do," she added, gesturing at the herd of cattle. "Something to focus on aside from how far away home is."

"For sure," Karen agreed with a smile. "We'd better get back to it, hey? Fancy that. You travel hundreds of years into the past and thousands of miles from home and you still wind up herding dumb animals into quarantine to stop them from getting sick."

"At least these dumb animals stay in quarantine when we put them there," she laughed, gesturing to the cattle. "Humans are much harder to control. I'd take a sick cow over a sick human any day."

CHAPTER 18

I t was a long, hard day. By the end of it, her body was sore and aching — but they'd successfully quarantined all the ill cattle from their fellows. Karen suggested running regular checks on the remaining cattle in order to catch any of the animals for whom the pox was still incubating and not yet showing symptoms, but Maggie just chuckled at that, explaining that she was fairly certain she'd gotten all of the sick ones, not just the ones who were showing symptoms. Remembering what Kay had said about Maggie being a half- fae, Karen just nodded her assent, happy to trust the woman. After all, if magic had brought her here, was it really so outlandish to assume that magic could tell a sick cow from a well one?

They talked a little about the way the infection had jumped to humans. All four of them had been wearing thick leather gloves all day while handling the cattle, just in case, and Maggie didn't seem surprised to hear that a handful of milkmaids had already fallen ill — she rummaged in the depths of the ratty cardigan that she was wearing as the top layer over all her other clothing and withdrew a little pot, which she pressed into Karen's hands after a moment.

"You'll be visiting the maids again, yes? That's for the lesions. Helps them heal and stops them itching."

"Great," Karen said thankfully, tucking it away. "If you have any more, the herdsmen might need some."

"The herdsmen?" Maggie looked up sharply at that, a frown on her face. "Men've caught it?"

"A couple of them, yes. We saw the lesions at the inn a few nights back."

"Don't like that," Maggie muttered to herself, a dark look on her face — but when pressed, she grew cagey, refusing to explain what she meant. But Karen couldn't help drawing a connection with the unease she'd felt when she'd visited with Mary.

Something here didn't add up… and she was deter-mined to figure out what it was.

The salve was as good an excuse as any to get up bright and early the next day to head over and visit with Mary again. It was a pleasant ride despite her aching muscles from the work the day before — it was surprising how much strength it took to wrangle sick cows. She rode past the quarantine paddock on her way up, smiling to herself at the way the cattle were peacefully grazing. Even all coming from different herds, they already looked like the best of friends. There was something lovable about cows, and she hoped very much that the creatures weren't in too much discomfort as a result of their sores.

Cameron answered the door to the cottage, just as she'd expected. The boy was bright-eyed and bursting with energy, and quickly showed Karen inside, rattling on about how carefully he'd looked after Mary, about how he'd washed his hands every time and been very careful about touching her sores. He seemed fascinated by the nature of the disease and how it was conveyed, and she couldn't help but smile, answering his questions with as much patience as she could. She recognized that enthusiasm, that interest

— it was exactly how she'd been as a child, exactly what had brought her to the study of medicine as an adult. Perhaps the village's next doctor was right here in this room, chattering away to her about his sister.

But the warmth she felt for Cameron was quickly eclipsed by her dismay for Mary's sorry state. When she headed up the stairs to her room, her heart sank at how dark and dank it was in the room. Cameron and his mother had clearly done their best to cheer the place up — the place was tidy, at least, and there was a bunch of flowers on the bedside table. But the misery surrounding Mary was almost palpable.

"Mary? I've brought some salve for your lesions," Karen said timidly, creeping a little closer and reaching out to pull the blanket away from the huddled lump on the bed. She heard a muffled cry, and the blanket was snatched back with an incoherent instruction not to touch her. "Woah, woah," she said soothingly, taking a few steps back and exchanging worried glances with Cameron, who was standing stoic in the doorway. "Sorry, Mary. I won't touch, okay? I'm just going to put this little pot of salve by the bed for you. It will help them stop hurting and heal faster, and stop them from itching too much, too, okay?"

A muffled grunt from the bedclothes. Mary seemed even more uncommunicative and miserable than she had a few days prior — which was strange, given that her fellow maids had been chatty enough. Was she really feeling this bad? Or was something else entirely going on?

"You'll start to feel better soon, I promise," she said softly, wanting to reach out to touch her shoulder through the blanket but mindful of how sharply she had resisted being touched earlier. "Just make sure you're keeping your sores clean and covered... Cameron here has offered to help you with that, hasn't he?"

"I have, I have," Cameron said urgently, all but vibrating with his desire to help. But there was no response from Mary.

"We'll leave you to rest, okay, Mary?" Karen said softly, knowing a lost cause when she saw one. And with that, she and Cameron left the room, gently closing the door behind them.

Cameron was quiet as they headed down the stairs. As she lingered at the doorway, he bit his lip, clearly conflicted about something. "Mary's been sad for ages," he said softly, looking up at her. "She got sick... then she got sad."

"She got sad because she got sick?" Karen

asked, tilting her head. But the little boy shook his head, his face worried.

"N-o, I don't think so," he mumbled. "She got those sores on her hands and started getting sick… but it wasn't until a bit later that she got sad like that. I was scared she was angry with me, but she's like that with everyone. Do you know what could be wrong with her?"

"Sorry, Cameron. I don't," Karen said heavily. "But if I think of anything, I'll let you know, okay? And if you think of anything, you tell me."

The little boy seemed cheered — at least a little — that she was on his side, that the two of them were working on helping his big sister feel better. But Karen gnawed on her lip as she walked down the cottage's little path toward where she'd tethered her horse. There was definitely something wrong here… some information she was missing, something that had happened. Something to do with the girl's fall, perhaps? But as she walked, she was distracted from her reflections by the sight of a familiar face peering through some bushes in the front yard. It took her a moment to recognize the young man, and a pang of dread ran through her. It was Danny — the lad from the bar the other night, the one who'd threatened her in such an ugly tone of voice.

"Hey," she said, surprised more than anything to see him. What was he doing here? Could he be a friend of Mary's, perhaps? Unlikely… they seemed several years apart in age. But as she looked at him, she saw the lesions on his hands and was reminded that he, like Mary, had come down with the disease. "Oh! I wanted to talk to you about —"

But as she took a step toward him, he turned on his heel and disappeared. She shouted after him as he sprinted down the path toward town, but it wasn't long before he was gone from sight. Karen rolled her eyes, debating whether it would be worth it to chase after him. Probably not.

"Just wanted to tell you how to avoid getting all your creepy friends sick," she muttered to herself as she swung up onto her horse's back. But Danny's appearance bothered her all the way home. Just what had he been doing there, camped out outside Mary's cottage like that? Could he have followed Karen there?

But why?

CHAPTER 19

A few days passed. Karen found herself fairly busy — Connor kept coming by, offering to bring her with him on various errands that didn't really feel like they needed her to complete them… but she was hardly going to point that out if it risked the opportunity to spend more time with him. The crush she was nursing on him was getting worse and worse… and it was made all the more acute by Kay's casual observation that he liked her, too. Was it possible? She read into everything he said, every sidelong glance, the way he smiled at her when he saw her first thing in the morning, the lingering way he said goodnight… but it was impossible to tell, she told herself firmly. She wasn't exactly au fait with social norms of this time and place… what if he was just being polite?

At any rate, there was an epidemic to worry about before she started fussing over her love life. Word had spread among the villagers that the pox was afoot, and Connor and Karen found themselves besieged with questions from the village folk every time they rode out. Rumors, too, were flying about the disease — most of them patently false and downright ridiculous. When Connor caught an enterprising young man selling small jars of what looked like mud with weeds mixed into it, claiming to his customers that the slop (when applied liberally to the hands) would protect them from pox, it seemed he'd had enough.

"This is nonsense, right?" he asked Karen, raising an eyebrow at her as he gestured to the jars of mud. The guilty look on the young man's face told her all she needed to know, and she nodded.

"We need a town meeting," Connor said with a roll of his eyes once the young man had been clipped around the ears and sent off to make repayments and apologies to every single one of his hapless customers. "It's clear we need to get the right information to as many people as possible, as quickly as possible, in one hit."

And so, a special meeting was arranged — to be held in the church up on the hill, which seemed to be the only room in the village that was large enough to hold everyone at once. Karen helped Connor spread the word about the meeting, inviting as many villagers as possible to come along, and by the time the evening of the meeting came, she was feeling oddly nervous about addressing everyone. Though she'd met plenty of the villagers in the week she'd spent there, she still felt a little apprehensive about addressing them all en masse. There had been — varying responses to her claims of being a medical professional that was for sure. Some villagers had scoffed at the very idea — others had been delighted. What would the crowd at large think?

They headed up the hill as the sun was setting. Karen was interested, despite her nervousness, to see what the little church was like on the inside. It had been a long time since she'd been inside a church... and to her amusement, the medieval church wasn't so different to the ones she'd been to in her childhood. Rows of pews, an altar up at the front with a great crucifix, even the stained glass windows seemed oddly familiar... but this church, unlike the ones from her childhood, was lit by torchlight, not electricity. She headed up to the front of the room with Connor, who introduced her to a few other members of the Watch, including Brendan, the Captain.

"Brendan's wife Elena came from your time," Connor explained with a smile.

"She sends her apologies for not being here," Brendan said. "I'm sure she'll be thrilled to meet you."

To Karen's surprise, the village priest was there, too — and was much younger than she'd expected him to be. He was barely in his early twenties, with a pale, peaky look to him, though he seemed on friendly enough terms with all the guards and he greeted her politely, too. Connor had explained that Father Caleb was something of a hard-won ally of the people of the Keep — though the talk of faeries and magic were antithetical to his religion, he managed to broker a peace between the faith of the villagers and the supernatural work done by the Sept. A difficult line to walk, Karen could imagine, looking with new respect at this young priest.

The villagers all filed in and sat obediently in the pews, and the meeting began. It was warm in the church, and rather pleasant to look out over the sea of faces, to hear the announcements and discussions that went on. It wasn't long before she was called up to speak about the pox. Feeling her stomach flutter nervously, she headed for the pulpit, where Father Caleb smiled and gestured for her to begin.

"Uh — good evening," she said, trying to calm her nerves. "I've met some of you already, but for those of you who don't know, my name is Karen. I've been helping control the spread of cowpox, and … well, I have a lot of experience in handling diseases like this, so I thought I'd share what I know with you all so that we've got a good shot at keeping as many people as possible from getting sick."

The villagers were glancing at each other, and even from her position at the pulpit she could tell she didn't have their trust. Then Father Caleb was at her side, raising his voice effortlessly to call over the murmuring crowd.

"I have every confidence in Karen's wisdom," he said firmly. "She is a skilled healer with much to teach us all, and I'd invite you to open your ears and minds to what she has to say." He gave her a little nod, and she smiled her appreciation. The villagers didn't look especially impressed, now — but at least they stayed quiet as she continued to speak.

"The disease is cowpox. It's capable of spreading from cows to humans — that's how this outbreak started, unfortunately, with some young women milking sick cows and the disease spreading to their hands. We've been able to separate the sick cows, and they should recover soon."

"What about the milkmaids?" someone called, an old woman with a voice full of worry. "Will they die?"

A murmur of fear went up, and Karen raised her hands for quiet, grateful for the opportunity to put this particular misconception down. "Not at all," she said firmly. "Cowpox is an unpleasant disease, but very rarely fatal. They'll feel fairly unwell for about eight weeks, but they'll make a full recovery soon. And they won't ever get the disease again," she added. "Once you catch it, you'll be immune." She was tempted to tell them that they'd also be immune to smallpox… but that might have been a bit too much for one meeting.

"How do we avoid getting it?" the same woman called.

"Well, the disease is passed on by touching. So long as you avoid touching anyone who's sick, you should be fine. That includes touching things they've touched with their lesions — like clothing and bandages — or sleeping next to them. It's called quarantine," she said firmly. "If you notice symptoms — feeling sick or feverish, or seeing little round sores on your body — you should shut yourself away until you get well. We'll help keep you fed and safe until you're better. You definitely shouldn't go to work," she added.

There was a kerfuffle up the back at that. Half a dozen men were standing, and she could see angry expressions on their face even from here — and with a jolt, she recognized them as the cowherders from the bar the other night. Giving her ugly looks, the six of them turned and stormed out of the church, slamming the great doors hard behind them as they stormed into the night.

Well, she thought faintly, as the villagers tittered and murmured amongst themselves. She supposed her little speech could have gone worse.

CHAPTER 20

"They're just annoyed about having to do their own washing," Connor consoled her. It was an hour or so after the town meeting — she was still irritated that the herdsmen had stormed out of her talk about keeping each other safe during the epidemic. "That's all it is."

"They're not going to do what they have to do to keep themselves safe," she grumbled. "And that means they're going to infect other people. This thing has an incubation period, Connor. You know what that means, right?"

"Not precisely."

"It means that if you catch it, it takes a week to show up. That means we won't be seeing how quickly it's spread until… well, a few days from now." She rubbed her face, exasperated and tired. They were sitting outside the church, the dark, cloudy sky above them — the villagers had all gone home, and they were alone here. If she hadn't been so annoyed about the reaction from the villagers to her talk about controlling infection she'd have been overthinking how close Connor had chosen to sit to her, the heat of his body warming her arm… but even Connor's distracting presence wasn't enough to take her mind off how annoyed she was with those herdsmen.

"They want to work," he said with a shrug. "They don't like being told what to do… least of all by a woman, I'm afraid." She glared daggers at him, and he raised his hands. "Not me! I love being ordered around by women."

Karen couldn't help but laugh at that — at the worry on his face, at the reassurance in his voice. She got to her feet, rubbing her face, and thinking fondly of her cozy little bed back at the inn. A gust of wind distracted her, and she blinked, staggering a little in the force of the breeze. The evening was cooler than the day had been, but that wind was strange. It came from the west, and it was hot and fierce, leaving her feeling oddly clammy. Connor had noticed it, too — she saw him frowning as he stared up into the sky.

"Odd weather," he said softly, his eyes on the dark clouds above them. "That west wind…"

"Is it a storm?"

"Air's dry," he said, shrugging as he held out a hand. "Doesn't look like it to me. Looks like… I don't know what it looks like." Another gust of wind came, stronger this time, blowing gritty dust into their faces and making Karen wince and scrub at her eyes.

"Looks like time to go home," she said firmly.

Connor nodded.

The two of them headed down the street toward the inn — the church was within walking distance, so neither of them had bothered to ride. Probably a good thing, too, she thought with a frown as the wind picked up, howling through the streets and causing the two of them to stumble a little as the force of it threw their balance around. She could feel it dragging at her clothing, flapping at the cloak she was wearing around her shoulders, and she could hear Connor swearing softly under his breath as he, too, struggled with the windstorm.

By the time they'd reached the inn, the storm had

hit with a vengeance. Karen had never seen weather like this in her life, and she cringed a little in shock at the howling and screaming of the wind through the trees, through the village, flapping at open windows. She could hear cries of alarm from the townsfolk, many of whom were out in the street, staring with matching looks of horror into the sky. Connor was looking around with his jaw tight and his eyes clouded.

"I think I might be on duty tonight," he told her in a low voice. "You get inside and make sure your window's shut tight, alright?"

She nodded — and he was gone, jogging off across the street and calling to a woman who'd just emerge from her cottage, shouting in dismay as some laundry that had been hanging from her window went flying off into the night, gripped by the wind. Karen followed the garment with her eyes, watching it get whipped up into the sky and flung out of sight… then her eyes widened. The wind was still screeching and moaning through the trees, but there was something else in the sky… something past the clouds, something obscured by shifting shadows. She narrowed her eyes, trying to make out the shapes she could see flapping and shifting in the wind… it looked for all the world like great leathery wings, but she couldn't get a proper look at them in the gloom. As she listened, the shrieking of the wind came again… but this time, perhaps because of the wing-like shapes she'd seen, she couldn't help but imagine it as the shriek of some great, horrible bird…

Her mind was playing tricks on her, she told herself firmly, pulling her cloak around her shoulders and turning on her heel to head inside the inn. Thomas was downstairs, a look of acute worry on his face as he struggled with the shutters on the windows — Karen set about helping him get them shut and he shot her a grateful look. They worked together to get the place closed up and locked down, and she helped him check the windows on the upper stories too, ensuring that even the empty rooms' windows were shut and barred.

Then there was nothing to do but go to her bedroom and lie down in the dark. She was itching to stare out through the window, but it was shut and locked… she dwelled on the images she'd seen, trying to work out what they could have been. Bats, perhaps? They'd been broad and leathery, from what she could make out… but why would bats be flying in such terrible weather? And that screeching… now that the thought had occurred to her, she couldn't shake the impression that the high-pitched sounds were the screams of some kind of wild creature.

Despite the noise and her residual fear, she found herself dozing off eventually — it had been a long, exhausting day, and even the storm couldn't keep her from her sleep for long. She tucked herself deep into bed, though, some primitive part of her sure that she'd be safe as long as the blanket was tucked around her. As she drifted in and out of a shallow sleep, she almost fancied she could hear other sounds, mingling with the shrieking of the wind… calls and cries that were much more human than that, for all the world like the high-pitched shrieking of men in mortal danger. Once or twice, she sat up in bed, not sure whether the scream had been part of her dream… or the thing that had brought her out of it.

By the time dawn came, she wasn't well rested… but at least the wind had died down out there. She got up just after dawn, well aware that she wasn't going to get much more sleep… and besides, she wanted to find Connor, to check how he'd gone in the storm out there. Part of her was worried about him… worried about the cries she couldn't quite convince herself had been part of her dreams. But when she headed out onto the main street, she breathed a sigh of relief. There was Connor, working with another couple of guards to clear the street that led out of town of a huge tree that seemed to have fallen then been dragged some distance by the wind.

Seeing her, he straightened and waved, and she ran to him, too giddy to see him safe and well to worry about what his friends might think about her running into his arms. He held her close for a moment, clearly surprised by the force of her greeting — then she pulled back, clearing her throat hard.

"Are you alright?" he asked, looking at her as he held her by the shoulders.

"Fine," she said, staring around at the somewhat bedraggled town. "Which is more than I can say for the town, it seems." The place was scattered with tree branches, and she could see considerable damage to at least a few of the cottages — broken windows, damaged roofs… but there was something else wrong. Something deeper… something about the faces of the people moving disconsolately through the battered town that made her hesitate.

"It's worse than that, I'm afraid," Connor said heavily.

The look on his face filled her with dread.

CHAPTER 21

"W hat's wrong?" she said cautiously, her heart suddenly pounding as her chest filled with worry. "What happened?"

"Last night," he said, his eyes avoiding hers. "Something… something happened. It wasn't good."

"What happened?" she said, aware that her voice was getting louder, frustration building in her chest at the evasive way Connor was looking at her. "Connor?"

"Come inside," he said, his voice low and taut. His eyes kept darting to the villagers moving past them, and she was aware that they were being watched — and there was something new in the expressions on the faces of the villagers passing by. Something... curious, and afraid, and a little bit hostile. She couldn't shake the feeling that they were looking at her. Did it have something to do with what she'd said at the meeting last night? Did they resent her for telling the herdsmen to stay home from work, to do their own laundry, to quarantine themselves? Annoyance flared up in her ... but it was quickly quashed by worry. What if something more serious had happened with one of the sick people, and the townsfolk blamed her? Complications were very rare with cowpox, especially when the patients were otherwise young and healthy, but it was entirely possible that something unexpected could have gone wrong. And the more she thought about it, the more it seemed that the atmosphere in town suggested that somebody had died.

Connor hurried her into the inn. The innkeeper and barmaids were nowhere to be seen — she supposed it was possible Thomas was in town, trying to help clear some of the considerable damage that had occurred overnight. Connor looked exhausted, now that she got a good look at him — had he been up all night? she wondered. Annoyed as she was about the straight answer he was utterly refusing to give her about what was going on, she couldn't help a flare of sympathy and worry. Maybe she'd put him to bed in her little room, if she could convince him to get some sleep… but knowing him, he'd keep working until the village was back in good shape.

He called out for the innkeeper, but when no response was forthcoming, he shrugged and let himself into the kitchen, returning with a couple of bread rolls she recognized from dinner the night before. Better bread than nothing, she supposed… but food was the last thing on her mind with the look on Connor's worried face. They sat down together at their usual table. There was something eerie about eating in the deserted inn, with all the windows still shut and barred from the night before… but she doubted Connor had stopped for food the night before, so she wanted to encourage him to eat.

"What's going on?" she said softly once he'd finished a few mouthfuls of bread with butter slathered generously on it. Not exactly a complete meal, but it would do.

He took a deep breath, his face shadowed. "Last night. During the storm. We… we lost some people."

Her eyes widened. "Lost them how?" It had

been a ferocious windstorm that was for sure… but how had it caused deaths? Visions of horror danced across her vision — fallen branches crushing people, roofs collapsing on sleeping families… but there was something on Connor's face that suggested that he hadn't told the full story yet, so she bit her tongue.

"We don't exactly know what happened," he said softly, his face lined with worry. "All we know is… six young men were found on the hillside outside of town, just past the dairy farm we were visiting the other day. All badly battered and torn up… and all dead."

She stared at him, not understanding, the tragedy of the loss for a moment taking a backseat to her complete confusion. "Why? What were they — doing out there?" Had an animal attacked them, or something? But Connor was shaking his head.

"We don't know. We don't know why they were there, or how they got there. All we know is that the bodies are… they're a shocking sight," he said softly. "The Watch is spending most of its time making sure the villagers are kept away from the scene. The expressions on their faces…" He shuddered, and on impulse she reached across the table to take his hand in hers, wanting to comfort him somehow.

From the expression on his face it was clear he'd gotten a good look at the bodies... and that it hadn't been a pleasant sight.

She could remember the first time she'd seen a body — and the first time she'd seen one outside of the teaching hospital where she'd first worked on a cadaver. The cadavers they studied were different, somehow — sanitized, clean, distant from the people they'd been. But the first time a patient had died on her watch... that had been another experience entirely. He'd been an elderly man who'd succumbed, finally, to a troubling case of flu that his body was simply too old to fight off. She'd always expected the dead to look peaceful... but that hadn't been the case. What she remembered, even years later, was how frightened his expression had been. Something about it stuck with a person. She squeezed his hand tightly, trying to let him know she was there — he wasn't alone in this. He smiled back at her, and she felt her heart do that familiar backflip.

"Do you know what caused it?" she said softly. But that made him shift in his seat, clearly uncomfortable.

"Nothing natural, that's for certain," he muttered, frowning. "It's... unpleasant, Karen. I don't want to disturb you unnecessarily." Was he seriously trying to protect her?

"Connor. I'm a medical professional. You can speak bluntly to me — you're not going to damage my delicate feminine sensibilities," she said, exasperated by his protectiveness… even though it did send a little thrill down her spine that he was so concerned with her feelings.

"Sorry," he said, shrugging his shoulders with an exhausted smile. "Old habit, I suppose. They…" He rubbed his face with one hand, clearly exhausted. "Witnesses reported seeing two of the men dragged through the western windows of their homes. The other four went running into the paddocks to calm their herds — they weren't seen again until we found the bodies."

She blinked hard. "Dragged out of their windows? By what?"

"That's just the thing," he said heavily. "We don't know."

"Some kind of… wild animal?" She was struggling to visualize it. She was no wildlife expert, but she'd never heard of a wolf or a bear dragging someone through a window…

"I don't think so," he said heavily. "Everything we've seen points to a supernatural creature. And the men's injuries... they seem to have been dropped from a great height. That would explain the terror on their faces."

"Wait — they were dragged out of their homes and into the sky?"

"Aye, they were," Connor said heavily.

She sat back in her chair, shocked. "Does that mean —"

"It does. Whatever did this... it didn't come from this side of the Burgh."

CHAPTER 22

She was stunned. The existence of magic was one thing — she'd reluctantly had to accept that there was no other explanation for what had brought her here. She'd even been able to accept that Old Maggie was somehow able to tell a sick cow from a well one without anything more than a passing glance. But the idea of some kind of supernatural creature that yanked men out of their windows and into the sky… that was utterly unthinkable. She gnawed at her bread roll, though hunger was the furthest thing from what she was feeling right now, trying to give herself space to process what she'd been told.

"Has this happened before?" she asked finally, remembering what he'd said about the men of the

Watch and the Sept being responsible for defending the world from monsters from beyond the Burgh. "Do you know what kind of — what kind of monster would have done it?" No wonder he'd wanted to have this conversation inside, away from the ears of the townsfolk. She felt ridiculous speaking about supernatural beasts like this. But he only shook his head.

"Nothing like this has happened before," he said heavily. "Redcaps and goblins and the like will steal a child through a window if it's left unattended… but these are fully grown men. And goblins don't fly."

She recalled a flash of what she'd seen in the clouds the night before — the dark, leathery, flapping wings, half obscured by shadow — and a chill ran down her spine. She explained what she'd seen to Connor, who gritted his teeth hard.

"Aye, it does sound like something that might have caused this," he said heavily. "I was worried this would happen."

"What?"

"When you came through." He sighed heavily, scrubbing at his face. "The Burgh is like a gateway. When something comes through… it often isn't alone. It's possible these creatures, whatever they are, slipped through when you did."

Her eyes widened again. "They came through when I did?" She bit her lip. "So, it's my fault."

"No," he said firmly, grabbing her hand the way she'd grabbed his. "Absolutely not, Karen. This has nothing to do with you."

"Let me look at the bodies," she said firmly, coming to a decision.

He blanched. "No. It's a horrible sight, Karen —"

"I've seen dead bodies before," she said firmly. "I'm an epidemiologist. We examine the dead. I might be able to learn something that can help us figure out what happened."

He looked horrified, but she wasn't going to give in. They argued for a few minutes, but she hadn't gotten to the position she'd been in back in the future without knowing how to argue with men who thought women weren't cut out for unpleasant work like examining bodies… and to Connor's credit, he saw reason relatively quickly. He didn't like it, but he still rode by her side through the village, out toward the hillside where the bodies had been dropped. Sure enough, there were guards stationed on the road, clearly there to turn back curious onlookers — they gave Connor a nod, and shot Karen some curious looks, but they let them pass.

What he hadn't mentioned were the specific identities of the six men who'd been killed in this awful way... but once they reached the hillside, her eyes widened in shock. The bodies were spread out over a reasonably wide area, though all were within sight of one another — and the first one they came to was none other than Danny, the young man who'd given her so much trouble in the bar that first night. She frowned as she stared down at him, feeling a peculiar sympathy for his passing... though he'd been an unpleasant person all around, the look of abject horror on his face made her pity him in a strange way. Nobody deserved a death like this.

Connor was watching her closely, and she schooled her expression, not wanting to give him any indication that she couldn't handle the situation. The way he was lying, it was clear he'd been dropped from a considerable height — his body was broken and twisted, consistent with a fall as Connor had suggested. What was more, he was covered in deep slashes that had oozed a little blood — they looked like the claw marks of some great animal, though she had no idea what kind of creature could cause that kind of damage and also be strong enough to carry an adult man into the sky. She frowned to herself, examining him closely. Sure enough, there were the cowpox lesions she'd noticed that first night, covering his hands … but as she gently pried away his torn and slashed clothing, being careful not to touch the lesions, she realized that they weren't limited to his hands. There were lesions on his chest and shoulders, dotted amongst the deep slashes from whatever creature had carried him out of his window the night before… and she frowned a little, noticing something else too.

"What is it?" Connor asked, his voice hoarse. He was squatting beside her, taking careful note of the examination she was conducting of the body — and to his credit, he wasn't trying to interfere, despite his clear worry about showing her such an unpleasant sight.

"These scratches," she said thoughtfully. "They're odd."

"Aye, probably inflicted by whatever seized him and carried him aloft," Connor said, his eyes clearly on the deep gouges around Danny's shoulders. But she shook her head.

"Not the fresh ones. Here — these ones. Half-healed. They look maybe a week old?" He leaned in, looking more closely at the wounds she was indicating. Long, narrow gouges, most of them on his shoulders and chest, one going from his collarbone straight down, and evenly spaced — she held her hand up to the wounds, not touching his chest.

"Fingernails," Connor said thoughtfully. "So, the monsters have human hands?"

"I don't think these were done by the monster," she said thoughtfully. "They've healed over a little. I think these happened a week ago."

"Young lads roughhousing," Connor said with a shrug.

"With their shirts off?"

Connor shrugged.

She frowned to herself… but there were five more bodies to investigate. Sure enough, each and every one of the corpses belonged to the men who had been causing such a commotion in the bar the other night. And to her surprise, as she continued to examine them, she noticed that they had a few more things in common, too.

"All six of these men have the pox," she told Connor as she straightened up from examining the last man. Connor was looking down at him, clearly distracted, and she nudged him gently.

"Hmm? Sorry," he said, shaking his head. "This

man… William… he had a family. A wife, a young son. I'm not looking forward to breaking that news," he said softly. "He's one of the ones who ran off to check on the herd once the storm got serious…"

"He's got lesions all over him, too," Karen said with a frown, straightening up from the investigation. "Chest and shoulders and all. The lesions usually don't spread from the hands. And he's got the same scratches as Danny and all the others," she added.

"Maybe he scratched his chest and shoulders with an infected hand, or had a fall or something?" Connor suggested, clearly still preoccupied with the man's tragic loss. "The same way Mary's lesions spread to the rest of her body?"

She frowned. "Maybe … but the lesions on Mary's hands were clearly a little older than the ones on the rest of her. These are all the same age — they've healed the same amount, can't you see? At a guess I'd say — the lesions turned up a week ago, and the scratches maybe a week before that. Then the deeper wounds, last night," she added, biting her lip as she realized she'd forgotten what she was actually looking at. "At any rate… it doesn't paint a pretty picture of what killed them."

"Have you finished looking?" he asked softly, his

eyes distracted. "I'd like to have the men start carrying the bodies back into town. There'll be funerals to prepare for."

She sighed. There was no way of taking photos, nothing but her memory of what she'd seen to rely on… but she had an excellent memory, and she supposed it would have to do. "Alright," she said, nodding.

He gave her a brief, wan smile then turned and headed back across the hillside, his long strides carrying him away from her. She watched him go, her mind troubled. Hopefully, the information she'd gleaned from the bodies could help figure out what supernatural creatures had done this terrible thing… but some part of her felt like there was more to the story than just a random attack. Why these six men? Why did they all have the exact same old injuries — and the exact same distribution of cowpox lesions, even though they were extremely unlikely to have come into contact with infected cows in that way? She remembered Old Maggie's suspicion about the prevalence of pox in the men of the village and frowned.

Something was going on, here. And she was more determined than ever to get to the bottom of it.

CHAPTER 23

That night, an emergency town meeting was called, and Karen was asked to come along and speak a little about what she'd learned from investigating the bodies. It was Father Caleb who asked, surprising her — she hadn't seen the priest outside of his church before, and it was strange to see him in his robes, poking his head into the inn.

It was busy in the inn — it seemed the towns-folk, in the wake of the great tragedy, had come together to talk it over. Karen felt a little out of place amongst all the grief. She'd only been here for a week — she'd never met these people before, barely knew the men who had died — aside from her rather unpleasant encounter with them that first

night… and of course the odd run-in with Danny
outside of Mary's house the other day, which for
some reason she couldn't stop thinking about. What
had he been doing there? But they were six young
men in the prime of their life, one of them a
husband and father, and the grief in the village was
palpable.

Maybe that was why she felt like such an
outsider. She'd tried to sit at the bar, wanting to be
with the people of her new home in their time of
grief, wondering if any of them wanted information
about the deaths that she could provide — but
nobody had seemed interested in talking to her.
Locked in their grief, she supposed… though she
couldn't help but feel an odd hostility that wasn't
quite in keeping with what she thought was motivating her exclusion. She'd headed upstairs to her
room after a quick lunch and found herself at a
loose end until the priest was tapping on her door.

"Father Caleb, hello," she said, a little surprised.
He gave her an odd little bow and she couldn't help
but smile at the fussiness of the gesture.

"Miss Frakes, my apologies for disturbing you."

If anyone looked disturbed, it was him — it
took her a minute to realize why he looked so
embarrassed, until she realized her spare clothing

was laid out on the bed behind her, including her newly washed underthings. For a priest, she supposed, that was as good as seeing a woman naked — so she stepped out into the hallway to talk to him, gently shutting the door behind her and hiding a smile at the look of vivid gratitude on his face.

"You must be busy with the dead," she said softly, detecting a look of worry on his face, and he nodded solemnly.

"Indeed, I have been. The funerals will be tomorrow, but of course the bodies were in need of… some care." His expression was bleak.

She nodded agreement.

"Ah, of course. You — examined them. I did wonder whether you'd attend another gathering tonight? Perhaps you can — share some words of comfort with the people?"

There was nothing comforting about what she'd learned out there on the hillside that morning, but she nodded regardless. Father Caleb was the village's priest — clearly someone who had earned their trust and respect. If he thought her attendance was a good idea, if it were something that could help in some small way… she was more than willing to do it.

But Connor didn't seem to feel quite the same way about her attendance. He came along with her happily enough, walking side by side, but there was a tension in his body as they headed up to the great church at sunset that made her curious. She was tempted to write it off as a symptom of his exhaustion — predictably, instead of getting some much-needed rest, the man had spent the entire day charging around the village, doing what he could to ease the grief and repair the damage of the night before. She could see the weariness in his face. But there was something else there… something in the worried way he kept glancing at the villagers around them who were also walking up to the church for the meeting.

The atmosphere in the church hall was tense and awful. She sat in one of the pews toward the front, grateful to have Connor at her side… she still felt that odd sense of isolation, of not belonging in this place the same way the other people did. Even Kay, who like her had come from another time and place entirely, seemed to fit in better than she did… and was she imagining the sidelong looks she was catching from the villagers? There was hostility here. She tried to ascribe it to grief, but she was beginning to suspect that there was something more going on.

Father Caleb spoke, and his words went some way to calming the people — he gave an impromptu sermon about grief, about death, and about the afterlife. Karen listened quietly, impressed by the priest and the quiet sincerity of his words. It was a beautiful speech... but at the end of it, she saw Connor grit his teeth as he got up to speak.

He gave a short summary of what had happened, of the results of the investigation they'd conducted. There wasn't much information, unfortunately, save for the names of the men affected. There was a woman sitting in the front row dressed head to toe in black. Karen suspected she knew who this was... and the choked sob she uttered when William's name was listed among the dead confirmed it. Sitting by her side was a little boy of maybe three or four years old, tears streaming down his cheeks as he stared up at his mother. William's wife Rosemary, Connor had mentioned her ... and his little son Malcolm. Karen felt a lump rise in her throat as she looked at the two of them. She couldn't imagine what the two were going through... or how frightening it must be, not to know what had been to blame for what had taken their husband and father from them.

Connor finished his description of events, and an uneasy murmuring went up among the villagers — a murmuring that revealed fear, as well as anger. They were frightened — of course they were. Such a senseless, random attack with no explanation? But Karen wasn't expecting Rosemary to get to her feet, lifting her chin defiantly even as her body shook with suppressed tears. She was a young woman — maybe twenty-five, if that — though her grief made her look old beyond her years.

"What caused this?" she demanded, her voice thin — but there was a chorus of agreement from the villagers behind her, clearly strengthening her. "What took our men from their beds? What took my William from his work?"

"We don't know," Connor said softly, his face a mask of sadness. "We're doing everything we can to find out."

"I know," Rosemary said unexpectedly, her voice like ice. "I know exactly what happened." She took a deep breath, and raised her voice, and what she said sent a chill down Karen's spine.

"It was witchcraft."

CHAPTER 24

The room erupted immediately. This had clearly been a topic of hot debate all day — the explosion of noise sounded like about forty arguments being immediately reawakened. Shocked by the volume, Karen listened in vain to the dozens of voices even as Connor shouted for quiet, trying to bring the noise down to a reasonable level again. Some villages were shouting in defense of the idea, saying it was the clearest example of witchcraft they'd ever seen — others were calling them fools and charlatans. Finally, with the help of Father Caleb, Connor was able to get the crowd under control again.

"I'll remind you there are no witches in our village," Connor said firmly.

Father Caleb nodded solemnly at his side.

"We have evidence to suggest that creatures from the Burgh may be responsible — with the help of the scholars of the Sept, we'll be looking into —"

"Look into witches!" someone shouted from the back of the room, and there was a chorus of agreement. Karen scanned the faces of the crowds, feeling sick low in her stomach. This was always a fear when it came to public health — that fear and anxiety would run away with the public, leading them to jump at shadows. It happened with every serious epidemic, in some form or another. She remembered a virus that first came to prominence in Africa, and quickly spread around the continent. For months, people reacted with attacks against the sick people — even those who were merely suspected of having the virus had been attacked. Fear and anxiety had a way of awakening people's deeply-held beliefs… and as the argument raged around her, she realized that witches were a real fear here.

She remembered reading about witch hunts, a long time ago. The fear, it seemed, was twofold — one, of things not yet understood (especially medicine and disease — that had been the subject of the book she'd been reading, in fact) and the other —

of women. The knowledge and power of women had always been a threat to patriarchal institutions like monarchies and churches…. and as a result, a lot of misogynistic rumors were spread about evil women, witches, who did harm to those around her. She remembered thinking how grateful she was to have been born in a more civilized time.

Little did she know that witchcraft might be about to become a much more serious problem for her personally…

"What about her?" Rosemary said.

Karen realized with a shock that the woman's tearstained eyes were resting on her. She looked around, feeling the crowd of villagers turn their attention to her, and she shrank in her seat. "Who is she, anyway? She arrived in town a week ago, nobody knows where she came from or who her family is… she started lecturing us about cowpox and telling us how to conduct our business, supported entirely by the Watch…"

"What are you suggesting?" Connor asked, his voice suddenly low and deadly. "I remind you, you're speaking in a public place, about a woman who's done nothing but try to help us. Why, it was Karen who examined the bodies of the dead this morning."

This didn't seem to have the effect Connor was after on the villagers — a low murmur went up, the villagers nudging each other and shooting her hostile glances. Clearly, the idea of a stranger examining the bodies of their dead had not gone over well.

"I think she should be investigated, that's all," Rosemary said primly, clearly aware of the impact Connor's words had had. There was an ugly look on her face when she looked at Karen, but she could see the fear and the grief underlying the anger and spite that seemed to be motivating her. "If she's not a witch, she'll have nothing to hide, isn't that right?"

Connor exploded. "How dare you," he almost roared, his voice echoing from the walls of the church. Silence fell immediately, the villagers all recoiling at the anger on the usually cheerful and friendly watchman's face. "How dare you cast aspersions on a woman who's done nothing but help? May I remind you of every single other time you've collectively decided to let your imaginations run away with you and start levelling accusations of witchcraft? Had the Watch not intervened, you'd have run Old Maggie herself out of town! Old

Maggie! Whom among us doesn't owe our life or our health to that woman?"

There was a guilty murmur and a shuffling of feet. Karen was staring at Connor, absolutely shocked by this new side of him… and her heart was fluttering furiously at how oddly attractive she found it. All that rage, all that fury… all to defend her? It was enough to make a girl swoon… if she hadn't been so worried about being hauled out onto the hill for witchcraft that was.

"Every time you've convinced yourselves of witchcraft," Connor continued, his voice low and deadly, "or been led by some con artist or other to that conclusion, the problem has gotten a hundred times worse. For once, I implore you to let the Watch do our damn jobs. Sorry, Father Caleb," he added.

The priest waved a hand, clearly more interested in having the uprising quelled than he was in the mild blasphemy being spoken under his roof.

"Why does the Watch exist? To investigate and protect you from things like this. Supernatural forces. Things from beyond the Burgh. Whether or not you believe in it is irrelevant — call it what you will, demons or the ungodly, we know how to fight it.

Trust us. And don't turn on one another," he added sharply. "Accusing random women of witchcraft is an excellent road to chaos. Is that understood?"

There was a resentful murmur from the crowd.

Connor nodded grimly. "Good. This is Watch business, you understand? We've encountered dangerous creatures before, and we'll encounter them again. Leave us to do our work. And if I hear any more talk of witchcraft, you'll have me to answer to, understand?"

The villagers settled down completely at that. The rest of the meeting passed in relative peace — Karen could tell that this flare of anger from Connor had utterly surprised all of them, and she felt a secret glow of pleasure deep in her chest that he'd spoken so strongly in her defense. Could it have something to do with his feelings for her? Ever since Kay had said what she'd said, she'd been working on the theory that he was as attracted to her as she was to him… but she'd still been too shy to actually do anything about it. *More evidence filed away… maybe in a few years I'll actually bring it up*, she thought with a roll of her eyes.

But as the meeting wore on, she realized that Connor's anger hadn't quite succeeded as much as he might have hoped. Though the villagers were quiet, she could still feel their eyes resting on her when she wasn't looking… that prickle on the back of her neck that indicated she was being watched. And when the meeting was finally drawn to a close, the villagers all hurried out ahead of her, casting suspicious glances over their shoulders as though worried she was going to follow them home and cast a spell on them. Exasperated, but not especially surprised, she lingered in the church, getting a sympathetic smile from Father Caleb as he bustled about tidying the hall up. Connor was deep in conversation with the other men of the Watch — she could tell from the tension in his body how annoyed he was with the villagers.

An awful day, all told, she thought as she walked outside into the gathering dark. Mysterious deaths, rumors of monsters and witchcraft… and she herself a suspect. What was she going to do?

CHAPTER 25

Karen started walking back toward the inn, wanting to get a good night's sleep, but halfway there she knew in her bones that she wasn't going to be able to get any sleep. She still felt restless and worried, so she wandered the streets of the village for a little while, avoiding eye contact with anyone she walked past… which wasn't difficult, given the suspicious looks they were shooting her. It felt oddly lonely, and she found herself wishing Connor were with her. He had a way of cheering her up… and unlike everyone else in the village, she knew he wouldn't suspect her of being a witch.

Or would he? That was a horrible thought. Had he been avoiding talking to her earlier, after the meeting, because he was worried that she was responsible for the deaths of the men? Was that even possible? Surely not... surely, he knew better than that. After all, he'd defended her so vocally in front of everyone. But her anxiety was creeping in, casting aspersions on her certainty. What if he'd only been trying to convince himself? What if he'd been angry with the suggestion that Karen was a witch because he, too, was worried it was true? He was a sixteenth century soldier, and she'd been very open with him about everything she knew about medicine, about the spread of diseases... what if he suspected her?

The thought was so stressful that she found herself halfway to the church, the last place she'd seen him, before she realized how silly that was — he'd be home by now, probably fast asleep given how exhausted he'd been. She hesitated, almost wanting to go straight to his house, but not wanting to wake him from his sorely needed sleep. Still, her feet took her to his cottage... but she needn't have worried. He clearly hadn't been home yet. Then, where was he?

She found him eventually — on the very hillside where the bodies had been discovered that morning. Thankfully, there was no sign remaining of the corpses — they'd been carefully carried back up to the church to be prepared for burial, and the hillside, lit by moonlight, was clear of anything but grass and heather and the occasional tree. It was by one of these trees that she found Connor, focused deeply on something in his hand that she realized with a start was the sling he always carried at his belt. He hadn't noticed her yet, and she hovered, torn between not wanting to bother him and not wanting to startle him when he was wielding a deadly weapon…

And a frightening weapon it was. He had a pocketful of small stones, which he put into the sling's pouch over and over, whirling it then sending the stone flying toward the tree that stood some distance away. Each time, the stone struck the tree with a solid thunk — even in the moonlight, and at a considerable distance, his accuracy with the weapon was amazing. She watched quietly as he flung stone after stone at the tree, and when his little supply ran out, she cleared her throat softly to alert him to her presence.

"Karen! What on Earth are you doing out so late?" He was clearly pleased to see her, despite his scolding tone.

She smiled, already reassured a little that he

wasn't furious with her for being a witch. "I could ask you the same question. Aren't you running on no sleep whatsoever?"

"Had to vent some anger," he said with a shrug, gesturing with the sling in his hand. As she stepped closer to him, she blinked, smelling a familiar scent… and as he noticed her inhaling, he grinned, reaching into his pocket to pull out a sizable flask that sloshed when he shook it. "What's better for a temper than whisky?"

She couldn't help but laugh. "You're a good shot with that for a drunk," she observed, nodding to the sling in his hand.

He pretended offence. "Drunk! I'd need four of these at least to be drunk. You insult my tolerance," he said, taking a deep swig of the drink then offering it to her.

She grinned, accepting it. The idea of a drink sounded amazing right about now. Maybe it would help soothe her ragged nerves a little. She'd always tried to steer clear of alcohol as stress medication — that was a slippery slope she wasn't interested in sliding down — but right now, she decided, she definitely needed it. The whisky was delicious — it burned pleasantly all the way down her throat, setting off a warm glow in her chest that was only accentuated by the way Connor was smiling at her.

"I haven't seen anyone else with one of those," she said, still interested in the sling. "They all have swords or bows."

"Aye, I've gotten my fair share of ribbing for wielding what they call a child's toy as a weapon," Connor agreed, shrugging his shoulders. "But I like it. It's deadly as anything if you're accurate enough — which I am — and it keeps your foe much further away than even a broadsword." He reached into his pocket, then sighed. "A sword doesn't run out of ammunition, though."

"Did you make it yourself?" she asked, curious. Connor sat down heavily on the hillside, stretching his legs out in front of him and inviting her to sit beside him with a gesture of his hand.

"No, no. A merchant came to the village when I was just a boy. Said he was from Greece — saw me with a child's slingshot, complimented my aim and sold me this, the adult version I suppose." He grinned. "I've been practicing with it ever since. I'm better with it than a bow or a sword."

"Maybe I should learn how to fight with something," she said softly, gazing into the sky. It was a clear night after last night's storm, and the stars and moon shone down so brightly that it was almost as bright as day. "Especially if the townsfolk are going to come after me for witchcraft…"

"They're not," Connor said sharply. "Don't you worry about that. The minute any one of them tries something, they'll have a sling bullet right between the eyes." He took another sip of the whisky and handed it to her, gazing out across the hillside. From their vantage point, they could see a little of the town, laid out before them. "They're just frightened," he said softly. "Frightened of death, of danger, of things they don't understand. So, they pin it on you, something else they don't understand."

"Do you?" she said softly, feeling the alcohol loosen her tongue. "Do you understand me? Do you think I'm —"

"Of course, I don't think you're a witch," he said fiercely. "Don't be ridiculous." To her surprise, she felt him throw an arm around her shoulders and pull her close to him, jostling her a little as though to shake the idea right out of her. "You're no witch, Karen Frakes. I know that. And even if you were… you'd never do something like this. I trust that."

She smiled, leaning close to him, grateful that

he didn't pull his arm away. Whether it was the alcohol talking or something else, she couldn't bring herself to interfere — it just felt so good to sit here with his arm around her, sheltering her from the cool night air. The smell of him was intoxicating, and she could feel her heart beating hard in her chest, urging her to do something about it… but she held herself still. A part of her was still frightened she was imagining the connection between them, the chemistry… that it was just wishful thinking, that she'd damage their friendship irreparably by doing anything as stupid as confessing her feelings for him.

Still, they sat for a long time on the hillside together before turning in for the night. And she certainly had a few dreams that night… dreams in which she was a whole lot less frightened about making it clear what she wanted from him.

CHAPTER 26

The next day dawned cloudy and overcast. The somber weather suited the mood of the villagers… with downcast eyes they headed for the church, where a memorial was being held for the lost men at midday. It seemed the choice had been made to burn the bodies rather than bury them — from what Karen could gather, the men's wounds were too severe to make an open casket an option, and cremation had been opted for instead.

Thankfully, Connor had seen fit to organize more clothes for her than simply the pairs she had borrowed from the innkeeper's daughter. She had a reasonably varied wardrobe now, including a simple black dress that seemed appropriate for a funeral…

even though, as she looked down at it, it reminded her a little of a witch's costume. She wasn't a witch, though, she told herself firmly. She was a regular woman who was going to a funeral to pay her respects to the dead, and she wasn't going to be stopped from doing that by silly superstition.

Still, she felt a little out of place at the memorial, so she sat in the back, trying to draw as little attention as possible. Though she drew a few cool looks from passing villagers, it seemed the focus wasn't on her today... or perhaps Connor's harsh words the night before had gotten through to them, and they'd all resolved to leave her well enough alone. She sat and listened as the villagers shared stories about the six lost men — there was a sermon from Father Caleb, too, oddly touching, and a few of the villagers even sang songs. Still, she felt like an outsider. She hadn't known these men... hadn't grown up with them the way so many people around here had. All she'd known was the unpleasant way they'd treated her at the bar... but that wasn't any indication of who they really were, was it? She took a moment to say a little prayer, feeling odd about it. She'd never really been a practicing Catholic, and her medical career had driven a lot of what religious thought she had out of her.

But in this moment, in this church, it felt appropriate to hope that the six men were at peace.

She avoided the crowds as they left the church after the ceremony, not wanting to antagonize anyone — especially the widow, Rosemary, who had sobbed throughout the whole service. She found herself almost hiding behind the church, waiting for the crowds to disperse… which was where Connor found her. He, too, was dressed in black, looking rather dashing — or was it just that he was wearing something different?

"Are you alright?" he wanted to know, moving to her side.

She couldn't help but think of the evening before, the time they'd spent together on the hillside… the warmth of his arm around her… she shivered a little, annoyed by how strong her crush on him was getting. It was distracting… and she had other things to think about right now.

"I'm fine," she said with a shrug. "Just trying to keep out of everyone's way."

"Nobody's been bothering you, have they?" The protectiveness in his eyes sent a surge of warmth through her, but she shook her head.

"No, no. Everything's fine. I just… it's not really my grief, you know? I didn't know those men. I can't imagine how everyone's feeling." She sighed. "I can't stop thinking about the investigation."

"Aye, I'm in the same boat," Connor said, shaking his head. "Hard to grieve when I'm so focused on figuring out what did this — and how to stop it striking again."

"I can't help but wonder how they got those lesions all over them, too," she said, glancing over her shoulder to ensure they weren't being over-heard. "It's just not how the disease generally works... it only attacks the part of their bodies that would have come into contact with the diseased part of the cow. So how did they have them on their chests and shoulders?"

"How did they get it at all, is what I'm wonder-ing," Connor said with a frown. He put his arm around her shoulders, surprising her, and led her away from the church, down a winding path she knew led eventually to the paddock where the quar-antined cows were being kept. The casual intimacy of the touch was distracting, but she tried to focus. He just wanted to walk away from the church while they talked, that was all. No need to read into it...

"What do you mean?" she said, realizing he'd spoken.

He looked thoughtful. "I mean, most herdsmen

I know don't touch the animals at all — let alone their udders, where the pox are seen. That's why it's milkmaids who generally come down with the pox, right? Herdsmen don't do any milking unless they're pressed — and from what the farmers have all said, none of them stepped in to help out with the milking."

"Old Maggie was curious about that, too," Karen said with a nod. "Curious and a bit suspicious."

"I'm not surprised. I've been meaning to go and visit with her, actually," he said, clicking his fingers as he remembered. "She may have some insight into what happened the other night… or at least she'll be able to tell us where to start looking."

"Could there be a supernatural explanation for the men coming down with the pox in that strange way?" she asked, the thought occurring to her suddenly. "A — a curse, or something?"

"It's possible," he shrugged… then an amused look came into his eye. "I mean, there are other explanations, too, for how a man might come to have contact with an illness like that in so many intimate places…"

"What do you mean?" She blinked… then realized what he was getting at. "Oh! Of course — if they had contact with the milkmaids…" She wrinkled her nose a little. "I still don't see why anyone would sleep with someone who was covered in lesions… doesn't seem especially romantic. Maybe we should visit the sick maids again?"

"Aye, a good idea. Probably best for you to go alone this time," he said with a twinkle in his eye. "I'd imagine women would be more likely to share their secrets if there wasn't a member of the Watch present…"

"Ah, yes. The secret ways of women… very clandestine," she said solemnly, drawing a laugh from him that made her heart glow with warmth. He was such pleasant company… even after a funeral, with everything that was going on, being in his presence was making her feel more content than she could remember feeling in a long time. They continued to walk for another hour or so, strolling at a pleasant pace through the countryside. She was worried that he had duties he was neglecting to be with her… but couldn't quite bring herself to bring it up for fear of reminding him and sending him away.

Finally, they reached the inn, and he bid her good afternoon. She headed inside, at a bit of a loss for how to spend the rest of her afternoon. The inn was packed with mourners, and she hesitated a little before quickly grabbing some food and taking it up to her room, not wanting to intrude on the town's grief any more than she had. She'd leave her visit to the young women until the next day, she decided, settling into her room with her lunch. It would be good to see how they were mending from their illness… and to see if they had any insight into what could have caused the odd spread of the pox to those six young men. She was glad Connor wouldn't be with her. It might be something of a sensitive subject… after all, one of the men in question was married, and from what she'd seen of Rosemary, who didn't have any lesions anywhere on her body, it wasn't his wife he'd contracted the pox from…

But all of that would need to wait until tomorrow. For now, all she could do was sit and think, her mind worrying away at the problem like a dog with a bone. There was information she was missing; she was sure of it. And one way or another, she was going to find it.

CHAPTER 27

She passed the afternoon pleasantly enough, and got an early night, tucking herself into bed to be ready to get up bright and early the next day to go and visit with the young women. She'd drop in on Mary and see how she was feeling, though she didn't hold out much hope that the girl would be any more willing to talk than she had been… she had more hope for the sisters, who seemed much more social, more likely to be on friendlier terms with the young men who'd passed away.

There weren't many people about when she headed out to the stables to collect her horse, which she was glad of. The grief in the village was still palpable, and she didn't want to feel like she had to avoid people's eyes, feeling guilty for even being there in the first place. She was going to solve the mystery — that had been her decision the night before. That was what she could do for the villagers. She couldn't cure their sick of the pox, only slow its spread, and she certainly couldn't bring back the lost young men... but she could use her knowledge, her skills and her dedication to help find out what had happened and make sure it never happened again.

It was a pleasant ride up to the little cottage Mary shared with her family. She peered up at the window she now knew belonged to Mary, trying to see if the girl had decided to let any light in — but sure enough, the window was shut and bolted, the curtains drawn tight. What was worse, when she knocked on the door, Mary's mother answered, looking sad and drawn. She explained that Mary wasn't letting anyone into her room — she was barely opening the door long enough to accept a meal once a day, so visitors were definitely out of the question. Karen stayed long enough to have a brief chat with the worried woman and to answer a few of her questions about the girl's sickness... but there wasn't a lot she could say that was very useful. Cowpox shouldn't be causing such intense depression in the girl — as unpleasant as it was to be unwell, it was clear that something else was going on with Mary.

She just wished she knew what. And did it have something to do with the night she'd seen Danny lurking in the bushes outside the cottage? She asked Mary's mother a little about the girl's relationship with the cowherders, but the woman just shrugged, saying that she didn't think her daughter had any suitors among the lads of the village. Besides, her depression had started well before the deaths of the young men.

Still feeling at a loss, she headed down the street to visit with Anne and Rhianne instead. The girls' mother answered the door, looking tired but happy enough to see Karen. It seemed the work of looking after the sick girls was beginning to wear her down, on top of everything else — Karen offered to help by changing the girls' bandages for her, an offer she accepted gratefully.

Sure enough, the girls were still in bed, looking much as they had the last time she'd seen them — though it looked like Anne had been crying. Rhianne was dozing, drifting in and out of consciousness as they chatted.

"I wish I could have been at the funeral," Anne

said softly when the topic of the lost herdsmen came up. It seemed she and her sister had found out quickly what had been happening — they'd heard the shouting of the herdsmen outside their window when the storm had come, and Anne reported hearing shrieks and screams much like the ones Karen had heard in the village. They exchanged worried glances, a shiver running down Karen's spine as she remembered that night.

"What took them?" Anne murmured; her eyes full of fear. "What was it that would do a thing like that? Carry them up into the sky and…" A tear ran down her cheek and she dashed it away.

Karen sighed, turning her eyes down to the lesions she was carefully dressing, not quite sure how to answer the question.

"I don't know yet, and neither do the Watch," she admitted softly, feeling a pang of sadness at the grief that twisted Anne's young face. "But we're doing everything we can to find out." She hesitated, wanting to broach the subject of any contact the girls might have had with the herdsmen, but not quite sure how to go about it without offending or embarrassing them. They were very young… when she'd been a teenager, anything like a conversation about sex would have sent her running for cover.

"Did you know any of them?" she asked finally, feeling like she was prying. "The young men?"

"Aye, we did," Anne said softly, twisting at the bedsheets between her hands. "They were always around when we worked, bringing the cows to us for milking... we were friends, I suppose. We'd known them for years and years."

"Were you close with any of them?" she asked gently, not wanting to pry too much... but a blush came to Anne's face that piqued her interest.

"Kind of," she said faintly. "I — well, there was Galen…"

"Anne was in love with Galen," came Rhianne's voice from the other side of the room, slurry with sleep but her eyes glinting with amusement as they slid open. "Absolutely obsessed, it was disgusting."

"Rhi!" Now Anne was blushing furiously. "I had a bit of a thing for him, that was all. He — " She shrugged her shoulders, and now Karen could see the sadness in her eyes. "He was always sweet to me, that's all. We weren't seeing each other, or anything."

"Did you —" She hesitated, biting her lip. It was so hard to ask these questions without risking embarrassing the girls... "Anne, can I ask you some personal questions? I promise I won't tell anyone —

it's just to help with the investigation, to help find out what's going on."

"I didn't sleep with him, if that's what you're asking," Anne said frankly, drawing a feverish little giggle from her sister on the other side of the room. "Wish I had."

Karen almost smiled in relief… but held the expression back, mindful of the somber mood. "Did you — touch each other, at all? We noticed that he had pox, that's all," she explained, thinking back to the body of the one Connor had told her was called Galen. He had been a fine-looking young man… the injustice of such an early death twinged at her and she shook her head sadly. "We were wondering whether —"

"I didn't give it to him," she said indignantly. "As soon as I noticed the sores, I covered them up. Didn't want him thinking I was disgusting." She tilted her head, curious. "How'd he get sores? The herdsmen never touched the cows where they get the pox."

"That's what we're wondering," Karen said, disappointed by this new dead end. "You're sure neither of you had any close contact with any of the young men?"

"Definitely not."

"What about Mary?"

Rhianne giggled weakly. "Absolutely not. She *hated* all six of them. They used to pick on her for being short… then when she got taller, they picked on her for, you know… developing." Rhianne made a gesture to her chest that indicated pretty clearly that she was talking about breasts.

Karen resisted the urge to roll her eyes. It seemed young men never changed.

"No, she'd never have touched any of them."

Then how on Earth had they gotten the pox? Karen wondered, frowning. Here she was, stuck again at yet another dead end.

CHAPTER 28

She spent another half hour or so with the girls. They seemed to enjoy her company — she imagined any distraction from the boredom of being stuck in bed was a welcome one — so she lingered on, chatting away with them and assuaging a few of their fears about the virus they'd come down with. It seemed news had reached them of how insular and shut-in Mary was being... they were worried she was much sicker than they were, and that there was a chance they might be about to get much, much worse.

"I don't want to die of pox," Anne said, sounding miserable. "I want to get married first, at least."

"The pox will go nicely with your wedding

dress." Rhianne giggled. The girl was utterly delirious — and the joke didn't seem to impress her sister, who scowled and then turned pleading eyes to Karen.

"Don't worry," she said, trying to sound as reassuring as she could. "Honestly, the worst part of this disease is how long it lasts. You won't get any worse than this… and you'll be all better in eight weeks or so. I promise. You're definitely not going to die of it."

"I bet Mam wishes we'd die of it," Anne said darkly, though there was a look in her eye that told Karen she was just being hyperbolic for the sake of it. "She's so fed up with looking after us…"

"She'll keep you safe," Karen said with a smile. "That's her job. That's what moms are for. When she gets old and frail, you'll do just the same for her."

The girls nodded, which made Karen smile — she'd expected a groan of resistance, but it seemed these two girls were more than willing to care for their mother in her old age. There was something sweet about that… and something that made her feel a pang of grief for her own mother. At least she'd had a generous life insurance policy. That money should go a long way to caring for her parents as they got older… hardly a substitute for having their daughter with them, but there wasn't much she could do about that now, was there? She sighed heavily, feeling grief creeping around her mind. What she wouldn't give to talk to her mother again…

So, she was in a somber mood as she rode away from the row of cottages. No new answers about how the men had gotten the pox… let alone answers about what it had been that had taken their lives the other night in such a horrible way. The expressions on their faces still stayed with her — utter, heart-stopping fear. She hadn't been able to ascertain cause of death with any real precision — it could have been the fall or the wounds, but part of her suspected that it might have actually been fright. Fear could do a lot of dreadful things to people… including stopping their hearts, if the fear were strong and immediate enough.

And fear seemed to be the dominant mood in the village as the days wore on. The village remained in mourning, quiet and morose as time passed. Karen stayed as quiet as she could, keeping out of the way of the townsfolk, wanting to leave them to their grief… and, if she was honest, there was an element of fear there, too, a worry that occasionally stopped her from sleeping. She'd read about what happened to women with knowledge that went beyond the average in medieval times… she had a few dreams about fire, about the villagers hauling her out over crimes they'd imagined, and though she wasn't proud of it, she was afraid.

She trusted Connor to protect her, of course. Connor knew she wasn't a witch, at least — she had at least one solid ally. More, too, if you counted the people at the Keep… but she couldn't exactly rely on them. The castle wasn't exactly far away — about half an hour's ride, from what she'd heard — but far enough to be of no help whatsoever if the villagers turned on her. So, she kept to herself, doing what she could to help… and as much as possible, only coming out when she had the company of people who knew she wasn't responsible for the awful tragedy of the deaths of all those young herdsmen.

It was reassuring to know that the measures they'd put in place to control the infection were working, though. It seemed the herds were safe now that the sick ones had been quarantined. A week after the day they'd sorted the herds, Karen and Kay visited every herd in the village to check the animals for pox — despite their most thorough

search, they found no sign of the disease whatsoever. That was an excellent sign — it meant that
once the little quarantined herd down in the
paddock they'd designated were well again, there
would be no more source of pox.

Unfortunately, the spread had not slowed quite
so successfully in the human beings in town. She'd
been expecting more cases, but part of her had still
hoped for a complete cessation of the spread... so
when another couple of milkmaids reported lesions
and illness, as well as a couple more herdsmen, she
was disappointed. Still, it could have been worse.
She'd at least been successful in conveying the
nature of the disease to the villagers — they knew
not to touch one another, especially if they'd been
in contact with an infected person or their belong-
ings, and she had faith that the spread of the pox
would slow and then stop once the current cases
had gotten well again.

She was still worried about Mary, though. The
young girl was still refusing to open her door when
Karen visited, but her mother and little brother
reassured her it wasn't personal... it seemed Mary
had refused to see or speak to anyone ever since the
night of the storm. That worried Karen, kept her
up at night sometimes, wondering what on Earth

could have gotten into the girl. She'd been incredibly dejected and depressed before the storm that was true — but why had it gotten so much worse? Had there been some kind of connection between her and one or more of the dead herdsmen? But her friends Anne and Rhianne had said that she'd hated them all… why would she be reacting so strangely to their deaths? It was a mystery that she was no closer to solving as the days wore on, and though she knew it was technically none of her business, she couldn't help thinking that it might be some part of the broader mystery of just what had happened to those herdsmen that night.

CHAPTER 29

The biggest concern with the spread of the pox was that it had found its way to a child. Little Malcolm, the son of William, one of the dead herdsmen, had fallen sick — she found that out from Connor one morning about a week after the funeral service. It seemed he'd been visiting with Rosemary regularly, making sure she was coping okay in the wake of her husband's death, keeping her spirits up as much as he could. Karen felt a tiny bit jealous... but not enough to risk insisting on going with him. What claim did she have to his company, after all? Besides, Rosemary had made it quite clear that she didn't like or trust Karen — visiting her and her sick child would only make things worse. But

Connor kept her in the loop, visiting her often to chat about how the infection was spreading and to assure her he was doing his best to educate the villagers on how to reduce transmission.

"It's worrying that it's spread to such a small child," Karen said over lunch one day. Connor had collected her from the inn and they'd ridden out into the countryside, ostensibly to check in on a few herds of cattle out this way to make sure that they remained pox-free ... but Karen had her suspicions that that was an excuse to get her away from the village and have a little picnic. He'd brought sandwiches of roasted meat and even a little bundle of freshly baked fruit buns, which were absolutely delicious. "I hope she's keeping a close eye on him."

"Aye, she's being careful, too," Connor explained around his mouthful of food, his gray eyes intent as he reassured her. "I made sure she knows just how the illness is transferred, too, so she's making sure to protect her skin when she washes his clothes and bandages. I trust she'll be safe."

"And the little boy? He's being kept indoors and stuff? Kids are unbelievably fast disease vectors... if he goes and plays with anyone, I'd bet my life on him spreading the disease —"

Connor nodded. "Poor little guy's too sick to

play anyway — but I made sure Rosemary knew to keep him well away from his friends until the sores have healed."

"It'll be a long time," Karen sighed, thinking back to how long it had taken for time to pass when she was little. A summer lasted a thousand years… being stuck in bed with a fever for a month or two would be rough on a small child. "How did he catch it, anyway?"

"Must have been his father," Connor said heavily, shaking his head. "William came down with the pox around the same time as you arrived — before you'd spread the word to avoid touching each other if you've got it. He was keeping the sores bandaged by that time — well, by the end — but his son must've touched them at some point."

"Is Rosemary alright?" As much as she didn't like the woman for accusing her of witchcraft at the town meeting, Karen still had an interest in keeping the townsfolk safe. "Did you check her for lesions too?"

"Not myself," he said, raising an eyebrow. "That wouldn't be appropriate." His eyes were twinkling, and she fought the urge to blush, well aware she'd been fishing for a reassurance that he wasn't interested in the widow. Not that Connor, from what she knew about him, would be so callous as to go after a woman in mourning… "But I asked her if she'd noticed any sores or signs of fever, and she said she was well so far."

"If Malcolm's showing symptoms already and she's not, she's probably safe," Karen said thoughtfully. "Still…"

"I'll keep an eye on her," Connor said firmly, but there was a slight hesitation in his voice. "If you don't mind."

"Why would I mind?" Her heart was pounding at what he seemed to be about to suggest…

But he avoided her gaze, leaning back and turning his face up to the sky. The sunlight had been patchy all day, with clouds scudding across the sun at regular intervals, but at the moment the sun was clear and the warmth of it was very pleasant. She could feel her heart fluttering, the adrenaline tingling through her body — and she scolded herself, feeling ridiculous for reacting so strongly to such a subtle implication of … what? Of commitment? He was mindful of her growing jealous of him spending time around other women… and more to the point, he was interested in reassuring her that there were no intentions underlying his actions. What did that mean? Were they … dating?

Courting, or something? Impossible to know… and she realized, with gritted teeth, that she'd missed her chance to casually raise the issue when he moved on to another subject of conversation.

"I visited the castle this week," he said, and she leaned forward, interested in this. He'd said he was going to check in with the scholars up there about what could have caused the deaths of the men — there was an enormous archive of books up there, he'd told her, full of stories and accounts of supernatural encounters, and dozens of scholars who made it their life's work to catalogue them.

"Did you find anything?"

"Nothing particularly concrete," he admitted, shaking his head, "but those scholars move slowly when it comes to this kind of thing, I'm afraid. I'm hoping that my enquiry will prompt them to do a deeper dive in the archives, but it may take them some time. They've had an influx of new information lately, it seems."

"Really?" She blinked. "Have there been more supernatural encounters than usual lately?"

"Over the last few years, absolutely. When I was a young man, we'd encounter a goblin every few months and not much more than that. The last few years have been… well, very different. Ever since

Anna arrived, actually. I remember heading out through the forest to hunt a great wolf — Unseelie creature, eyes like embers, extremely dangerous. It had been hunting the villagers' flocks. Ever since then, there've been dozens of creatures like it, it seems. You've chosen a dangerous time to join us, Karen," he added with a smile that she couldn't help but return, even though worry was twisting at her stomach.

"Any idea why?" she said with a frown. "Why the last few years?"

"No idea," he admitted. "It could have something to do with Anna and the other women — the women like you," he added apologetically — "coming through the Burgh. Maybe the door's getting more use, drawing more attention from the kinds of creatures that love to creep through and cause havoc on this side of the doorway…"

"But correlation isn't causation," Karen argued, setting down her half-eaten bun as she considered the issue more thoroughly. "Did the women cause the things coming through — or did the things coming through cause the women turning up?"

He frowned — this clearly wasn't something that had occurred to him. "Surely not," he protested.

"I mean, think about it. The Sidhe bring women through who have been on the verge of death in their own time, right? But there are only half a dozen of us. I can guarantee you that more women die before their time than that. There's something about us — something special, something that makes the Sidhe bring us here. I mean, I'm an infectious disease specialist. Is it a coincidence that an infectious disease is spreading through the village right when I turn up?"

He looked flabbergasted. "I hadn't thought of it like that at all."

"I mean, it's all conjecture," she said, lowering her eyes as she felt a blush rising to her cheeks — he was looking at her with such frank admiration that it was making her feel uncharacteristically shy. She was usually so good at taking compliments… but when it came to Connor, she felt like a teenager again. "I don't have any more information on this than you do." She tilted her head, a thought occurring to her. "What about Old Maggie? Have you asked her about what's going on?"

"I stopped by on my way to the castle, but she wasn't answering her door." He shrugged. "Out gathering herbs, perhaps. Nobody's really sure how Maggie spends her time."

"Would it be alright if I came with you?" she asked, the thought occurring to her suddenly. "Would she mind? I have a few questions of my own."

"I don't see why not." Connor shrugged. Then he smiled at her, almost knocking her over. "And I'd take any excuse to spend a little more time with you."

The glow in her chest lasted for the rest of the day.

CHAPTER 30

They arranged to visit Maggie the next morning. On their way back into town, they ran into Kaitlyn, Maggie's little apprentice, who was able to fill them in on the old woman's schedule, or as much of it as she understood, anyway — it seemed even Maggie's apprentices didn't get much information about her comings and goings.

"Midmorning's usually your best bet," Kaitlyn explained brightly, falling into step with the three of them. She had a bundle in her arms and was clearly on her way out of town — probably heading for Maggie's cottage. "She sleeps in sometimes and disturbing her from her sleep's probably the best way to get on her bad side and stay there."

Karen laughed at that — there was an expression on Kaitlyn's face that indicated she'd learned this particular fact from experience. "Well, we'll come tomorrow midmorning, then. Are you heading there now? Maybe you could let her know we're visiting, make sure it's okay with her?"

"Aye, I can do that," the girl said brightly. "No promises, but I'd imagine she'll be happy enough to see you. She acts all tough and standoffish, but I think she secretly likes visitors. Besides, when it's about something that's threatening people's lives, she's always willing to help. You didn't hear it from me, but she's a big old softie, truly." The girl winked, then turned on her heel with a cheery wave and headed off down the road that headed out of town. Connor shook his head, smiling.

"She's a plucky girl and no mistake," Karen commented with a smile. "Bet she's beating the boys off with a stick."

"Oh, aye. But they keep a respectful distance, her would-be suitors," Connor said with a broad grin. "The last one who tried anything too forward with her wound up breaking his leg when he was walking through the woods. The most curious thing — he claimed a root crept out and tripped him up."

A suspicion flared to life in Karen's mind. "He

wouldn't have been walking near Maggie's cottage, would he?"

"Aye, how'd you know?" Connor's eyes were twinkling. They said their goodbyes until the next morning and Karen headed up the stairs, smiling to herself… but a little unnerved by this information. Old Maggie had a considerable amount of power that was clear. She just hoped she wouldn't get on the woman's bad side.

It was strange, she thought as she drifted off to sleep. Strange how quickly she'd adjusted to her entire world being torn away from her and replaced with something completely new and different. Time travel, magic, witchcraft, magical dimensions between worlds… if anyone had told her about any of this a month ago, she'd have laughed at them. But here she was, planning a visit to a magical being who lived in a cottage in the woods… on the shore of Loch Ness, where she knew for a fact an enormous monster lived— Connor had seen it himself — and why would she refuse to believe that, when she'd accepted so much other wild information? The human capacity for adaptation was remarkable — that was her conclusion, as she drifted off into a comfortable sleep.

With their trip not scheduled until midmorning,

she treated herself to a bit of a lie-in. It was well past dawn when she got up and dressed, heading down the stairs with a spring in her step. She told herself it was because she was going to see Old Maggie, and maybe get some answers about what was going on around here… it had nothing to do with spending the day with Connor, with going on a ride with him and presumably stopping for lunch somewhere…

To her surprise, Thomas was waiting for her downstairs, a covered basket in his arms. He put it on the bar when she approached him, pushing it toward her. "Connor mentioned you're going to see Old Maggie? This is for her; if you don't mind taking it along."

"Sure," she said, a little surprised. "What is it?"

He grinned. "Shortbread. Her favorite. I got the recipe from Blair, up at the Keep — mine's not quite as good as hers, but it'll do in a pinch I think."

Karen took the bundle, smiling a little as she realized it was still warm. It smelled fragrant and delicious, and she quietly hoped Maggie might see her way clear to sharing a little of the gift with her guests.

"She helped me out a few weeks back," Thomas explained. "Had a terrible pain in my back — she gave me this miraculous ointment, told me to rub it in and lay flat on my back for a night, and in the morning, I was good as new. Magic," he said firmly.

"Sounds like it," Karen said diplomatically. To her mind, rubbing sore muscles then resting them sounded like a fairly non-magical cure for a condition like that… but she had a suspicion that a fair bit of Old Maggie's so-called magic relied on a combination of common sense and the placebo effect. And how could she criticize that? She used it herself fairly regularly — if patients felt that they were doing something that would help them, more often than not, it would help whether it had any actual medical impact.

Connor arrived shortly afterwards, and they tacked up their horses together, Connor showing her a way of tying the little bundle of shortbread onto the horse's saddle so she wouldn't have to carry it as they rode. He did the same for his own gift for Maggie — a bottle of some kind of dark liquid that sloshed back and forth when he showed it to her. Mead, he explained — a favorite of hers.

"Does everyone just — send Maggie gifts?"

"She's Fae," Connor said blankly, as though it was the most obvious thing in the world. "You don't visit Fae without a gift. Everyone knows that."

"Why not?" she asked as they set off, the horses' hooves clopping pleasantly against the cobblestones of the road that led out of town, before the sound was replaced by the duller thuds of the hooves against the dirt road.

"Bad luck," he said with a shrug. "It's … difficult to explain. I think the scholars have a better sense of it — Old Maggie explained it once. It's a kind of … system of favors and obligations they've got. You have to be careful around them. If you accept a gift — or even some help — without being careful about the wording, you can wind up owing them a debt that you'll never get clear of."

Karen shivered at that. It sounded an awful lot like her own student loans… albeit a slightly more magical version. "So, Maggie — what, is owed huge debts by the townsfolk?"

He grinned. "Not exactly. She doesn't play those games — not the same way the Fae do. But we tend to err on the side of caution regardless. Besides, it's only fair — she's helped us so much over the years, the least we can do is bring her things she likes. It's a good idea to stay on her good side."

They rode in pleasant quiet along the road, Karen gazing out over the placid waters of the

Loch. Connor glanced over at her as she stared at the waves, grinning a little.

"Looking for the Monster?"

"Maybe," she said a little defensively… then relented. "Yes. Of course, I am. The Loch Ness Monster's famous! I can't believe she's actually real."

"You're not likely to see her any time soon, I'm afraid. She's been a bit shy ever since a fisherman wounded her with iron a few months ago." He heaved a sigh. "Nasty business. She's an ally of ours — keeps a lot of the nasties that come through the Burgh from ever reaching our shores. Here we are," he added.

She started in surprise. There, on the other side of the road, was a little cottage, just clear of the treeline. An old oak tree in the front yard, a rickety porch with a rocking chair on it… yes, Karen thought with a chill running down her spine.

This looked just like a witch's cottage that was for sure.

CHAPTER 31

They tethered their horses to the tree out the front of the house, which had a low-hanging branch that seemed ideal for the purpose. Karen carefully untied the bundle of shortbread from the innkeeper, hoping it was still warm. They were almost up to the porch, Karen bracing herself to knock, when the door flew open, revealing the short-statured figure of Maggie grinning at them from her threshold.

"I'd heard I was to be expecting visitors," she said brightly, her eyes shining from her wrinkled face.

Suddenly, the apprehension Karen had been feeling vanished, replaced by a feeling of warmth and comfort. Why had she been so worried about visiting Maggie? She'd met her already — she was a friendly old woman who only wanted to help. Sure, she might have her quirks, too, but who didn't? Was this how Karen had been received by the villagers? she wondered. Were the reasons for their suspicions as simple as that?

"I've been wanting to talk to you," Maggie said, pointing one crooked finger straight at Karen in a way that made her feel a little uneasy. "To welcome you properly. We didn't have much of a chance to talk last week, did we?" Her beady eyes rested on the bundle in Karen's hands, and she started forward, smiling.

"These are from Thomas, the innkeeper," she explained, presenting them to Maggie. "He was telling me you helped heal his back?"

"Oh, that old fool," Maggie said dismissively, waving her hand. "No magic required at all, there. I gave him some oil and told him to lie still on a hard surface. His imagination did the rest."

Karen laughed, delighted that she'd correctly guessed the real nature of the cure. "The placebo effect! I had my suspicions."

Maggie's eyes were twinkling. "Maybe one in ten of the problems brought to me requires anything else," she said cheerfully. "But I'm pleased that word's getting around of my penchant for shortbread. Come in, you're both welcome." She liberated the bundle from Karen's hands, making an approving sound when she felt that it was still warm, then bustled inside with a vague gesture that indicated they should follow.

Connor grinned down at her when she hesitated, nudged her in the ribs and mouthed, "She likes you."

That was all the encouragement she needed — she took a deep breath, then stepped over the threshold of Maggie's cottage.

The first thing that struck her was how unbelievably crowded it was. It felt like an old furniture store, so cluttered with shelves and tables that she could barely find a path through the chaos... and every piece of furniture was absolutely jam-packed with decorations, or jars full of mysterious substances, or candles, or herbs, or miscellany... for Karen, who preferred a more minimalistic decor, the place was exhausting to even look at. She could feel Connor by her side, grinning down at her as she took the place in.

"Don't mind the mess," Maggie called cheerfully. She was bustling about, holding three mismatched glasses in one hand and a few plates in the other. There was a small table over by the hearth, surrounded by three squashed armchairs, and this seemed to be where they were being invited to sit down — obediently, she took the seat Maggie had offered her, feeling the warmth of the fireplace wash over her. It was strange — the place felt dark and close, but she didn't have any trouble seeing, even though the light through the windows was rather weak. How did Maggie move about so quickly without knocking everything over? Karen felt like she didn't even want to breathe, she was so worried about upsetting the careful balance of the little room.

"Is Darter about?" Connor asked, glancing sideways at Karen as though a little worried about her. "Karen hasn't met anyone… like him."

"He's asleep upstairs," Maggie said, her eyes twinkling thoughtfully as she fixed her gaze on Karen. "You'll meet another time, I'd warrant."

"Who's Darter?" Karen asked, glancing between them. "Another apprentice, like Kaitlyn?"

They both chuckled as though she'd said something funny. "Aye, in a way," Maggie said thoughtfully. "Though not very like Kaitlyn."

The glasses were all lined up, and Maggie pinned an expectant gaze on Connor, who grinned and pulled the bottle of mead out of his satchel. The old woman clasped her hands together, visibly pleased, and Karen couldn't help but blink — had Connor mentioned the gift? How had she known it was in his bag? But she decided against questioning it as Connor poured them each a generous helping, and they toasted each other before she sipped cautiously at the liquid. It was absolutely delicious — like spiced honey that sent a warming buzz right through her whole body. Maggie unwrapped the bundle of shortbread, too, inviting them to take some. Not the healthiest morning tea she'd ever had, she thought with a grin, but when in Rome...

"Now, how are those cows getting on?" Maggie asked briskly when they'd all had a piece of shortbread, as though bringing their little meeting to order.

"Just fine, Maggie," Connor said around a mouthful of shortbread. "You caught each and every one of the sick ones, and every check we've made of the rest of the herds has come up clean."

"Good," Maggie said with satisfaction. "You let me know once the pox have disappeared from the sick ones and I'll come up and see which ones can be returned to their herds without risk of reinfection."

"How do you do that?" Karen asked, curious despite herself. "How do you tell which ones are sick?"

"There's a knack to it," Maggie said briskly… and Karen got the sense that this particular piece of information wasn't one that Maggie was willing to share. "How about the other patients? How are they faring?"

Connor glanced at Karen, clearly deferring to her — that pleased her, and she finished her piece of shortbread as she sat forwards. "Not too badly," she said thoughtfully. "We've got five sick milkmaids altogether — the first three, obviously, with two more diagnosed more recently — and maybe ten cowherders, plus little Malcolm who caught it from his father. With the cattle quarantined we shouldn't see any more cases of animal-to-human transmission… that just leaves community transmission to worry about. That's cases spreading between people who haven't had contact with the cows," she added when Connor looked nonplussed — though Maggie seemed to be following the jargon just fine. "And of course, … we lost six of the patients."

Maggie tilted her head, a thoughtful look on her face. "Lost them?"

"The storm last week," Connor said heavily. "The six young men who were killed…"

"Ah, yes," Maggie said, an odd expression on her face. "An interesting event. You're saying all six had the pox?"

"That's right," Karen said, frowning a little. "We found it when we examined their bodies. Pox all over them — not just on their hands."

"Very strange indeed," Maggie said, and Karen could still see her mind working away over something — but somehow, she got the feeling that prying about it was a bad idea. If Maggie had something to share, she'd share it when she was ready and not a minute before. "Any idea what killed them?"

"That's what we were hoping to ask you about," Connor said. "I've asked the scholars at the castle, but no conclusive ideas."

"Well, I have a theory," Maggie said softly. "But I can guarantee you're not going to like it."

CHAPTER 32

Karen and Connor exchanged worried glances. The expression on Maggie's face was somber, and she even lowered the piece of shortbread she was halfway through.

"Something came through," she said softly. "A few weeks ago — the Monster told me about it, but I'd hoped it was just Karen here."

Karen's eyes widened. "The Monster — talks to you?"

"Aye, in her way," Maggie said, as though it was the most natural thing in the world.

A thousand more questions rose to Karen's mind — but Maggie seemed a little annoyed to have been interrupted, so she suppressed them, sitting back in her seat, and taking another steadying sip of the mead. It was so delicious… she made a note to find out where Connor had gotten it so she could think about getting hold of some for her own stores.

"She keeps an eye on the Burgh down there — eats up any small Unseelie creatures that sneak through and comes to fetch me when something more serious happens. She helped you to the surface, too," she added, giving Karen a beady-eyed stare. "Said you were fast asleep, though."

Karen stared. She'd been wondering how she got from the Burgh, which by all accounts was at the bottom of the Loch, to the grassy lake shore she'd woken up on. The idea that the Loch Ness Monster itself had carried her up to the surface was… well, wild, to say the least. "I should thank her," she said softly, glancing over at Connor. "I could take her a gift of fish, maybe?"

"Fish, or meat are good gifts for Nessie." He smiled and then turned back to Maggie, a more somber look on his face. "What came through?" Connor asked. "Did the Monster say?"

"She hadn't seen them before," Maggie said, shaking her head. "So, the image I got was confused. But I've got my theories. First — tell me exactly what you know about the attack."

"Two of the men were dragged from their beds through the windows of their houses," Connor explained. "The other four were out checking on the herds — it was as though something swooped down on them and carried them off."

"They were covered in wounds," Karen chimed in, wanting to help Maggie with as much information as possible. "Deep slashes, like claw marks from an animal, as well as the injuries associated with hitting the ground from a great height… and their expressions were terrified, too. I wouldn't have been surprised if they'd died of fright — some kind of cardiac event, not just the injuries and the fall itself." She hesitated, thinking of what she'd seen that night when she'd looked up into the clouds… the hot wind, the stinking smell in the air… "And I think I saw… I mean, I might have been imagining it, I'm not sure, but I swear I saw something like… wings, up in the clouds. Wings wrapped in shadows."

"A few of the villagers said the same thing," Connor said abruptly, leaning forward with a look of sharp interest in his gray eyes. "I thought they were imagining it — they're a susceptible lot, and what with all this talk of people being carried off… but you saw wings?"

"I think so," she said. "But it was hard to see… almost as though the clouds were casting shadows over them, or something." She looked at Maggie, who was taking all this in, quietly working her way through the shortbread. "Does that help at all?"

"It confirms a few suspicions, that's for sure," Maggie said heavily. "Have either of you ever heard of the Sluagh?"

Karen's face went blank. It wasn't a word she'd ever heard before, let alone a creature she recognized by name… but a shiver ran down her spine regardless at the heavy way Maggie spoke the word. Connor swore softly under his breath, and Maggie nodded grimly.

"What's a Sluagh?"

"Trouble," Maggie said flatly. "And hard to hit. They're incredibly fast and agile in the air… and those shadows they're cloaked in make them incredibly hard to hit. The Watch still has a stock of iron-tipped arrows, don't they?"

"Aye, stored at the castle. I've put in a request to have some distributed to the watch here in the village — might suggest that a few of the Keep's best archers come down as well, if it's Sluagh we're dealing with. Are you sure?" he added, frowning. "I thought they were drawn by war."

"They're drawn by misery in all its forms," Maggie said, shaking her head. "War's a common one… but there are no end of causes of despair."

Karen bit her lip, hoping someone was going to explain just what the hell a Sluagh was. It seemed serious, whatever it was — both Maggie and Connor looked utterly dismayed about whatever the creatures were, and she could tell by the tension in Connor's jaw that he was more worried now than he had been before hearing Maggie's theory. This was bad. "What's a Sluagh?" she tried again, feeling a little out of her depth.

"Of course. You don't know." Connor scrubbed at his face. "They're… well, Maggie, you know better than I do. I've never run into one face to face."

"I have," Maggie said flatly. "Nasty creatures. Some of the worst among the Unseelie… and the enormous flocks they travel in don't help. No wonder the Monster had trouble telling me what she'd seen — those shadows are hard to see through at the best of times. You did well to make out wings," she added, giving Karen a nod. "When you get hold of one, they look like a cross between a rotting corpse and a raven. Great big wings with the feathers falling off them in chunks, flesh that stinks like it's been in the sun for days, more bone visible than skin... ugly creatures, and spiteful. They ride the west wind, and they're ruthless when it comes to hunting."

She shivered, not liking the image this was summoning. "They pull people out of their beds?"

"Aye, if their quarry is abed, they'll burst in through a west window and carry him away," Maggie said heavily. "That's what happened to those young men, I'd warrant."

"Why those six?" Connor wanted to know, leaning forward. "Why did they take those men and nobody else?"

"They're drawn to despair and misery," she said, frowning. "Plague victims, the sick and dying, usually."

Karen's eyes widened. "The pox. Could it be the cowpox that attracted them?"

"I suppose so," Maggie said, but there was something oddly hesitant in her face... and Karen made the connection soon enough.

"But why didn't they take everyone with the pox?" she said softly, half to herself. She thought of Mary, for some reason — the poor girl had far more lesions than any of the men who'd been taken, and she seemed a great deal more despairing than they were. If the Sluagh were drawn to despair, why hadn't they taken the girl as well?

"Much more to learn," Maggie said, frankly. "But what you need to know is that the only thing that kills Sluagh is iron, fire or sunlight. Once you're chosen as their victim, they'll hunt you until dawn… or until you name someone else to die in your place. They'll carry you aloft, drain the life from you, then drop you."

Karen shook her head, thinking of the looks of utter horror on the faces of the men. Just as she'd suspected — they'd been dead before they'd hit the ground, the life drained out of them by these monsters.

The rest of their morning tea passed in somber silence, and Karen felt thoroughly shaken when Maggie showed them to the door. She'd hoped that talking to Maggie about what was attacking them would help… but more information hadn't helped. It had only made her feel more powerless, more afraid… and more confused about what exactly was going on.

CHAPTER 33

"Well," Connor said, breaking a long silence. They were riding their horses aimlessly back toward town, though she wasn't exactly looking forward to getting back. "At least we've got a bit more of an idea of what we're dealing with."

"But no way to fight it," Karen said heavily. "What if those creatures come back tonight? What are we going to do to keep the villagers safe?"

"Tell them to stay inside and bar their west-facing windows," Connor said with a grim shake of his head. "Especially the ones with pox. We ought to visit the sick on our way back."

It felt good to have something to do, at least. They rode up the hill to where Anne and Rhianne lived — both the girls were asleep, but they gave their mother the warning to keep the west windows shut. Karen was a little hesitant about explaining why, but Connor didn't flinch from explaining that they had a theory that a supernatural creature that rode the west wind had been responsible for the deaths of the young men a week earlier. Anne and Rhianne's mother listened wide-eyed, and before they'd even finished, she was bolting her western windows shut, shaking her head in dismay.

They visited Mary's house again, too — as before, Mary was refusing all visitors, but they passed the message on to Cameron and his mother. The boy, undaunted, brandished a butter knife and told them that if anything came for his sister, it would have him to deal with. They visited the more recently infected milkmaids, too, and the herdsmen who remained — which left only Rosemary and her son Malcolm. For that particular visit, Karen waited outside the fence, feeling strange. It seemed the villagers were clumping together more as they passed her, shooting suspicious glances over their shoulders at her. She sighed. She'd hoped that keeping to herself and staying out of the villagers' way would help them realize she wasn't any kind of threat... but it seemed that suspicions of her were only growing.

Was there any way to prove she wasn't a witch, she wondered as Connor headed back out to meet her? Could she publicly bathe in holy water, perhaps? Wear a silver cross around her neck to prove it didn't melt or bubble her skin? How did a person go about proving that they weren't a witch, anyway? Wasn't the whole point of witches that they were hard to spot? She sighed, leaving the thought alone. No use dwelling on something she couldn't change. Like her mother had always said — what other people thought of her was none of her business.

But it rapidly became her business when they reached the inn. It was late afternoon, and she could tell from the street that the inn was packed and busy — but there was something strange going on. Many of the patrons seemed to have congre-gated by the windows and were peering out at the street as though waiting for something to happen. She frowned, glancing up at Connor, who also looked nonplussed.

But that wasn't all. Thomas was waiting outside the inn, his arms folded and a tight look on his face — some mix between embarrassment and annoyance. And she realized with a shock that the wooden crate at his feet contained the clothes she'd packed carefully away in her room — she recognized the fabric of a dress she hadn't gotten around to wearing yet, a gift from Connor. Why were her things out here on the ground outside the inn? And what did Thomas want from her? She had a horrible suspicion she knew what was about to happen...

"Good afternoon, Thomas," she said, narrowing her eyes suspiciously. "Is everything okay?"

"It's not, I'm afraid," Thomas said heavily, glancing behind him to the patrons in the windows — all of whom did a poor job of pretending that they weren't trying to listen to this conversation. "It's the townsfolk. They're not happy about you staying here."

"What do you mean?" she asked, trying to keep her voice level although she could feel anger singing in her blood.

Thomas shook his head. "You know as well as I do that there's — suspicion raging about your connection to the pox going around... and to those poor young men's deaths."

"Thomas, what are you suggesting?" That was

Connor at her side, anger in his voice — but above all, he looked shocked.

Thomas spread his hands, and she could tell he was conflicted. This wasn't something he wanted to do, she realized. This was something he'd been strong-armed into — by who? By his clientele?

"You know I don't believe it," he said in a low voice, clearly not wanting the listeners to hear this part. "I know you're no witch. But — I can't afford to have my patrons abandon me. And they won't be comfortable here while you're upstairs — not until you can clear your name, at any rate."

"And how am I meant to do that?" she snapped, feeling anger flaring to life in her chest. "Just how am I supposed to prove a negative? That I'm not a witch?"

"I don't know," Thomas said, shaking his head regretfully. "But you're no longer welcome in this establishment," he added firmly, raising his voice so they'd hear him inside — she scowled as a raucous cheer went up inside the building.

"Great," she snapped. "I do everything I can to help slow the spread of this disease, to teach you what I know about it — and I'm called a witch?"

"They don't think you're a witch, they're just — scared," Thomas said with a grimace.

Connor was shaking with anger at her side, and she put a hand on his arm as he started forward, clearly about to give the innkeeper a piece of his mind.

"Connor — don't. Thomas is right. They're just scared. And making a fuss is only going to scare them more," she said, fighting her own fury. "We should just — go. I don't want them thinking I've bewitched you," she added with a roll of her eyes.

And with that, they turned and walked away from the inn, leaving an apologetic Thomas and a leering, booing crowd behind them. Connor was carrying her box full of clothing for her, and she could see from the whiteness of his knuckles on the box that he was gripping it hard enough to hurt. Still angry with Thomas… and she couldn't bring herself to talk him down from that anger, either. As much empathy as she might try to exercise for the villagers, grieving and frightened, the injustice of it all was what was most frustrating. She hadn't done anything wrong… she'd been trying to help… and what, they were going to run her out of town?

"Where am I going to stay?" she asked blankly, staring around the streets of the village, which felt curiously deserted. Was everyone at the inn, celebrating her expulsion from it? A flare of anger struck at that thought… her frustration was getting worse and worse. And Connor looked angry, too, shaking his head.

"That coward," he said in a low voice.

"I mean… he was letting me stay for free," she pointed out, trying to be reasonable, though part of her was secretly thrilled that he was so angry on her behalf. "It wasn't like I was a paying customer."

"Stay with me," he said abruptly, his gray eyes fierce. "I've a cottage all to myself here in town, you'll be more than welcome there."

CHAPTER 34

K aren looked up at him, a little surprised by the offer. She'd gotten the idea that he was a little worried about the village gossips when it came to the amount of time they spent together... whatever would they say if she stayed with him? "Aren't you worried about what people might say?"

"Aye, I used to worry about that," he said, his jaw tight with anger. "But now I don't give a toss what they think. Bunch of utter fools, spurning the woman who's trying to help them..." He hesitated. "But if you're not comfortable with that, Karen... we can ride straight up to the castle now. They've always got spare quarters somewhere — you'd have your own space."

She cleared her throat, feeling a pang of sadness at the idea of being so far away from him. "I kind of need to be in the village," she said quickly, telling herself that what she was saying was true, that she wasn't just trying to come up with excuses that would let her stay with him, alone, in his cottage, where his bed was… "If I'm going to keep an eye on the epidemic…"

"Aye, that's true," he said, looking at her with unmistakable hope in his eyes. "I mean, I know it's not ideal, but I'm a reasonably tidy man. You won't be picking up after me if that's what you're worried about. And it's only for a short time — until Thomas sees sense, or I beat some into him," he added darkly, shooting a glance back over his shoulder toward the inn.

"If you don't mind," she said softly, shrugging a little helplessly. "I'd love to stay with you, Connor."

"Then it's settled." He smiled at her, the anger and frustration still clear on his face — but then he offered her his arm and she took it, feeling a little thrill run down her spine at the heat of his body. They walked together through the streets in pleasant silence, and he soon stopped at the door to a quaint little cottage like many of the others, if a little more run-down looking. There was a little stone path that led to the door and the front yard was neatly kept.

"It's not much," he said with a shrug. "An old man lived here for the longest time — I'd just moved to a permanent position in the Watch here in town when he passed away, and his family were happy for me to take the place over."

It was a tiny little cottage, feeling somehow even more crowded than Maggie's despite there being far less furniture… but it was cozy, and she was grateful to have a place to stay. He cleared out space in a drawer for her to store her clothes and showed her to the bedroom, where she hesitated before he leapt to assure her that he'd be sleeping on the floor and she'd be taking the bed. She protested — but he was adamant. A treacherous part of her remarked that there was a much easier solution that wouldn't leave either of them with a bad back from sleeping on the cold ground… but she shushed it firmly, her heart pounding. Being alone with him was one thing… being alone with him in the privacy of his cottage was quite another.

"I tell you what," he said once she'd put her things away. They were standing in the cozy little main room, Connor knelt by the fire and coaxing it to life. The afternoon had come over chilly, and she appreciated the warmth of the fire.

"What?"

"I could use a drink after all that," he said with his gray eyes twinkling, reaching into a basket beside the fire and withdrawing a bottle that looked just like the one they'd taken as a gift to Maggie. Her eyes widened.

"God, me too," she breathed.

He grinned at her, handing the bottle to her as he settled into a chair by the fire. She sat beside him and they passed the bottle back and forth, warming themselves with sips of spicy mead and the flickering warmth of the little fire. As frustrated and exhausted as she was from the conflict outside the inn, part of her was absolutely thrilled with how this had turned out. Now she had even more excuses to see him, to talk to him, to spend long evenings together… and she could tell by the sidelong looks he was shooting her that he felt the same way.

"I suppose I should figure out my own place at some point," she said softly, her mind drifting away toward the future. "As well as something to do with myself…"

"You plan to stay in town?" he asked, glancing over at her.

She nodded, then shrugged her shoulders. "I mean, it's not as though I know where else to go," she admitted. "And as frustrating as it is that everyone thinks I'm a witch… they're wrong, and they'll see that sooner rather than later. I'm not going to leave town just because they've made such a stupid mistake. That would be letting them win. Besides, it's pretty clear this town's in bad need of a doctor."

He tilted his head, looking curious, a smile dancing across his lips. "You're a remarkable woman, Karen Frakes."

"Is that so?" She forced herself to make eye contact despite how hard her heart was pounding. The mead was helping, making her feel more brave…

He nodded, not looking away. "Aye, it is. These villagers have been hostile, ignorant cowards… and you're still thinking about how you're going to help them once they've gotten over their own stupidity. Plenty of other people would have just left… myself included. You're inspiring."

She blushed, feeling a little embarrassed by the warmth of his gaze. "Well, I swore an oath," she murmured, thinking back to her med school days. "I mean, I didn't officially swear it, but… doctors are meant to help. That's our whole job — the whole reason we exist, why we do what we do, is to help people. We don't do it for acclaim, or gratitude, or money…" She sighed. "Lord knows med school's the most expensive thing I've ever done. I'd have gone to business school if I'd wanted to make money. No, I want to help. And sometimes helping means being patient with people who don't understand the nature of that help."

He smiled, something clearly occurring to him. "That's exactly how I feel about my own work — the Clan's work."

"What do you mean?" She turned to him, a little surprised by the comparison, and he leaned forward to explain.

"We do what we do to protect the people of the village, right? It's about keeping them safe from the creatures on the other side of the Burgh. Half the time they don't even know how close those beasties came to harming or killing them or someone they loved… and they grumble and complain about us riding around town, taking up space, bossing them around… but we protect them because it's our sworn duty, not because we need their praise. Or even their approval."

"I hear that," she said softly with a smile. "You know, in my time we've all but eradicated a lot of very serious diseases? All you need is a tiny little injection when you're little, and you'll never get polio, or whooping cough, or measles... But there's a group of people who've decided that that injection is evil, and that doctors are lying to them about how important it is, and they refuse to get it done. They'd rather have polio."

"That's absurd," he said, shaking his head. "But not surprising."

"No?"

"I mean, look at how these people are responding to you." He sighed, shaking his head. "I suppose five hundred years isn't long enough to change people."

They sat in gloomy silence for a long time, gazing into the fire. As much as Karen was warmed by Connor's sympathy and understanding, she couldn't help but feel pretty dejected and miserable about the whole situation. It was difficult enough dealing with what faced them... now they had to contend with hostile villagers, too?

CHAPTER 35

They kept chatting as the afternoon wore on, and she felt her spirits begin to lift despite her dejection. Connor was just such pleasant company… and the mead was helping, too, easing the anxiety she usually felt around him and loosening her tongue. They found themselves talking about love and romance — she was a little embarrassed to admit how few stories she had to tell.

"Truly? Nobody serious? A woman like you wasn't snapped up by some lucky man the minute he met you?"

Connor's cheeks were flushed, and his hair had come down a little and was falling in his handsome face — he looked so gorgeously disheveled that she could barely bring herself to look at him for fear of what her face might give away.

"I never had time," she protested with a laugh, waving a hand. "I mean, I went on dates here and there, had a few reasonably long-term relationships… but never much longer than a year. I mean, it's hard to date a doctor who travels all the time. I was always stressed and exhausted from work or traveling all over the country for internships or placements or study programs… and by the time I got my current position, well." She sighed, taking another sip of mead, and discovering to her surprise that the bottle was nearly empty. Had they really finished the whole thing between them? "Married to the job, I guess," she concluded heavily. "What about you? What's your excuse?"

"What excuse do I need to live the romantic life of a bachelor?" he countered her, gesturing around his little cottage in an imperious way that made her giggle. But his smile faded a little and he shrugged his shoulders, suddenly looking a little solemn. "I'll admit, Karen, I used to be a bit of a cad. I don't know if you've heard stories, but as a young man I was always chasing women."

"And catching them, so I've heard," she said before she could stop herself.

He raised an eyebrow at her, and she lowered her gaze, a little embarrassed.

"Am I wrong?"

"Didn't know you'd been investigating me so thoroughly," he said, but his voice was amused and not annoyed so she let herself relax. "Anyone would think you had an ulterior motive."

"Would they now?" she challenged him, looking straight back at him. And maybe it was the mead loosening her inhibitions, or just the force of the built-up anticipation of the weeks they'd spend with each other, but suddenly, looking in his eyes, she knew that he wanted her exactly as much as she wanted him... and it felt utterly ridiculous that neither of them had acted on it yet. So, before she could stop herself, or hesitate, or overthink it, she leaned over and closed the space between them, sealing their lips together in a kiss.

She could sense how shocked he was in the way he seemed to freeze when she kissed him, and for a long, frightening moment she was convinced she'd misread things catastrophically. What if he wasn't interested at all? What if this was a terrible mistake — what if she were about to make thing horrendously awkward for them both? She'd have to leave, she thought dizzily — have to move to another

village and forget that any of this had happened…
but then, giving her a sense of relief stronger than
she'd ever felt before, she felt his hand come up to
cup the back of her neck and pull her closer to him,
his other hand on her shoulder as he deepened the
kiss, his lips somehow rough and soft and exactly
what she needed. They kissed for what felt like
hours before he broke away, his hand still on her
neck, and she could feel his breath hot and
scorching against her lips and her whole body
vibrating with delight at what had finally, finally
happened —

"I've been wanting to do that since we met," he
said softly, his voice hoarse in the quiet atmosphere
of the cottage.

She felt a smile break out across her face. "Me
too," she admitted, hearing her own voice tremble a
little with the force of what she was holding back. "I
thought — I don't know. I thought you were just
being polite."

He laughed breathlessly, then pulled her to him.
"I suppose I'd best stop being so polite, then," he
growled, sending lightning shooting down her spine
— and then he was kissing her again, and somehow
they found their way out of the chairs and onto the
floor in front of the fire, where somehow he'd

managed to spread out his cloak to protect them from the cold floor.

It felt unbelievably good to be in his arms like this, to have his body pressed up against hers… she sighed with pleasure as he held her close, laying her down on the cloak and pressing himself down against her as they kissed.

Without even realizing it, she felt her hands moving as though they had a life of their own, stealing across his back, across his chest, unfastening the clothing he was wearing — needing little encouragement, he reached up to help her, and it wasn't long before she'd successfully disrobed him. Looking up at him was… overwhelming. He smiled down at her, his hair loose from its restraints, his gray eyes shining… she ran her hands tentatively across his shoulders, the broad muscles of his back, his powerful chest, his muscular torso…

Then they were kissing again, more urgently than before, and any shyness she might have felt was banished by the warm buzz of the mead and the overwhelming knowledge that she trusted this man more than many others she'd met. He moved slowly and carefully, never pressing any boundary she even hinted at, not pushing her to do anything she didn't volunteer to do… and it wasn't long before she sat up, impatient with how gentlemanly he was being, and ripped off the tunic she was wearing, baring her body before him. He gazed at her for a long moment, the firelight flickering from their skin — and then he was on top of her again, his hands roaming, his lips against hers, then breaking away to kiss her throat, her chest, to take her nipples into his mouth and send lightning waves of pleasure shooting down her body...

Clothes were ridiculous, she decided as she kicked her boots off and struggled with her pants. Why did anyone bother with them? They just got in the way... held her back from what she really wanted, which was Connor's hands all over her. She felt like she'd been holding herself back for a thousand years, and now that he was finally here, finally as close to her as she wanted him, she could barely restrain herself, impatiently dragging at his clothes until they were both as naked as they day they were born. His arms around her, his lips on her throat... her whole body thrilled to his touch, and when his hand slid down her hip and curled around to her sex, it was all she could do not to groan at the gentle, careful way he teased her lips apart and began to pleasure her...

It was too much — she couldn't wait for him,

not for another second. She took his ear in her mouth and nibbled at the sensitive lobe, drawing a choked-off moan from him as she reached down with one hand to grasp his manhood firmly, to whisper a plea in his ear that he was all too happy to oblige. Before she knew it, she felt him slide himself inside her and her eyes rolled back in her head with how good it felt, how utterly indulgent the sensation was of him inside her...

So, the afternoon wore on as they explored each other, finally giving way to what both of them had wanted since they'd met. And when she finally drifted off into an exhausted post-coital nap, she felt at peace for perhaps the first time since she'd gotten here.

CHAPTER 36

She woke up feeling disoriented. There was a loud knocking that had pulled her from her sleep… but something was strange. This wasn't her little room at the inn… it was too big, and the fireplace was too close… and what was more, there were arms around her, a sleeping form in the bed beside her… wait, not the bed. She was lying on the floor, wrapped in a cloak and the arms of a sleeping man… and someone was trying to beat the door down. Karen sat up blearily as the last few hours returned to her, feeling her mind slowly surfacing from a deep, hypnotic sleep. She smiled a little as she looked at Connor, the memory of their lovemaking not far from her mind… but frowned as the knocking recommenced, louder this time and accompanied by angry shouts.

"What's going on?" Connor said blearily as he sat up, looking absolutely magnificent with the cloak around his waist and the low light of the dying fire dancing from his muscles. God, this was a view she could get used to… even the knocking at the door wasn't enough to distract her from his physique. She was just about to reach out for him when he got to his feet, an irritated expression on his face as he reached for his pants and hauled them over his sleek, muscular legs. A dreadful shame, she thought idly, pulling the cloak up around herself to protect herself from the chilly late afternoon air.

"Who's at the door?" she said, curious but too lazy and sleepy to worry about getting up. He shook his head, frowning as he padded over to the door barefoot and slammed it open. From her vantage point on the floor she could see a little way out the door over Connor's shoulder, but his body should block her from being seen by whoever it was.

"What the hell do you want?" he demanded, voice low and gruff. There was a murmur of sound outside, and Karen's eyes widened as she craned her neck to try to see what was going on. It seemed for all the world like an angry mob had come to the door — she could hear them shouting, and worry began to gnaw at her. They knew she was here, it seemed — that made sense. They'd walked through the streets together, and it was no secret that she and Connor had been getting close over the last few weeks… it made sense that she'd be taking shelter here. But they'd driven her from the inn, she thought with mounting frustration. Where had they expected her to go?

Were they trying to get her kicked out of town altogether? That seemed likelier and likelier as she heard the shouting grow louder. Despair began to sink into her stomach, reawakening the anger that had been so pleasantly quashed by her time with Connor by the fire… they seriously believed she was a witch? They wanted her gone?

A familiar voice rose above the crowd, and it was all she could do not to surge to her feet and spring out there to give the crowd a piece of her mind. Why, that was Rosemary, William's widow — the woman with a sick child, the woman who should be grateful to have a doctor in the village, not calling for her removal. Seething, Karen moved a little closer to the door, careful to stay out of view of the crowd outside, trying to get a better sense of what was going on. Connor had stepped through the door and closed it behind him, but she was able to peer through a window, staying hidden while getting a good vantage on the confrontation.

Connor looked terrifying. He stood there, half-naked, the late afternoon sun dancing off his muscular physique. In one hand he held a sword — she hadn't even seen him pick it up. It was still in its sheath, held easily at his side, but the message was clear — he was more than willing to defend himself, and her, if he needed to. That sent a surge of warmth through her, his protectiveness. She'd always been the kind of woman who protected herself, but having Connor on her side, in her corner, ready to fight for her... there was something about that that made her feel a way she'd never felt before.

"What exactly do you want?" he demanded of Rosemary, who'd stepped to the front of the group. Still clad all in black, still looking haggard, the woman lifted her chin, pinning her furious gaze on Connor. Some people's grief turned to despair, Karen reflected sadly, thinking back on the families she'd had to break bad news to... and some people's grief turned to anger. Rosemary seemed to be of the latter category. She was channeling her loss, the sadness about her husband's death, into attacking an innocent person. Knowing that went some way to stilling Karen's anger, transforming it into pity… though it was still frustrating to be disturbed like this for no good reason, especially when she'd finally gotten her hands on that gorgeous man out there…

"It's perfectly simple, Connor Grant," Rosemary snapped, her voice authoritative even though it shook a little. "We have reasonable suspicion that there is a witch living amongst us. We want you to tell us where it is, so we might hold it for trial."

"It? Her name is Karen," he snarled, and Karen saw Rosemary recoil at the fury on his face. "And she's done more for this village, to protect it and keep it safe, than you have in your entire miserable life —"

"Maybe she has," Rosemary said firmly, cutting him off. "And maybe she's the cause of the problems she's pretending to help us fix, did you think of that? The pox was nowhere near this bad until she turned up." The villagers murmured their angry agreement — to Karen's dismay, she saw a few among them with lesions on their hands and arms. She just hoped they hadn't been stupid enough to touch one another on this daft mission of theirs.

"That's a coincidence," Connor said through gritted teeth. "I'm not telling you where she is so you can conduct some farcical trial, that's for certain."

"She'll have to answer for her crimes eventually," Rosemary said, her voice low and deadly.

"Look," Connor said, clearly frustrated. He ran the hand not holding his sword through his hair, pushing it out of his face. "You're all being utter fools. I understand you're grieving, and I'm with you there. I knew those boys — their deaths were a great shame. But that doesn't give you the right to hassle an innocent woman who's helping us."

"If she's innocent, let her prove it," Rosemary snapped. "Bring her to the church yourself, if you don't trust us to convey her there safely." There was an ugly jeer from the crowd at this point that made it pretty clear that that lack of trust was entirely justified.

"The church? Father Caleb's involved with all of this?"

"Who better to test a witch?" Rosemary replied smugly, her eyes gleaming.

But Connor was nodding. "And if Father Caleb clears Karen of witchcraft, you'll all agree to leave her alone?"

"Of course."

"Fine," he said, gritting his teeth. "That's fine.

You all go back to your homes, and I'll bring Karen up to the church later this evening and we'll figure out some way to put your daft minds at ease. Alright?"

Rosemary gave a stiff little nod, and the crowed, at her signal, began to disperse. Connor stood in the front yard until they'd gone, shaking his head, before he came back inside and shut the door. Karen went to him and he took her into his arms, holding her close.

"Damn fools," he muttered into her throat.

She nodded. "Thanks for sticking up for me."

"Of course," he said blankly.

She smiled and kissed him… but she felt as troubled as he looked. Clearly, the villagers were unhappy with her being here. Tensions were coming to a boiling point… what were they going to do?

CHAPTER 37

For now, it seemed, they were going to go back to bed. She'd only intended their kiss to be brief, but he was just so magnetic, and it wasn't long until they were entwined in a passionate embrace again, Connor's powerful arms around her waist, drawing her close… the cloak fell to the ground between them and she shivered in the cool air, leaning into him, instinctively seeking the comfort of his body in the wake of the uncertainty and chaos of everything that was happening, the literal angry mob that had come to his door to drag her off to be tested for witchcraft…

But she couldn't think about any of that with his hands on her body, his lips against hers, crushing her to him as their kiss deepened. She could feel his passion stirring, feel his manhood hard against her body, and she shivered with desire, feeling her own body respond in some deep, instinctive way she barely understood but knew well enough to follow… and then she gasped as he lifted her in his arms, effortlessly powerful, and carried her toward his bed.

Connor half threw, half placed her onto the bed, and she giggled as she sank into the quilts, grinning as he hurled himself down on top of her and renewed kissing her with considerable vigor. They lost themselves in one another again, using their hands and mouths to coax pleasure from one another — she grew bolder as the afternoon gave way to early evening, pressing him back against the bed and straddling him, her hands flattened against his broad, muscular chest as she sat back to contemplate the gorgeous man spread out beneath her. His hands were resting on her hips, caressing her, sending shivers of pleasure up and down her body as he rocked his hips, urging her to do what they both so clearly wanted… and with a grin, she slid herself down on top of him, impaling herself on his manhood and gasping at the new sensation.

In this position, the angle was even better, and she rocked her hips experimentally, groaning at the feeling of him inside her… and surprising even him with how good it felt to move together. It wasn't long before he was utterly lost, groaning as he bucked his hips furiously, trying to get more sensation, to drive himself deeper and deeper into her… and she moaned as she felt her own climax drawing closer, supporting herself with her palms flattened against his chest, rocking her hips back and forth to coax every inch of pleasure from him…

She was on the edge before she knew it, but there was no need to hold herself back, to wait for him — he was groaning as his own climax neared, clearly fighting to hold himself back, to wait for her, and she had to fight back a scream as she let her orgasm crash over her like a great wave, aftershocks of pleasure rocketing through her as her lover groaned beneath her, his hands clutching desperately at her hips as his own climax struck him.

Karen all but fell into bed beside him and he gathered her closer to him, pressing soft kisses to the side of her head as their breathing settled. Connor pulled the quilt over them both and they lay close, their bodies still damp with perspiration. He smelled utterly intoxicating... that powerful, masculine musk, something deep and powerful about it, something that made her just want to kiss him over and over and never leave the warmth of his embrace...

They lay there in that twilight a long time before the real world came creeping back into her memory, and she sighed heavily, drawing a puzzled look from him. His eyes had been sliding shut as he drifted off into a half-sleep, but he propped himself up on one elbow now, looking down at her thoughtfully.

"What's the matter?"

"The villagers think I'm a witch."

"Well, you've certainly cast a spell on me," he murmured huskily, and she couldn't help but laugh as she looked up at him. "It's true," he said softly. "I've never felt this way about another woman, Karen Frakes."

"Neither have I," she said, weakened by that smile, by the afterglow of their lovemaking, by the scent of him. "And I've never..." She was blushing, but she fought to keep speaking, that dazzling smile of his keeping her going. "I've never had sex this good in my life."

He laughed, pulling her into his arms and

hugging her tightly, and she giggled too, feeling utterly euphoric. "Can I stay here?" she said breathlessly, not caring if it was too much, too soon, too ridiculous. "Can I —"

"I never want you to leave," he murmured, squeezing her before looking her meaningfully in the eye, his face alive with feeling. "I want you to stay with me as long as you want. Forever, if you want to."

She ducked her head, a little overwhelmed, and they lay together for a long time, her head pillowed on his chest and his arm around her shoulders. She could have laid there forever, it felt like… but her memory of what the villagers had said kept creeping in around the edges of her bliss, and eventually she sighed, sitting up in bed despite his protests and attempts to pull her back into his arms.

"We have an important appointment," she said heavily, reaching down to push that beautiful hair of his out of his face.

He scowled. "With a bunch of fools."

"The sooner I prove I'm not a witch, the sooner we can get back to figuring out what's happening around here. The more they'll trust me to stop them from getting sick. The more likely I might be to have a future as a doctor here," she added, shaking his shoulder a little. "Come on, Connor. Father Caleb's alright, isn't he?"

"I suppose," Connor said grumpily, still not looking thrilled at the idea. "He'll be fair, at least."

"We'll go to him now, find out what I need to do to prove my innocence… then we'll come back to bed. Deal?"

"If we must," Connor said heavily, dragging himself reluctantly out of bed with an expression so dejected she couldn't help but laugh.

Despite the fact that she was getting dressed and ready to go up to a literal witch trial, she couldn't help but feel utter joy in her chest. She wanted to sing, to dance, to scream her joy to the rooftops. She'd wanted him for so long… and he wanted her too. Not just for sex — forever, he'd said. And even though she'd only known him for a few weeks, something about that didn't feel overwhelming, or like it was too much commitment too soon. Something about it just felt… right.

She smiled to herself as she finished dressing. He was ready and waiting for her by the door, his hair pulled back in its usual neat tie, his expression a mixture of annoyance at having to go out… and delight at the way she reached out to take his hand in hers. They set out together into the gathering dusk, hand in hand, and Karen knew that no matter what the villagers might have in store for her — no matter what kind of ridiculous trial they might expect her to go through to prove that she wasn't a witch — she could face whatever it was a hundred times over if she had Connor at her side.

CHAPTER 38

T he late afternoon sun made the village glow warmly in that golden-hour way that Karen was getting more and more fond of. It might have been the leftover sex endorphins, it might have been the giddy rush still lingering from their respective confessions of their feelings, or it might have just been that she felt good after a nap… but somehow, Karen couldn't bring herself to worry too much about just where it was they were headed. A witch trial… or something like it. But what did she have to fear? She wasn't a witch — that ought to be easy enough to prove. These people were scared, they weren't malicious — she'd done nothing to anger any of them except know a few more things than they did and turn up at a time when a lot of strange and frightening things were going on. She'd find a way to convince them she was a friend, not a threat. And quietly, she looked forward to receiving a few sincere apologies once they figured out who their friends really were.

Connor was stony-faced as they approached the church, where torches were already burning in anticipation of the coming night. Dozens of villagers were there — not quite as many as the meeting the other night, but enough to send a prickle of unease running down her spine. Were this many villagers really convinced she was a witch — or at the very least, interested in seeing the proof to the contrary? What proof was she going to have to offer? She remembered reading about a witch trial that had been favored a long time ago... women would be bound and thrown into a body of water. If they floated, they were witches, and would be burned — if they sank, they were innocent, but of course, they'd drown, so it was something of a hollow victory. What if they threw her into the Loch with her hands bound? Would the Loch Ness Monster save her again? She almost laughed at that mental image. What result did that indicate, on the witch test?

She noticed that while many villagers who'd

been peering at her through the inn's windows were present, Thomas was not. She wasn't sure how to take that. He'd seemed fairly sympathetic to her — had offered her free room and board until the pressure from the village got to be too much for him to handle. Did his absence mean he supported her? Or was he just feeling too guilty for casting her out to be here? She frowned to herself. He'd been happy enough to accept the work of 'witches' when he'd accepted Maggie's cure — even though Maggie herself had admitted there was nothing magic about it, he hadn't known that. It was frustrating, how willing the villagers were to accept 'magic' when it suited them... but when it came to something they didn't understand...

She headed up to the front of the church, reasoning that if she were the reason for the meeting, she may as well get up where everyone could see her. Father Caleb gave her a wan little smile, clearly deeply uncomfortable with what was going on here. Was he on her side? she wondered. It would be a relief to have an ally in the priest... and he'd certainly shown no signs that he distrusted her in any way. Maybe she could just splash some holy water on her face in full view of everybody and be done with it... would wearing a crucifix help? She made a point of standing close to the huge cross that stood at the back of the church, hoping that her proximity to it might put some minds at ease. See, she wanted to say? No sizzling skin. Now can we stop wasting everyone's time when there's an epidemic afoot and monstrous creatures hunting us in the night?

The village leaders were seated in the front row — she recognized a few of them from having spoken at the meeting a few nights previous. They were stony faced when they looked at her, the whole council, and she sighed, irritated despite herself. Was it their fault that this was happening, or were they simply responding to the demands of their people? Rosemary was sitting in the row behind them, her face set with determination, and Karen suppressed the flare of irritation that went up in her chest when she looked at her. She had to remind herself that grief could make people act out in strange ways... and this woman had just lost her husband.

"Right then," Father Caleb said from the pulpit, raising his voice a little anxiously. "Now, I understand we've all called this — this uh, impromptu meeting, I suppose — to discuss some troubling accusations that have been made."

"Baseless accusations," Connor cut in, his voice snapping and bristling with anger. A murmur went up among the assembled villagers, all of them exchanging glances, and Karen bit her lip, reaching out to put a steadying hand on Connor's arm. She hoped he didn't make too much of a point of defending her. The harder he fought the idea that she was a witch, she knew, the more strongly inclined the villagers would be to believe he was ensorcelled by her, that she was controlling him in the interests of protecting her. The best approach, she decided, was to treat the accusation as though it was ridiculous and easily dismissed. Which was why she smiled as she stepped up beside Father Caleb, giving the room a reassuring little nod as he continued.

"Karen is new to us, a — a guest in our town, from quite some distance away. Obviously, none of us want to accuse her of any wrongdoing," he said firmly, giving the villagers a warning glance. "But in the interests of ruling out the possibility that some of these… these awful events that have been tran-spiring lately… might be linked to her, with or without her knowledge…"

She wanted to reach out to squeeze Connor's hand — he looked like he was about to explode with rage. As much as she appreciated him sticking up for her, she couldn't help but worry that he wasn't helping the cause much…

"This matter was brought to me early this afternoon," Father Caleb said firmly. "I take my role as spiritual leader here very seriously, and I've been reflecting and praying on the best way to proceed, to thoroughly clear our guest of any suspicion so that we might continue our fight against the real issues that trouble us." He was being very diplomatic, and she appreciated it — appreciated the implication that this was a clearing of her name, not a trial. "So, I'd like to propose a method of clearing Karen's name of any wrongdoing. The first step is having her set foot in a church — as we all know, the Lord hates evil, and it cannot bear to be in his presence. So —" He gestured to her, and she felt a bizarre urge to take a bow. Here she was, standing in a church. Strike one for the witch theory.

"And furthermore," he continued, gaining confidence as he saw a few of the villagers nodding their approval of this first step of the plan, "Karen will be invited to take communion, go through confession, and be interviewed here by myself and a member of the Watch."

"Best choose someone other than Connor," Rosemary called out, her eyes burning. "If she's a witch, she's gotten to him already."

Connor started forward, his eyes blazing, but Father Caleb cleared his throat hard, raising a hand for silence — Karen was grateful to see her lover gain control of himself, though she could see the tension emphasized by every line of his body.

"I've asked Captain Brendan to conduct the interview," Caleb continued stiffly. "I trust that these steps will be enough to assure you all that Karen is no witch?"

There was a general murmur, but Father Caleb remained stalwart, asking the same question of each of the village leaders. They all nodded their approval stiffly, and Karen could tell from the expressions of the crowd that confession and communion would be enough to calm their fears.

"Karen?" Caleb turned to her, a little hesitantly. "You've been rather quiet. Does all of this seem — acceptable, to you?"

She hesitated. How best to play this? What she really wanted to do was tell them all off for being superstitious idiots — but hostility wouldn't help anything. They'd see how wrong they were soon enough — some of them were already beginning to realize they were being ridiculous, she could tell by the shifting expressions on their faces, their refusal to look straight at her. She stepped to his side at the pulpit, raising her voice to address the congregation.

"I'm a little upset to be accused of this, as anyone would be," she said, trying to keep the anger out of her voice. "But what I want more than anything is to keep the peace — to be able to help you all deal with what faces us. To have your trust, and your respect. And if this will help ease your minds, convince you that I'm just a regular person who wants to help, then I'm more than willing to do it."

CHAPTER 39

She'd hoped, quietly, for a round of applause — Father Caleb clapped his hands together a few times, then cleared his throat and stopped when it became clear that nobody else was going to join in. All she got were stares... but it would do, she decided as the meeting was adjourned, and the villagers began to trail out of the church. She could tell from the energy in the room that a great deal of the momentum of the witch hunt had been arrested by this little gathering, by the priest's slightly pompous address... and, more to the point, by how Karen had gone along with everything they'd requested without so much as a peep. It had been the right move, she decided. And though she hadn't taken communion or given confession since she was a child, she was happy enough to partake in that familiar old ritual if it would help the people trust her again.

"Karen, are you sure you're willing to go through all this?" Connor said softly, stepping to her side as the village leaders filed out of the church, talking amongst themselves in an effort to avoid making eye contact with Karen. "None of them have any right to force you —"

"They don't need to force me, I'm happy to do it," she said softly, giving his hand a squeeze — she could sense Father Caleb's beady eyes taking that little gesture in, but for the time being she didn't care at all. "I'm Catholic, anyway — or at least, I used to be — it's not as if this is new stuff."

"Good to hear you're on your way back to the fold," Father Caleb said, giving her a sharp look — he clearly wasn't impressed by her use of the past tense regarding her faith.

She decided not to bring up the agnosticism of her father, or how little time she'd had lately for matters of faith — it didn't quite seem like the time. If playing the good little Catholic would help convince the people she wasn't a witch, then she could do it. Besides, it wasn't as if she didn't believe in God, exactly... more that she hadn't really given it much thought. If he was out there, she just hoped he approved of what she was doing with her life. Healing the sick was more or less in keeping with what the Lord encouraged people to do, wasn't it? Having premarital sex with Connor, on the other hand… that might be more of a gray area…

The appointment had been made — she would take communion the next morning, in a ceremony that had been arranged just for her. A few representatives from the village would be present as witnesses to this element of the process, though of course they wouldn't be listening in to her confession, and the interview with Brendan from the Watch would similarly be observed by the village leaders. Hopefully, she thought with gritted teeth, by this time tomorrow, the witch question would be entirely put to bed, and she could actually get on with her work.

But for now, the evening was drawing in, and when they left the church the dark was gathering. Father Caleb bid them a pleasant goodnight — she was glad to have the fussy priest on their side. It was clear that he didn't think she was a witch, and she appreciated that greatly. She also appreciated the way Connor slipped his hand into hers as they walked down the road in the twilight, the wind flapping at their clothing as it picked up. She frowned, peering up into the cloudy, overcast sky. It felt … dense and close, somehow. As though there was a storm coming.

Connor had taken the opportunity, at the end of the impromptu little meeting in the church, to instruct everyone to shut and bar their west windows for the time being — he'd encouraged them to go as far as nailing boards up over the windows just to make sure that nothing could get through. It was a superstitious instruction for sure, and Karen had expected resistance — but the villagers had just nodded as though it was the most natural thing in the world, and even as they walked down the street back toward Connor's cottage she could see villagers out in their yards, nailing planks over the west windows in their houses.

"I love that you tell people to nail their western windows shut and that's just fine, but I suggest avoiding touching infected sores and that's witchcraft," she pointed out with a roll of her eyes. There were certainly double standards at play. Was it because he'd lived here all his life and they trusted him already? Or was it because he was a man? Either way, she wasn't going to resent him for it. He'd done everything in his power to protect her, to use his privileges to amplify her voice and keep her safe. She couldn't hold it against him that the villagers trusted him more than they trusted her just yet. She'd earn their trust, one way or another. She'd just have to be patient.

When they got in, they had a quick dinner of bread and cheese that Connor prepared, quickly building the little fire back up from the embers that remained of it from their afternoon spent in front of it… she smiled to herself at the memory of it, gazing soft-eyed at him in the firelight. Come what may, she was unbelievably happy that this was happening… the new intimacy in their relationship was exactly what she needed to soothe her nerves and keep her going. And as the night closed in, they found themselves having a very early night indeed, finishing their bread and cheese before heading into Connor's little bedroom. She spent a little time pulling the bedsheets up, anticipation building deliciously in her body… but she also checked the west-facing windows before they went to bed, not liking the way the wind was howling through the eaves.

Then they were in bed together, mostly unclothed, and she sighed with happiness, losing herself in the scent and sensation of Connor's arms around her, his body against hers, the gentle tracing of his fingertips as they explored her body... gone was the hurried, explosive passion of that afternoon. Now, they had all the time in the world. She touched and caressed him, too, exploring in depth the parts of him she'd skimmed over earlier... the firm muscles of his forearms and shoulders, the occasional pearly scars that showed on his skin... she could feel her body shivering under his touch as they kissed lazily in the warmth of the bed, torn between the pleasant warmth of his arms around her, and a stirring, growing need for more contact, more pressure, for his hands to creep lower and lower to a place that was aching for his touch... she could barely hear the wind howling anymore, all she was aware of was Connor, his breath against her ear, his hands on her body, the scent of him, the intoxicating warmth of him... she could feel her heart pounding in her chest as her desire mounted, and she was just about to pounce on him and flatten him to the bed to take the pleasure she needed from him when their reverie was interrupted by what was unmistakably an alien, inhuman screech that echoed through the night like a gunshot.

CHAPTER 40

Connor's hands stilled, and he sat upright in bed, his body tense. One look at his face told her that he'd heard exactly what she had, and the two of them stared at each other, both of them hoping against hope that they'd been mistaken. Outside the window, she could see trees bending and swaying furiously in the wind that had picked up, and the low moaning and howling of the wind in the trees sent a shiver down her spine. Connor put an arm around her shoulders and squeezed her close to him in wordless reassurance, but she could tell from the expression on his face that he was worried, too.

"Is it them?" she said softly, her voice a little hoarse. "The Sluagh again?"

"That's a west wind," he said softly. "It could be that —"

But he was cut off by yet another unearthly shriek. This one was high and wild and set her teeth on edge as it seemed to rattle the very foundations of the house… and it was quickly joined by another, and another. Her eyes moved to the westward-facing window in the wall and she shuddered, unnerved by the utter darkness out there, by how little she could see beyond shadow. Shadows that seemed to move and shift before her eyes… shadows that she knew in her bones were concealing flapping wings and skeletal frames, the Sluagh keening and shrieking their awful song to the night.

"It's them," she murmured, sure of it.

Connor nodded, drawing her close to him. They huddled in the bed together, glad that the windows were all shut and barred, and listened as the storm closed in around them.

"I hope the villagers are all inside," Connor muttered a little later, clearly restless. There was no question of starting back up where they'd left off in their exploration of each other — the shrieking and howling of the wind and the Sluagh — difficult to tell one cry from another — had definitely killed the mood, and all she wanted from Connor was the warmth and reassurance of his body close to hers. He was tense against her, and she knew that some part of him wanted to charge out into the night with his sword to fight the things. But that was a fool's errand. From what Maggie had said, they were terrifically dangerous. And she couldn't risk losing him. Not when she'd only just truly found him…

"They'll be safe," she said firmly. "You told them to bolt their western windows — they were all doing it when we walked home. And besides, everyone knows what happened during the last attack… nobody would be foolish enough to go out until dawn."

"I hope so," Connor said softly. They lay in silence, holding each other close. It went without saying that sleep was out of the question — Connor leaned over to light a candle, which made the room a little cheerier, even if it did emphasize the contrast between the warm little room they were in and the howling and shrieking wind outside. Part of her wanted to go out there — she was itching to see a Sluagh for herself, to prove once and for all that monsters were real… but she knew that was a bad idea.

It must have been midnight when the new scream came. Despite their fear, Connor and Karen had dozed off a little into that curious half-sleep, dreams beginning to creep in around them... but Karen sat bolt upright when she heard that scream, so different from the shrieks and howls of the wind and the Sluagh. Connor had heard it too. It was real, and vivid, and full of the most heart-wrenching fear she had ever heard... and what was worse, it sounded like it belonged to a child. Having given out vaccinations, Karen was intimately familiar with the shriek of a child who was afraid, and this was just like that — but much, much worse than any fear that a simple injection could engender in even the most needle-phobic child.

Without saying a word, the two of them got dressed quickly. Connor lit a torch and they hurried out of the house, enveloped immediately by the hot wind that blew from the west, screaming through the village and setting their teeth on edge with that unearthly howling. Sure enough, they weren't alone in having heard it — the street was full of villagers in their nightclothes clutching torches and exchanging frightened looks. Connor and a few of the other watchmen took charge, asking the villagers what had happened, who had screamed.

Karen found herself praying that a child had simply been frightened by the storm... but it wasn't long before the truth of what had happened come out.

Rosemary burst out of her home, her eyes wild with terror and grief, gesturing wordlessly over her shoulder. Connor moved fast, running into the house and returning a few minutes later, shaking his head with a grim expression on his face. Rosemary had shut and barred her west-facing window... but it seemed that the lock had given way and the window was hanging open, almost wrenched from its frame by the force of the wind... or something else.

But it was worse than that. That window was in little Malcolm's room... and the boy was nowhere to be seen.

As if drawn by some awful magnet, the villagers turned as one toward the hillside where the men had been found. Rosemary screamed as she realized what the implication was, what they were expecting — a high, desperate sound — and before anyone could stop her, she took off running, her bare feet striking hard on the cobblestones as her nightdress flapped in the high winds. Connor and Karen ran after her, Karen grateful she'd stopped to put on her boots and grab a cloak to gather around her shoulders — the west wind was hot and reeking, but the night was cold. Connor called to Rosemary, begging her to slow down, to let them search for Malcolm, but she was like a woman possessed, running faster than Karen had ever believed possible up the street out of town. Despite their best efforts to catch her, she was well ahead of them by the time they reached the hillside.

With the clouds obscuring the moon and stars, it was almost pitch dark out here. The low keening of the wind and the flapping of their clothing distracted them as they stumbled out after Rosemary, who was quickly disappearing into the darkness. Connor held his torch aloft, shouting in vain after Rosemary... but she'd already vanished into the gloom. Karen stared wildly about her, trying to search the grassy hillside for any sign of what she prayed, so desperately, she wouldn't find...

But then a new scream ripped through the night, as the villagers caught up and gathered in an uneasy clump around Connor. A scream far worse than any that had come before it ... a scream that spoke of rage, of pain, of terrible, awful loss. A scream that sliced right through the murmuring of the crowd and put an identical stricken expression on every single face there as all of them at once came to the same awful, awful conclusion.

Rosemary had found her son on the hillside.

"Go back to your homes," Connor said in a low, flat voice. The villagers drew together, the expressions on their faces saying they understood completely — no woman would want a crowd at a time like this — and they began to trudge away across the hillside back toward the town, their torches held low. The scream had been replaced by a low keening wail that broke every few seconds for a gasping breath. It was easy enough to follow... and it wasn't long before they came upon Rosemary, collapsed on the hillside like a puppet with her strings cut. In her arms, a little figure, terrifyingly small, awfully still... and when she looked up at the approach of the torchlight, Karen saw all that she needed to see on her face.

She'd seen that face in a hundred hospital rooms. Even halfway across the world and five hundred years in the past, she recognized it instantly. It was the face of a mother who had lost absolutely everything.

It was the face of a mother clutching the dead body of her child.

CHAPTER 41

Things seemed to move in slow motion after that. There was no question of moving Rosemary between the two of them — she was all but comatose, rocking Malcolm's lifeless little body in her arms and uttering that low, keening wail of denial. Karen tried not to look too closely at the broken little shape of him, knowing that if she looked, she'd begin to diagnose what had happened... the wounds caused by the claws of the Sluagh, the broken limbs caused by the fall. And Malcolm was no longer someone she could help. That was the thing about being a doctor — in the face of death, there was absolutely no comfort she could offer. So, she stood back, and let Connor go to her.

Before long, another little group of villagers began trekking across the hillside toward them, torches held high. This group was just women, which Karen smiled a little at — a group of mothers from the village, all wearing identical expressions of grief and determination. They were here for their friend, here to support her in this, the darkest possible hour of her life, and Connor moved away from Rosemary's side automatically when they arrived, sensing that he had been relieved of his duty. The women closed in around her like a comforting blanket, holding her close, offering wordless sympathy and all the comfort they could give her.

Karen was surprised to see Old Maggie among their number, looking stalwart in her usual collection of cardigans with a thick winter cloak over the top that flapped in the wind. She waited until the women had gathered Rosemary up and wrapped the little body of Malcolm in a blanket they'd brought specifically for the purpose — Rosemary still clutched at it, wrapped up in its blanket, and Karen had a suspicion she'd be holding him for quite some time. Once the women had headed away across the hillside, Maggie turned her beady eyes onto Connor and Karen, who were standing by under the torch feeling a little useless.

"Sluagh," she said flatly, gesturing skyward. Karen had been avoiding looking at the clouds, but she followed Maggie's point up into the sky, where she could just make out the shadow-obscured edges of wings, exactly as she'd seen that first night… Connor could see it, too, and he uttered a low sound of disgust and anger, his hand moving to his sling. But Maggie clicked her tongue.

"You start a fight with them, and you won't be leaving it alive," she said in a low voice that stilled Connor's hand immediately. "They'll scoop you up into the sky, drain your life and drop you to the earth like an empty sack."

They stood for a while there under the dark, shadowy sky. Karen cleared her throat. "Are we in danger here, now?"

"They've fed," Maggie said bluntly, sending a chill down Karen's spine and a wince from the usually stalwart Connor. "No more will be taken tonight. But now they've a taste for the hunt, I'd warrant they'll be hunting more regularly."

"What can we do? How do we stop this?" Connor's voice was shaking with feeling, but Maggie just raised her arms.

"Iron, fire, sunlight. Bar the windows, tell everyone to stay indoors after sunset. Kill as many as you can. There's no easy way out of this, Connor Grant. They've been summoned, and they won't leave until they've fed on every last man, woman and child in the village."

Karen blinked; her curiosity piqued. "What do you mean by summoned?"

Maggie was silent for a long time before she spoke, her voice almost obscured by the low shrieking of the Sluagh above them and the hot, stinking howling of the west wind. "Sluagh feed on despair," she said softly. "They are called forth by the kind of grief that destroys a person, and they only grow stronger as it spreads and grow. Someone in the village in the depths of despair summoned these creatures to them… and then did the only thing that can stop the Sluagh from stalking their prey, once chosen. They named someone else to die in their place."

Karen felt a chill run down her spine even as her mind worked hard to make sense of this information — she could see Connor doing the same, a frown on his face in the flickering torchlight. Despair summoned the creatures to attack you…

did that mean the young men who'd died last week had been in despair? That didn't seem likely… which meant that it was someone else who had drawn the creatures, then named the men to die in their place. But why? Some kind of grudge? She could certainly believe that, given the way they'd conducted themselves at the inn… but would that kind of behavior be enough to warrant their deaths?

"Who would name a child to die?" Connor said softly, his face a mask of grief, and Karen nodded, confused by that element as well. Malcolm was by all accounts a bright, cheerful child — aside from the illness he'd been suffering as a result of the pox he'd caught from his father. But that hardly manifested as despair. And though his mother had been grieving her lost husband, she'd hardly been the picture of despair… even if she had been, why hadn't the Sluagh taken her and not her son?

"Doesn't have to be a name," Maggie said thoughtfully. "A description suits the purpose, too. What do the dead have in common? Come now, Karen. You're a sharp girl."

"Pox," Karen said blankly, remembering the lesions on the dead men she'd examined, remembering that little Malcolm had been suffering the disease too. "They all had the cowpox."

"Aye," Maggie said thoughtfully. "Victims of the pox could have been named. But then why didn't the creatures come for the milkmaids?"

"That's right," Connor said, frowning. "The first attack happened when nobody was bothering barring their windows. There are dozens of these creatures — why didn't they take Rhianne, or Anne, or Mary? Her window faces west," he added. Karen nodded, remembering the house's layout.

"It's just men," she said slowly — and Maggie nodded firmly, her eyes shadowed.

"Aye, it's men with the pox that's the pattern. Someone in the depths of abject despair named every male in the village who's suffering the pox to be killed."

Maggie pulled her cloak around her shoulders as though drawing their meeting to an end. "Now what are you going to do about it?"

"I don't know," Connor said bleakly, staring at her. "I don't know what we can do."

"Well, you'd best figure it out, young man," Maggie said seriously as she began the trek across the hillside toward where her cottage lay. "Because

I'd warrant more men are going to come down with the pox before all of this is over."

They stood for a long time, watching Maggie's retreating form vanish into the gloom. Even without a torch, she walked with a surprising confidence, not tripping or stumbling over any hidden rocks or roots on the hillside — Karen found herself wondering if that had something to do with magic, too, her mind clearly wanting to recoil from the awful situation they were in.

"Despair," she said softly, and Connor looked down at her with a troubled frown. "I think we ought to pay Mary another visit."

His eyes widened. "You don't think she has something to do with this?"

Ever since Maggie had spoken the girl's name, Karen's mind had been racing. The depression the girl was clearly lost in, the misery that seemed to emanate from her like a palpable force... she had to have something to do with it, didn't she? Karen was beginning to draw some rather awful conclusions from the evidence they'd assembled before them... but right now, she was utterly exhausted, and she felt herself swaying, hardly able to bring herself to speak out loud what she was thinking.

Connor put his arm around her, his expression

set. "We need some sleep," he told her softly. "We'll deal with this in the morning, alright?"

They made their way back across the hillside, their heads bowed. Things would look better in the morning, she tried to tell herself... daylight usually improved things. But somehow, right now, she was finding it very difficult to believe that.

CHAPTER 42

They all but collapsed into bed when they reached Connor's cottage again, barely stopping to remove their boots and outer garments before they'd fallen into each other's arms. More sex was out of the question... they were both so tense and exhausted that the idea of lovemaking seemed a thousand miles away. As she curled into Connor's arms, she realized she was crying... and with that realization, she found to her alarm that she couldn't stop. The tears shook her body, sobs wrenching at her shoulders, and all she could do was weep as Connor held her close and murmured reassurances in her ear.

"It's just so awful," she said, finally, when the worst of her sobbing had eased. "That poor child had nothing to do with any of this… he was four years old, Connor. No four year old should die so horribly."

"I feel for Rosemary," Connor said heavily. "I don't know how she'll go on. Losing her husband was bad enough… but to lose her child?"

"Her last connection to him," she said softly, wiping a tear from her cheek and curling into Connor's arms more tightly. "We ought to keep a close eye on her. If the Sluagh feed on despair…"

"She's a woman, though. And she doesn't have the pox." He was frowning. "At least, she doesn't yet. She might have… the way she was holding Malcolm's body, I'd imagine…"

Karen shut her eyes at the horror of that image. "It's possible," she said softly. "Though I'd imagine it would be the least of her worries at the moment.

"Aye, that's true enough," Connor said heavily. "We have to stop these things, Karen. I just don't know how."

"We have to focus on keeping everyone safe," Karen said steadily, trying to pull herself together enough to help come up with a plan. "Work on making sure everyone's windows can be shut and barred safely, make sure everyone knows to be inside well before dark… and can these things be killed? I'm not sure how Faerie creatures work, exactly…"

She felt him nod, his hair falling into her face as he did. "Aye, they can be killed. Iron and fire are the usual tools, and from what Maggie said those will do just fine this time. But they're airborne creatures… we'll need our best shots on guard each night. I'll ride to the castle tomorrow and check with Brendan about how many men he can spare."

"Just make sure they don't carry the pox back with them," Karen said quickly. "It's a bad enough disease at the best of times, but now that it's drawing the Sluagh to people…"

"Aye. That does add a new danger to it," Connor said heavily.

Karen frowned to herself. She'd spent so much time reassuring all the villagers that the disease was rarely fatal, that it was an inconvenience and nothing more… and now they'd have to tell them that having the pox meant you might be snatched up and killed by murderous Faerie monsters? Well, she supposed it would motivate them to be stricter about their quarantine guidelines… that was something, at any rate. But it wasn't much comfort.

"Maggie said they're going to hunt more often," Karen said softly.

Connor drew her closer to comfort her. They lay together for a long time, Connor drawing idle circles on the skin of her shoulder, and they were able to drift into a troubled sleep sometime later. It was clear they'd needed the rest — dawn had come and gone by the time they awoke, and Karen felt her body responding almost instinctively to Connor's presence, drawing him close, his hands roaming sleepily across her body even before he was fully awake. They made love in the early morning light, slow, and sleepy, and tender, and by the time they'd fallen back on the pillows, day had well and truly broken. The misery of the night before, the awful tragedy, was still upon them like a shroud… but with Connor's support and affection, she at least felt ready to get up and face the day.

She couldn't stop thinking about Mary. Her mind was finally starting to draw some rather horrible connections between seemingly unrelated events — the lesions she'd found all over the bodies of the dead men, the lesions all over Mary's body, the girl's absolute dejection and refusal to talk… she had an awful feeling that something had happened between Mary and the men, something much, much worse than a fall down some stairs that had served to spread the lesions all over Mary's body instead of just on her hands. It was almost too horrible to think of, and she kept her theory to herself, not wanting to share it with Connor because she prayed she was wrong.

But she knew she had to go to Mary, to speak to her honestly about what had happened those weeks ago. Because she had a suspicion, she knew... and if what she thought was true, the village was in a huge amount of danger.

But that would have to wait. As she got herself dressed, she could hear the unmistakable sounds of a crowd gathering outside of Connor's little cottage, and she frowned, confused by what she was hearing — what did they want from her? She had an appointment with Father Caleb up at the church later that morning — did the villagers want to see her before that? She headed out onto the porch and was met by a small but determined little group, their faces taut.

"What?" she asked blankly, too tired and stressed to try to be more polite than that. A man stepped forward — an older man who she recognized as one of the village leaders who'd been at the meeting the night before. God, that meeting felt like a thousand years ago... could it really only have been last night? Could so little time have passed? It felt farcical, to be going up to the church to be cleared of witchcraft when something so awful had happened... but it was clear from the faces of the assembled villagers that it was all the more important that she do as she'd agreed.

"We're just ensuring you don't miss your appointment," the village leader said, his eyes narrowed with suspicion.

"I'm on my way up there now," she said, fighting her frustration. Why did they think she needed an armed guard to go up to the church? Hadn't she gone up there willingly the night before?

"In the wake of everything that's happened, it's more important than ever that we prove —"

"Prove what? Do any of you honestly believe I summoned those creatures? What possible good does it do me?" she snapped, losing control of her anger a little. "I'm a doctor. I've dedicated my whole life to helping people get better from diseases that want to kill them. My life's work is helping people. Now, I'm playing along with this frankly insulting witch hunt of yours because I have nothing to hide, and if I can put your minds at rest, I'm willing to do that. But don't you *dare* treat me like a prisoner when I'm going of my own free will."

The village leader recoiled, clearly a little

shocked, and the villagers around him shuffled their feet. She'd spoken calmly and clearly, doing her best not to yell or rage — but it was clearly important to set some boundaries with these people. Sheepishly, the crowd dispersed, and she walked up to the church with Connor on one side and the village leader on the other. But it was a hollow victory, especially in the wake of last night's tragedy. How could anyone bring themselves to care about this silly test they were determined to conduct? Didn't they have more important things to focus on... like a grief-stricken woman? Like the funeral of a child?

CHAPTER 43

It had been a long time since she'd attended
Mass. It was a strange little gathering, with
only a dozen or so people present for the
sermon and the rituals and to observe that she
didn't turn into a pillar of salt or something,
presumably, and she sat quietly in the front row,
acutely aware that she was being observed and not
quite sure what to do with her face. Did she look
respectful enough? Or did she look like a witch
being forced to sit through a church service? Father
Caleb looked as uncomfortable as she felt. It
occurred to her, as she revisited the blurry childhood memories of church and communion, that
one of the rules was that you couldn't take communion if you'd committed a mortal sin. She was

pretty sure she hadn't — but at the same time, she'd been living an agnostic life for a long time. From what she understood, she'd be making her confession after mass — what if Father Caleb were angry with her for not revealing her sins beforehand?

She shook herself internally, a little surprised by how anxious the whole situation was making her... the old Catholic guilt rearing its ugly head again, making her shift nervously in her seat despite her determination to seem calm and serene. She hadn't done anything wrong, she told herself firmly. All she had to do was participate in this ritual... she tried to settle into it, reaching into herself and even offering a little prayer to a God she hadn't had much time for lately. She hoped he was proud of the work she did, at any rate. She was doing her best to do good... even if she felt a little guilty about how long it had been since she'd done anything like this...

Muscle memory drove her out of her seat when Father Caleb called for the gathered group to rise to take communion. She shut her eyes and opened her mouth, accepting the small piece of bread as it was given to her — as a child, she'd always preferred to take communion with her hands, worried about germs, about the priest accidentally touching her mouth with his hands... but right now she was much, much more frightened of the prospect of accidentally dropping the host, or of putting the wrong hand on top — she couldn't remember if it was right over left or left over right, and she didn't want to risk it. Feeling the gimlet gaze of the other parishioners on her, she took a sip of the consecrated wine, too, then returned to her seat to kneel and pray, reflecting on Jesus as she'd been instructed to do. It had been a long time since she'd reflected on Jesus. *How are you doing,* she felt herself asking the Lord — then almost laughed at how ridiculous she felt. There was an odd lightness in her chest. She'd taken communion — nothing had gone wrong, no sudden puff of smoke or calamity. Now all that remained was confession, and an interview.

Father Caleb had a small confession box on the other side of the church, and she felt a familiar pang of anxiety as she stepped inside it, kneeling by the grill through which she knew the priest would be sitting. She'd always hated this part as a child — worried that she wasn't confessing the right sins, or that she was confessing too much, not enough… it had been a great relief that she'd stopped going to church before her turbulent teen years began. Muscle memory stepped in again and she made the sign of the cross before she spoke, her voice oddly loud in the little booth.

"Forgive me Father, for I have sinned," she murmured, a half-smile on her lips as the memory came back to her. "It has been... twenty-two years since my last confession, maybe more."

She heard Father Caleb's voice murmuring something from the Bible through the screen and she shut her eyes to listen. Though her faith had never been particularly strong, she did like the ritual. She'd even given some thought to what sins she should confess, as she climbed the hill that morning. The rules of Catholicism were so strict that she knew she'd have no shortage of sins to volunteer.

"Firstly," she said, "I have to confess that... that God hasn't been high on my list of priorities for a long time. I've been focused on my work, on learning how to be a good doctor and doing that, but... my faith has taken a back seat."

"Yes, my child," Father Caleb said ponderously.

She couldn't help but smile a little. He was at least a decade younger than her — it felt a little strange to be confessing to him. But she pressed on a little, told him a little about her life as a doctor, the temptations of reckless ego and pride. It was odd, now that she thought about it, how much there was to say, how much to explore... and while she didn't exactly feel guilty about the personality flaws she was presenting, it was oddly satisfying to explain them all in detail, as though she was cleansing herself. She did catch herself using a little more medical jargon than necessary, though, and there was a definite vagueness to the way Father Caleb was responding. Well, fair enough. In a way, it was God she was talking to, not the priest. And surely God would understand what she was saying.

"But more recently... well, I suppose I should confess to the sin of — lust, I guess." A blush rose to her cheeks... it was very helpful that she couldn't see Father Caleb's face right now. "Um. I have indulged in sexual contact outside of marriage. With Connor Grant," she added, and she heard Father Caleb clear his throat hard. She could almost picture his face flushing furiously. Had he ever had any kind of experience with women, she wondered, a little amused despite herself.

"What is the nature of your relationship?" he managed to ask, and she could hear the timidity in his voice.

"Well. We've known each other for a little while... he's probably my closest friend here," she said thoughtfully, thinking of Connor as she spoke, imagining how he'd respond to these kinds of questions about their relationship. Did he do confession every week? Had he mentioned her to Father Caleb? "I like him," she said, feeling like a teenager.

"Ahem. Well. The Lord, as you well know, frowns on extramarital fornication," Father Caleb said severely. "So, if you are serious about this young man, and if this young man is serious about you… well, marriage is an obvious path to take. Before any further fornication transpires," he said sharply.

She nodded, realized he couldn't see her, then shook herself, grinning a little. That wasn't necessarily a promise she could make… but she wasn't going to say that, was she? The idea of marrying Connor… oddly enough, it didn't make her feel uncomfortable. Usually, commitment was a concept that either bored or worried her, but when it came to Connor… well, it was something to think about.

She confessed a few more things — most of them having to do with anger or frustration with the villagers for how they'd treated her. Father Caleb was rather diplomatic about those — she got the distinct sense that he felt she was justified in her anger, though he did solemnly advise her to be more Christlike in response to persecution — and then the confession was over. She recited the Hail Mary a few times as instructed, pleased that she remembered it as well as she did, and then she moved through to the manse beside the church, where the interview with Father Caleb and Captain Brendan was to take place.

That hadn't been so bad, had it? Now all she had to do was survive a conversation. Given the horror stories she'd heard about witch trials, Karen thought to herself, this one was going pretty well.

CHAPTER 44

Brendan was a burly, bear-like man with coppery hair and a beard — an intimidating figure in armor, but the smile on his face when he shook her hand was genuine and made her feel considerably more at ease. She recalled what Kay had told her about Brendan Grant the first time she'd met him — a cousin to Connor, and the Captain of the Watch up at the Keep. And he was married, more to the point, to a woman from her own time — Elena, an ex-cop from Baltimore. A good match, she thought with a smile… and reassuring to know that he'd at least understand where she was coming from.

Father Caleb joined them shortly — to her amusement, he was still a little pink in the face, clearly embarrassed by what she'd confessed to him in the booth. Was it really such an unusual state of affairs? From the gossip she'd heard around the village, premarital sex was hardly an unusual occurrence... maybe it was just Father Caleb who had trouble handling it. She fought the urge to smile, sitting up straight and proper as she looked at the two men sitting opposite her.

"So," Brendan said after introductions had been made. "I understand you're a witch."

Father Caleb clicked his tongue. "Captain Brendan —"

"Come on, Caleb, you know as well as I do that this is a farce," he said irritably. "She came into the church, and she did your little pageant... why do we have to pretend to interview her? You know as well as I do that she's about as far from a witch as she could be."

"The people of the village were worried," Caleb said stiffly. "It is my duty to serve them."

"Aye, sure," Brendan said irritably. "Karen, I do apologize for all of this. Sincerely. Similar tomfoolery was carried out when my Elena arrived, and I had as little patience for it then as I do now. Father Caleb, here's the only test worth a damn." The guard reached for his belt, drawing a long, black blade from a sheath there. It was about the length of her forearm and wickedly sharp, and she eyed it with some apprehension. Had she spoken too soon regarding barbaric witch-hunting rituals? Was he going to want blood from her?

"This is cold iron," he told her, shooting Caleb a disgruntled look as he spoke. "No creature from the Fae can stand to touch it. We use it to guard against them, to repel them, and to kill them. Any witch would sizzle and burn if they made contact with this blade. Do me a favor and touch it, will you?"

She nodded, reaching out to place the back of her hand against the cool metal surface of the blade. The two men looked at her hand, and she looked back at them, shrugging her shoulders. "Would it help if I wore an iron crucifix around my neck?" she suggested brightly, drawing a laugh from Brendan.

"Aye, perhaps, if we could convince the villagers to believe in the supernatural for more than five minutes," he said with a roll of his eyes. "I swear they alternate between demanding witch-hunts and refusing to acknowledge that there are real monsters about, depending entirely on what will most inconvenience us. I understand you're a woman of medicine, Karen?"

"Yes, that's right. A doctor."

"Brilliant. You're an asset to this place and we're lucky to have you. And we'll be twice as lucky if you have any interest in sharing your skills with us after the nonsense these town folk have put you through." He shook his head, rising to his feet and giving Caleb a look. "Is that enough of an interview? Have we sufficiently confirmed that this woman's about as much of a witch as you are?"

"I suppose so," Father Caleb said, clearly a little afraid of Brendan. The guard captain nodded, giving Karen a warm smile.

"Then we've taken up more than enough of your time, Karen. It was a pleasure to meet you. I look forward to seeing you again under less ridiculous circumstances. Father Caleb? Shall we make our announcement?"

The three of them headed out to the church yard together — where, Karen realized with a shock, it looked like more or less the entire village had gathered. Connor was there among the crowd, standing toward the front, an expression on his face that strongly suggested he was thinking about picking a fight if he needed to — he smiled and waved at her when he saw her, and she smiled back, her heart picking up as she remembered what Father Caleb had said about marriage…

"Thank you for coming," Father Caleb said, raising his voice to be heard. "I am pleased to report that upon thorough examination, Miss Karen Frakes is evidently not any kind of witch. She has taken communion and given a full confession, as any God-fearing woman would. Furthermore, Captain Brendan has thoroughly interviewed her and performed his own tests upon her, being something of an expert in the supernatural —"

"Aye, that's right," Brendan said roughly. "She's no witch, and anyone who thinks otherwise can take the matter up with the Watch."

With that, the crowd dispersed. Karen was pleased to see positive expressions on most of the faces, and a few villagers even came up to squeeze her hand and congratulate her on the result of the trial — she was pleased by their friendliness, but a little annoyed at the implication that there had been any doubt that she'd pass the tests. Then they were gone, and Connor was at her side, smiling down at her.

"So, you're not a witch after all. How disappointing."

"Sorry," she said with a sad little shrug. "I suppose that's the end of us?"

"Well, I'm only attracted to witches. It's a firm rule, I'm afraid."

Laughing, they headed down the hill together, hand in hand. It felt good to have been absolved like that — and to her surprise, she felt oddly good about having made a confession. It felt good, to talk through the things that were troubling you... to reflect honestly on your life, on what you'd done, the ways you wished you could be better. And though the act of forgiveness from the priest had been symbolic, there was still something about the feeling of having a blank slate to start from that was... well, reassuring.

And it made her all the more determined to get to the bottom of what was happening with the Sluagh, once and for all. They returned to Connor's cottage — she was rapidly beginning to think of the little place as home — and had a quick lunch of bread and cheese, but she could tell he was itching to get out and start work. They'd agreed to visit with Mary — it was time to try to get some answers from the young woman, as awful as those answers may be.

Their lunch done, they headed out, and Karen

found herself debating whether or not she should tell Connor about her theory regarding what was going on with Mary. Unless someone else in the village had been despairing when the Sluagh turned up — which didn't seem to be the case, having asked around — then it was likely that it was Mary who had summoned them. That meant that it was Mary who had sent them to attack someone else... specifically, men with cowpox, which earlier had been a description that only applied to the six men who'd died that first night. But what reason would Mary have for wanting those men dead? Karen worried that she knew... and that telling Connor would make him so angry at what had happened that he might interfere with the investigation. So, she kept the theory to herself as they rode.

One way or another, they were about to find out if she was right.

CHAPTER 45

I t was an overcast day, cold and blustery, and
she shivered a little, drawing her cloak tighter
about her shoulders as the two of them
approached Mary's little cottage. Her mother was in
the front yard, weeding a garden bed — the woman
straightened up with a tired smile, and Karen
recognized her as having been among the women
who'd come to fetch Rosemary from the hillside the
night before. They greeted each other, and Karen
asked after Rosemary, figuring that she was among
the last people the woman would want to see right
now. The news wasn't good.

"She's not speaking to anyone," Mary's mother
said heavily, leaning on the fencepost outside the
cottage as they discussed Rosemary. "We got her in

from the hillside and got her dressed a little more warmly, then put her to bed… but she won't say a word. I can't imagine what she's going through," she said heavily, the reflected grief clear in her eyes. "Can't imagine how she's going to recover from this. We've organized to have someone with her every minute of the day going forward, just in case… well, the despair…"

"Good thinking," Karen said, shaking her head. She'd had psych placements before — being on suicide watch was rather a terrifying responsibility. Her determination to get to the bottom of what was going on flared all the brighter in her chest. She'd make sure nobody else had to suffer what poor Rosemary had suffered. "We were hoping to speak to Mary if that's alright? I've brought some more salve from Old Maggie for her lesions, and we thought a visit might lift her spirits."

But the woman shook her head, a dejected expression crossing her face. "You'll have Cameron to contend with, I'm afraid. He's come over very peculiar of late. Says he's got to protect her from something — won't let me or anyone else anywhere near her door. I think she's put him up to it, but I've no idea why."

Connor and Karen exchanged glances, both

frowning. What possible reason could Cameron have for stopping people from visiting with his sister? The woman gestured them through as she returned to her work, and Karen let her, reasoning that she had more than enough on her plate for the time being. They'd go in and talk to Cameron.

Sure enough, there was the little boy, perched on the steps that led up to his sister's room. He was clutching a stout wooden branch he seemed to have gotten from outside somewhere — it showed some signs of having been inexpertly carved to a point and looked like a combination of a sword and a club. His expression was severe and determined when he looked up at them, but Karen could tell by the redness in his cheeks and the shine to his eyes that he'd been crying.

"Hullo, Cameron," Connor said with some surprise, dropping instinctively into a crouch to get on the little boy's level even as he got to his feet, his makeshift weapon ready. "Are you protecting your sister?"

"Aye," the boy said staunchly, lifting his chin. "I'm keeping her safe. Nobody's allowed up to see her, not anyone. Not the priest, or the village elders, or Mam, or even you!" He sounded equal parts determined and terrified.

Karen braced herself for Connor to push the child physically aside, or to just step around him. But to her surprise, he sat back on his haunches, giving the boy a smile.

"She's lucky to have a good protector like you, Cameron. You're a good, brave guard. I could use a few more men like you on the Watch, especially these days." Cameron looked surprised — and a little delighted by the praise, Karen noticed with a quiet smile. "Have you heard what's happening?"

"Yes," he said in a small voice. "Mam says there's monsters around and I mustn't go out after dark. And Da nailed the windows shut all along the west wall."

Karen and Connor exchanged glances — it was good to hear that their warnings were being taken seriously out here. She just hoped that every family was taking as much care as this one was. "Aye, monsters indeed," Connor said heavily. "Is it the monsters you're protecting Mary from?"

"Yes," Cameron said fiercely. "The monsters and the shadows and the bad men." He lifted the wooden club in his hand fiercely, as if to strike at some imagined enemy, and Karen made quiet note of the third thing on his list, resolving to ask Mary about it — if they ever got past her little bodyguard that was.

"Well, I tell you what. That weapon you've got there will do very well against the bad men," Connor said thoughtfully, reaching for his belt. "But I have something even better for monsters and shadows."

"You do?" Cameron had gone from defensive to curious, and Karen couldn't help but smile at how careful Connor was being with him. Validating his skills as a protector, offering him help… he was very good with children, it seemed. "What?"

"Cold iron," Connor explained, his eyes gleaming. "You know about faeries, right? I've seen that your parents hang up a horseshoe over the front door."

"To keep us safe from the Fair Folk, aye," the little boy said.

"Well, the reason for that is that it's made of iron. Iron's deadly to monsters from the Faerie world. Which is why I want you to have this knife." With that, Connor drew out a knife from his pocket — barely longer than a pocket knife, but definitely sharp enough to do some real damage. "Now, this is a serious weapon. Will you be careful with it, and treat it with respect?"

"Yes," Cameron whispered, his eyes enormous. Connor placed it hilt-first in the boy's outstretched palm, and he curled his fingers around it reverently.

"Now, I can give you a few lessons in how to fight with that, if you'd like," Connor suggested. "I often train with the men of the Watch — and seeing as you're keeping watch over your family, I think that includes you, too."

Cameron nodded; his eyes bright with excitement. But Karen could still see the worry on his face. "Can you teach me to fight six men at once?"

Connor tilted his head, looking thoughtful. "Aye, I can show you a few tricks. Why would you be fighting so many men yourself, though?"

"The bad men," Cameron said, sitting back down on the steps with an angry look on his little face. "They came last week, and I couldn't stop them."

"What bad men?" Connor asked, casual as anything, even though Karen knew as well as he did that this was a huge potential clue.

"There were six of them," he said, and there were tears in his eyes again. "I couldn't stop them. Mam was outside and she didn't see them, and I couldn't make them go away even though Mary was sick and hurt and didn't want to see anybody."

"That's okay, Cameron," Connor said softly. "Even grown-up Watchmen sometimes can't stop bad men from doing what they do."

He sniffled, squeezing the iron knife tight in his fist as he continued with Connor's encouragement. "I told them to go away but they wouldn't. They went up there and they all yelled at Mary, even though she was sick. They said… they said it was her fault, that she made them sick, that they were going to make her pay for it. Then they saw Da coming home along the path, and they all ran downstairs and away through the back door." He sniffed again, clearly distraught over this encounter, over his own powerlessness. Karen knew how he felt. "Then when I went to talk to Mary, she told me to go away. She was crying. And then that night, the storm came, and the wind kept screaming, and I could hear her yelling at it out of her window for ages. And now she won't talk to me, or Ma, or anyone at all."

CHAPTER 46

Karen and Connor stared at each other, and she could tell he was thinking as hard as she was about what had just been revealed. Cameron was still tearful, and Connor invited him outside to the garden so he could teach him the basics of knife fighting — something that seemed to intrigue him, though he hesitated a little at the prospect of leaving his perch at the bottom of the steps.

"Ah, a true guard, not wanting to leave his post," Connor said with a broad smile. "Tell you what — I'll put one of my best guards on to relieve you, alright? You know Karen. She's an expert in shadows and monsters."

"I promise I'll keep Mary safe," Karen said, giving the little boy a smile.

"Tell you what. I'll even leave an iron knife with Karen, too, to make sure she's ready to fight — and if we hear anything happening, we'll come straight back in, alright?"

Cameron seemed happy with that, and he got up to follow Connor out into the yard. Karen smiled at him as he went, nodding as he shot her a meaningful look — the plan was clear. She'd go up and try to talk to Mary while Connor kept her stalwart protector busy in the yard. It was a good idea... but part of her just wanted to go out and watch the knife-fighting lesson. There was something incredibly charming and sweet about watching her lover talk to the little boy...

But this was more important. She waited for them to go outside, then headed up the stairs, stepping carefully. Mary's door was shut, as she'd guessed — she knocked on it gently before letting herself in, glad that there didn't seem to be a lock on it.

The room was much worse than it had been when she'd last visited. The window was slammed shut, the curtains pulled tight over it, plunging the tiny space into darkness. It was clear that Mary wasn't taking good care of her lesions — from what Karen could make out of the slumped figure in the bed, her bandages hadn't been changed in several days, and there was an unpleasant, sour smell in the air that she knew came from unwashed bandages. In the corner, piles of plates and glasses lay in a haphazard mound — she could see that the food on the plates had barely been touched, and the room was at risk for attracting vermin. Mary was facing the wall, curled tight into a ball, and when Karen said her name she didn't respond.

"Mary," she tried again. "It's Karen. I'm here to talk."

Still nothing. Karen moved a little closer, reaching into the bag she carried. She might have been here for answers, but the sight of Mary had roused her medical instincts — those lesions were never going to heal if they weren't cared for. "Is it okay if I put some salve on your lesions? I bet they're troubling you…"

That earned her a response — a shrug of the shoulders, and when she reached for Mary, the girl didn't flinch away. Working carefully, sure to protect her hands from the lesions with a pair of gloves that Connor had brought for her, she took the bandages from the girl's arms and hands — the parts of her she could reach, that weren't covered in blankets. Carefully, she applied Maggie's soothing salve to the red, sore lesions, taking the soiled bandages away and leaving the lesions to get some air. No coverage was better than old, dirty coverings.

"Mary, I need to talk to you," she said again, hoping that the salve had brought the girl some measure of relief. "About what happened. About how you got these sores."

The girl sat up at that, and some life came into her dull eyes. Karen could barely see her in the dark of the room, but her eyes had adjusted enough to read fear and guilt into her expression. But still she didn't speak. Her face was puffy and swollen, and Karen knew she'd been crying… but her expression now was borderline catatonic.

"How about I talk instead?" she suggested softly. "I'm going to tell you all about what I think happened, and you don't even have to speak. You can nod or shake your head if you like… or you can just listen. It's up to you." Mary just stared at her, and she took a deep breath. "So, what I know is that the six men who died the night of the storm last week all had cowpox. They had it all over their bodies, not just on their hands, and they weren't working closely enough with cows to have caught it from the cows. I also know that they came here, Mary, and that they threatened you, and told you that you gave them the pox."

At that, Mary gave a deep, shuddering gasp, and Karen thought she was going to speak for a moment — but she stayed quiet, though tears began to roll down her cheeks, leaving tracks in the grime there. Karen kept talking, keeping her voice low and soothing, hoping to avoid upsetting the girl too severely.

"I saw those men's bodies, Mary. I know that the only way they could have gotten the pox was by coming into contact with someone with the lesions — all-over contact. I think they attacked someone who was sick, Mary. I think they attacked her, and hurt her very badly, and probably spread the lesions all over her body, too." She took a deep breath. "And I think those men are monsters for what they did, and I think they deserve what happened to them."

That seemed to get through to Mary. The girl took a deep breath — and then before she knew it words were tumbling out of her mouth even as tears flowed down her face. What she was saying wasn't especially coherent, but it wasn't long before Karen was able to assemble a pretty clear picture of what had happened... and it confirmed her worst fears. The six men had been bothering Mary for months, flirting with her despite her uneasiness, touching her without her permission, following her home, leering and yelling... behaviors that simply got written off as boys being boys. But then they'd taken it too far. They'd taken her out to the hillside late one night, when — unknown to them — she'd recently contracted the cowpox. She'd fought them, but what was one sixteen-year-old girl against a group of adult men?

"That shouldn't have happened to you," Karen kept saying, over and over again, like a prayer. Mary was barely listening, but she knew it was important to support her in the telling of this, to believe her unconditionally, to let her know that nothing was her fault. She was reeling with the reve- lation; with the monstrous thing those men had done. All six of them... even William, the married father of a small son? Even him? He seemed the worst of all — Mary haltingly mentioned that he'd left her his cloak when they'd abandoned her on the hillside, the only thing that had stopped her freezing to death out there. They'd raped her... then left her for dead, like a piece of fruit they'd finished with. Monsters, each and every one of them. She remembered the stricken expressions on their faces, how utterly horrified they'd looked, recalled how sad she'd felt at how terrified they'd clearly been in the moments before their death… but where before she'd felt sympathy, now all she felt was a grim satisfaction. It served them right, the misery that had been visited upon them. They deserved every single bit of it.

CHAPTER 47

"**I** only wanted them to kill them," Mary breathed now, her face streaked with tears and her eyes wild. This seemed to be a new topic, and Karen leaned forward to listen. "I only wanted the avenging angels to take them… I didn't want… I didn't want Malcolm to…" And then the sobs began to shake her body again.

Karen wanted to reach out, to hold her close and comfort her… but she knew physical contact was a bad idea right now for this poor girl.

"Mary, what did you tell them?"

"They won't go away," Mary breathed, and her face was a mask of despair. "They won't go … they won't stop, I begged them, I begged them to stop after Danny and the others, but they won't… they say they're hungry, they say they need to feed, that they'll take me if I try to stop them… and I don't want…" She collapsed into bed, uttering a high, desperate wailing that echoed through the house. Karen heard footsteps on the stairs and the door burst open. Cameron was standing there, his iron knife in his hand, looking every bit the fearsome protector as he rushed to his sister's side.

"You made her cry," he said accusingly, glaring daggers at Karen.

"It's okay," Mary breathed, reaching for her little brother. "We were just talking —"

Cameron was clearly thrilled to hear Mary speak — he turned to her, his eyes wide with shock, but then he turned back to Karen, his protective instincts clearly still flaring. "You should go," he said, a mix of defiance and worry in his voice. "She has to rest."

"That's a good idea, Cameron. I'll go. You're in safe hands with your little brother, Mary," Karen added, giving the girl a smile even though it felt like her heart was breaking. "I'm going to think about what you said and I'm going to come up with a way to make it all better, okay? I promise."

Cameron looked mystified — but Mary just nodded, her eyes full of tears and a desperate, broken hope. Karen shut the door to the little bedroom behind her, feeling her body trembling with the shock of what she'd just learned. Connor was waiting for her on the landing, a look of acute concern on his face.

"Is everything okay? I was teaching Cameron how to use the knife and then we heard Mary crying out and he just came tearing inside to save her…"

"He's a good kid," Karen said absently. "Come on. We'd better go. I'll fill you in on the road."

They headed out the front gate, waving goodbye to Cameron and Mary's mother on their way. Did she know? Karen wondered. Was she aware of the terrible thing that had happened to her daughter a few weeks ago? Did she realize that it was Mary who was responsible for all the deaths, for the flocks of winged monsters that were preying on the town? It didn't seem like she did… Karen bit her lip, wondering how the woman would react if she found out. Would she be on Mary's side? Or would she blame her daughter for the death of Malcolm, an innocent child?

She filled Connor in as they rode, relying on her medical training to keep her emotions out of the story, though her voice still shook when she got to what had happened to Mary on that hillside a few weeks ago. He was utterly thunderstruck. Part of her had worried that he would downplay what had happened, that sexual assault wasn't as big a deal in medieval times as it was in her own… but to her relief, he seemed even more furious than she was. He stopped his horse, dismounted, paced back and forth with his fists clenched at his sides.

"I can't believe they could do such a horrific thing," he kept saying, his face white with anger and fear. "Some of them are distant clansmen. My whole clan will bear that shame for eternity —"

"It's not your fault," Karen said, shaking her head as she dismounted her horse, too, going to his side. "You aren't responsible for other men's evil —"

"Where was I," he wondered, frowning. "Where was I that night? If I'd ridden past the hillside, I might have seen them — might have stopped it —"

"You couldn't have stopped them," she said firmly, grabbing him by the shoulders. "It happened, Connor. Those monsters did what they did… and they were punished for it."

"They deserved worse," he snarled. "I'm not interested in getting justice for them. As far as I'm concerned, justice has already been done."

"What about Malcolm?" she said softly, and he

stopped in his tracks, scrubbing his face with his hands, a picture of dejection.

"I forgot," he said softly. "Poor Malcolm. But —" He frowned. "If the Sluagh came to Mary in her despair… and she sent them after the men who victimized her… why would they have taken Malcolm?"

"I have a theory about that," Karen said, leaning against him as they stood by the side of the road. "From what she said, I don't think she knew the names of all six men. But she knew they'd fallen ill with the pox — the six of them visited her that day, the day the storm came. They threatened her, told her it was her fault they were all covered in pox. So, I think… I think that when the Sluagh came to her, she told them to pursue any male with cowpox."

His eyes widened. "But that means…"

"That means they're going to keep hunting," she said heavily. "And it means that cowpox is no longer a mild disease — not if you're a man, at any rate." She took a deep breath, looking out across the grassy field beside them to where some cattle were peacefully grazing. "What are we going to do?"

"The only thing we can do," Connor sighed. "We're going to kill all the Sluagh. Iron and fire, that's the solution. I just hope we can stop them from taking any more innocent lives."

"What about Mary?" Karen wanted to know. "What do we do about her? The Sluagh feed on despair… I've never seen a person in a worse state than her, and I've been at the bedsides of plenty of terminally ill patients…"

"I don't know," he said simply, looking at her with a look of dejection in his gray eyes. She moved toward him, put her arms around him instinctively, and he pulled her into his arms, holding her close as they stood by the road, gazing down into the little village below them. The day was bright, and the villagers were going about their business as though nothing was wrong… everything seemed fine from up here. It was hard to imagine the Sluagh coming back… hard to remember that the village was being stalked by murderous monsters who killed children and rapists with equal malice, equal disrespect for life. Their only hope was to keep the villagers safe until the Sluagh could be dealt with… and if that meant shooting every last one with an iron arrow, she supposed that was their only option.

"I'm glad I'm with you, Karen Frakes," Connor said unexpectedly.

She looked up at him with a smile, the serious

expression on his face making her feel strangely safe even in the face of the uncertainty and horror that faced them.

"I'm glad I'm with you," she echoed him with a fond smile. "I honestly don't think I'd have gotten through any of this without you."

"Come on, then," he said with a smile, swinging back aboard his horse. "Lunch at the inn? We've a successful witch trial to celebrate, after all."

She didn't feel much like celebrating… and neither did Connor, to judge by the sad look on his face. But no matter how awful the situation was, she knew she could face it with Connor Grant at her side.

CHAPTER 48

The rest of the day seemed to pass slowly. They headed for the inn first to eat a warm meal — she felt a little shy stepping through the door, crowded as the inn was with townsfolk who had until recently wanted her exiled from this place for being a witch. But to her gratitude, it seemed word had spread that she was no witch, and she even received a few friendly smiles and greetings from the townsfolk.

Thomas, too, offered her a full apology for kicking her out of the inn, and made it clear that neither she nor Connor would be paying for their meals here for some time. He brought their food out himself and hovered a little anxiously, explaining that her room was still free, and she was more than welcome to move back in at any time she saw fit. She hesitated for a moment, exchanging glances with Connor, who looked a little worried that she was going to take Thomas up on his offer... but she just smiled back up at the innkeeper, shaking her head.

"I've made other arrangements," she said smoothly, winning a smile from Connor on the other side of the table. "But thank you, Thomas, for the kind offer. And no hard feelings, okay? You did what you had to do."

"I'm still annoyed with him," Connor told her in an undertone once the innkeeper had bustled off, and she giggled, for a moment forgetting the gravity of the situation.

But it wasn't long before the memory of what had happened to Mary came back, and they passed the rest of the day in a rather somber mood. Connor had work to do — the watch was maintaining their patrol routes around the village, which was their habit when a supernatural threat was active as it currently was, and he invited her to ride with him as a way of passing the time. Neither of them acknowledged it, but they were waiting for sundown... waiting to see if the Sluagh would return to attempt to claim more victims.

On patrol, they visited with a lot of villagers to check their defenses, and they were both delighted by how the town had responded to the threat. Every west-facing window was well boarded, with the recent deaths clearly moving everyone to action, and there were groups of villagers assisting the less able-bodied members of the community to board up their own windows and doors to be safe from the threat. The pox, it seemed, was still spreading — Karen was dismayed to discover a handful of new cases among the villagers, some of them men — well, not men. Boys — three young boys between the ages of five and ten, whose parents were able to trace the infection to Malcolm.

"It's not Rosemary's fault," one of the mothers said, shaking her head fiercely. "She kept Malcolm's sores dressed and covered ever so carefully... but you know what children are like, he was always fidgeting at the bandages, and boys are so rough with on another..."

"It's an easy disease to spread," Karen said comfortingly. "It's nobody's fault. Just make sure you keep him inside at night — we have reason to believe these creatures target the sick." She exchanged a brief glance with Connor, a shadow crossing both of their faces. They'd agreed over lunch that it would be best to keep some of the situation to themselves… that while the villagers had a right to know that the threat of the Sluagh extended to people with pox, they wouldn't be well served by the full story. The last thing Mary needed was a tribe of angry villagers marching up to her door. So, they'd decided to spread the information that the Sluagh targeted the sick — after all, that was partially true, if not the full story, and made sense given their nature as predators on the miserable and despairing. The specific detail that the creatures were preying on male patients of the cowpox wasn't necessary… the worst that would happen would be that sick women would board their windows up, which they wanted everyone to do regardless.

Still, it felt a little uncomfortable to be withholding the truth from the villagers, especially when they were all finally being so friendly to her. It seemed her visit to the Church, her willing participation in the religious rituals of the place, had done the trick — not only had the villagers dropped all suspicions that she was a witch, they were actively interested in her medical knowledge now, asking for advice on avoiding the contagion, or on treating the ill who had come down with it. It was an unpleasant situation to be in, but for the first time she could see a future for herself here after the contagion. After all, it was clear the town needed a doctor. There would be other diseases, other plagues… not to mention the usual barrage of regular illness, injury, childbirth…

But for now, she reminded herself as they rode, they had one specific calamity to focus on. The village wouldn't be safe until the Sluagh had been dealt with… and from her understanding, the creatures were going to keep hunting until they'd taken every last person in the village and fed on their life forces, up there above the clouds. They couldn't be banished, couldn't be returned to whence they'd came — the only option was to kill each and every one of them.

That, Connor explained to her over dinner, was something the Watch was already working on. Brendan had spread the word among the Watch at the castle that there would be hunting trips each night, men put on duty in the village to watch for the Sluagh and kill as many as possible with arrows and slings. Fire and iron were their weapons, and the blacksmith in the village — as well as the blacksmith at the Keep — were both hard at work producing as many iron-tipped arrows as they were able. The best archers of the Watch were being organized into shifts, prioritizing the hours of the night that the Sluagh had attacked, and at Karen's suggestion, Connor ensured that several were placed near Mary's cottage, in case the creatures saw fit to visit the person who'd first summoned them there. This was done without revealing the reason, of course — his justification was that the creatures may revisit the hillside upon which they'd dropped their victims, and that Mary's cottage was a good vantage point.

With all that done, all that remained for the two of them was to wait. As the night drew in, they both grew restless… it had been a clear day and the night seemed bright and still, with stars shining peacefully down, no sign of the dark clouds or hot west wind that had heralded the approach of the Sluagh earlier. They decided to retire to bed, reasoning that it would be valuable to get some rest tonight if the Sluagh weren't coming… but it took a long time to get to sleep, wrapped tight in each other's arms. Somehow, though they had the time to themselves, neither of them felt much like sex… the memory of Mary's trauma was still fresh in both of their minds, and the comfort they needed was easy enough to get from physical touch and nothing more.

They must have dozed off for a few hours before Karen became aware that she was awake... but what had woken her? She stirred a little, hearing Connor's rhythmic breathing and feeling the soft rhythm of the rise and fall of his chest… but then she heard it again. The sound of the cottage's western windows, nailed shut, but still rattling as if in a high wind. And when she breathed through her nose, her eyes widened as she smelled the unmistakable scent — the high, awful reek that she'd first encountered the night those six rapists had met their just ends.

Connor was awake too, his gray eyes gleaming in the dark. They could both hear the wind howling, now, make out the distant shrieks of the creatures that had been plaguing the village.

The Sluagh were here again. But this time, they were prepared.

CHAPTER 49

They rose fast, moving around the room to get dressed with practiced ease. Connor had suspected this might happen and had made a point of laying out their clothes carefully so that they could get dressed as quickly as possible. It wasn't long before the two of them were heading out, Connor clad in his armor with his sling at his side, Karen wrapped in a warm winter cloak that she hoped would keep the chill from her bones. Connor had given her a knife, too — a long, wicked thing carved of iron that he encouraged her to keep on her person at all times.

"The Fae hate iron with all their hearts," he told her firmly. "Just having it on you should offer you some protection from them… just make sure you leave it at home if you go to visit Maggie," he'd added with a smile.

It was tucked away in the bodice of her dress now, and she reached in to give the handle a reassuring squeeze. Knowing it was there made her feel safer as she headed out into the night with Connor, a lit torch lifted high in her hands. Sure enough, the village was abuzz — the Watch was there in considerable numbers, including a number of unfamiliar faces she reasoned must be guards from the Keep. She spotted Brendan, too, the Captain holding a torch high as he squinted into the sky — when he saw Connor and Karen coming, he gave them a tense smile of recognition, though his mind was clearly on the battle at hand.

"Ah, good," he said, giving Karen a quick grin. "We've got a witch on our side."

"Very funny," she said with a roll of her eyes.

She liked Brendan. He had a quick wit and a warm smile — and she was very much looking forward to meeting his wife when all of this was over.

They headed for the church, which offered a decent vantage point over much of the village. From up here, it was rather a beautiful sight… the little houses all shut and barred for the night, the occasional point of light burning in a window as the villagers peered out to see what the Watch were up to out there. You just couldn't put a stop to good old human curiosity, it seemed, no matter the dangers... but if the creatures were in fact frightened of fire, a light in a window shouldn't be a risk. The torches held by watchmen lit up the streets... but that wasn't where her attention was. Karen turned her eyes to the cloudy skies over the town as that hot west wind flapped at her cloak.

Sure enough, there they were — those familiar shadows she'd seen in the clouds that first night, just dark enough to hide the skeletal shapes, the flapping of dark, feathery wings. She studied the groupings of the creatures, realizing that it was possible to see where they were by tracing the clumping of the shadows... and she realized, to her surprise, that they were moving not in one great flock, but in smaller groups.

"They're hunting in packs," Brendan breathed, clearly coming to the same conclusion she was.

A thought occurred to her, and she narrowed her eyes, scanning the rooftops...

"Connor, where does Rosemary live?" she asked, noticing a thicker clump of shadow above one particular house... and sure enough, her lover raised his arm to point to the house that the creatures were gathering over. She turned, certain she knew where else she'd see a concentration of Sluagh... and sure enough, there was a dense grouping of them where she knew Mary's cottage lay. She remembered the way Mary's mother had barricaded the windows shut and took a deep breath to steady her nerves. Everyone was safe — everyone was inside, making sure the Sluagh couldn't get them...

There was one more concentration of the creatures, and she realized with a start that they were circling low over the little cottage that she and Connor had visited just that afternoon — the cottage where a young boy with pox lived with his mother... she remembered the broken little figure of Malcolm on the hillside and felt an icy chill move through her. Connor was clearly thinking the same thing — her eyes widened as he set off down the hill toward the house, shouting for the guards he passed to come with him, insisting that they intervene in what was clearly an attack being planned. She hesitated before following him, not wanting to get in the way or distract him, and she and Brendan waited up on the hill, watching as the guards assembled by the house. Was the little boy awake? she wondered. Did he know what kinds of monsters were gathered outside? They'd done their best to avoid letting the children know that there were creatures stalking them... it was bad enough to be so unwell without adding that terrifying nightmare to the mix.

The creatures were swooping lower and lower. Even though they were tangled in shadow, knowing what she was looking for made it easier to make out the shapes of the creatures as they swooped and dived. She saw one make what looked like an attack on a group of guards, diving low as an unearthly howl of wind rose in the darkness... but as the guards lifted their swords to defend themselves, the creature fluttered away, recoiling from the iron as though it had been burned by even getting that close to it. She reached into her bodice for her own knife, squeezing it to reassure herself that she was safe, and Brendan glanced at her.

"You're armed with iron, then?"

"Connor gave me an iron dagger, yes," she said with a smile.

He nodded his approval. "Faeries are fiercely averse to it. Should keep you safe. Not that you should be risking your neck," he added warningly.

His eyes went to the flock of Sluagh, and she

realized the men on the ground were preparing bows and arrows. She watched as Connor called them to attention, then gave the order to draw then loosen their bows. The arrows went flying into the darkness, aimed high above the rooftops — as she listened, she heard the clatter of a few of them hitting the peak of their arc then falling down to the streets below.

But not all of them missed their mark, or so it seemed. The eerie howling of the wind seemed to reach a high point, and she heard a shriek that was quite unlike any that had come before. While the Sluagh's screeching had sounded like hunger and anticipation, this shriek was entirely different… this one spoke of pain, and anger, and rage. And as she sought the source of that dreadful sound, she saw a bundle of shadows plummeting from the sky with an arrow somehow jutting out of its middle. It hit the ground hard and she realized she was running toward it, Brendan on her heels. Had they really brought one down? Was it as simple as that — an arrow through the midsection and they were done for?

Part of her didn't believe that it had really happened — she expected to find a bundle of rags on the ground outside the little cottage when she reached it, or else nothing at all. Some part of her, she realized, was still in denial about the true nature of these things, desperately hanging onto the illusion of ignorance to shelter itself... despite the deaths, despite everything that had happened to prove once and for all that magic was real and so were monsters, her mind still couldn't accept it. Still didn't want to.

But then she approached the circle of guards who were standing around where the creature had fallen. They looked up at her, an odd mixture of expressions on their faces in the torchlight — some looked triumphant at their victory, others looked frightened by what they'd seen, still more just looked tired. Connor's eyes were already on the sky again, looking for more of the creatures, his mind clearly on the rest of the job of killing the whole flock... but they'd retreated a little, it seemed, hiding in the relative safety of the cloud cover as they coped with the fact that one of their own had been struck down in vengeance.

And Karen crept closer to the dead body of the first supernatural creature she'd ever seen.

CHAPTER 50

The monster was much bigger than she'd expected when she looked at it in the firelight. For some reason — perhaps the wings — she'd been expecting something roughly the size of a crow, maybe a little larger… like the winged monkeys from *The Wizard of Oz*, perhaps. She hadn't expected the Sluagh to be the size of an adult human, for sure, and it made her recoil a little, shocked by how human-like the corpse was. For a moment, she felt an odd thrill of dread at the association — what had they done? It was as though they'd struck down a person, not a monster…

But then the torchlight illuminated the crea-ture better, and she got a look at it that wasn't obscured by shadow, and that particular impression faded as quickly as it had arrived. This was no human. This was nothing close to human. Sure, it was loosely humanoid… it had four limbs, two legs and two arms, and a rounded head sitting on top of its shoulders. But that was the end of the human associations. Its body was skeletally thin, with bones jutting out through its corpse-pale skin. And its face was nothing short of monstrous. All she could look at as her eyes traveled to its face was its jaw — a mouth full of black teeth that jutted out in random directions, with the sickly appearance of rot … a narrow, pointed nose, and a pair of jet black eyes that stared horribly into nothingness, the life, or whatever passed for it, having clearly already fled its body.

She remembered the bodies she'd examined, the way they were slashed and scratched, and she scanned the monster for an indication of what had caused those wounds — and she found it, alright. There, at the ends of its painfully slender arms, were hands that were more claw than hand — it was as though five great curved blades jutted directly out of the creature's wrists. No wonder the men had been so badly sliced up — the creature wouldn't be able to lift anyone aloft without tearing their flesh if it had tried.

There, in its side, was the arrow that had brought it down. Karen dropped to her knees beside the creature to get a closer look, very interested in this particular part of the puzzle. The arrow had sunk into the creature's flesh as though it was liquid — she could tell that at least six inches of the arrow's length was in the Sluagh's side, maybe more. How had it struck with such power? It must have moved through the flesh like a hot knife through butter... and she wrinkled her nose as the faint smell of burning reached her. Sure enough, a tiny amount of smoke seemed to be creeping out of the wound that the arrow had left, and she reached down curiously to ease the arrow out of the creature's side. Sure enough, it came away easily, and she saw how deep the wound was, how it sizzled with contact with the iron arrowhead.

"Maggie wasn't joking," she said softly, shaking her head. "Iron really does end these creature's lives."

"Aye — tears them up and stops them flying," Connor said, and an echo of approval went up among the men.

It was heartening, to see their terrifying enemy

brought down like this… to know that the thing that had killed seven people could be killed itself, that they were more than equipped to win this battle.

"I've seen what happens when iron touches Fae creatures up close. It drains their energy as well as burning their flesh."

"We have plenty of iron arrows?" she asked, looking up at the men, and there was a chorus of agreement. "Good. Let's get as many of these out of the air as we can." She looked down at the creature again, curious now about the great wings that sprouted from its shoulders. It had fallen hard, and it was clear that plenty of bones in those wings had been broken — both by the fall, and by the guard who had kicked the creature over onto its back to be examined. She nudged it gently back the other way with her foot, wanting a better look at the wings, but not especially keen to touch its flesh with her bare hands. What she wouldn't give for a few pairs of rubber gloves…

The wings were covered in black feathers, but it was clear they weren't flight feathers from how bedraggled and droopy they were. Beneath them, the wings were black and leathery, more like a bat's wings than a bird's. They were enormous, too. Folded and broken beneath the creature's body it was hard to get a good look at the wings, but they were at least the length of the Sluagh's body, and from the looks of it they'd spread out to be a few times wider than the skeletal creature.

But those eyes... she kept coming back to the creature's face. Despite the mask of death that had frozen its face solid, she couldn't help but gaze into those black eyes. What she saw there was evil... and, what was worse, intelligent. These weren't simple carnivores, hunting their prey. These were intelligent creatures who knew what they were doing. Connor seemed to be thinking along the same lines — he put his arm around her as she got back to her feet, looking around at the men still gathered around the monster's body. She realized she could make out their faces better now, and with a shock realized that the dawn was approaching.

"We have our work cut out for us here," Connor said firmly, giving each man a sharp look. "There are dozens of these things — maybe more, it's hard to tell. They're intelligent, as shown by the way they backed right off when their friend here was killed, and they'll almost certainly be back with new tactics to try to get what they want without us killing them in return. We'll have to be careful in the face of their attacks… and we'll have to keep the villagers inside at all costs."

The guards nodded, their faces set and determined. But they were distracted by a tiny sound, like air escaping from an inflatable pool toy… a gentle hissing, just on the edges of hearing. For a moment, Karen was frightened that another Sluagh was about to ambush them — but then she realized that smoke was rising from the dead creature that lay at their feet, for all the world as though it had been set on fire. She was struck by confusion — hadn't she taken the iron out of the creature's wound? What could be happening to make it smoke like this? Then she realized what was happening. The sun was rising… and it was dissolving the monster before them as it did.

She stepped back, a little shocked to see how quickly the light of the rising sun was doing its work, and they stood around together in what felt like an odd little funeral procession as the monster's body slowly dissolved. The smoke rose into the dawn air, and within ten minutes it was as though the Sluagh had never been there… but for the image of its gaunt body and awful face, burned into Karen's memory in a way she knew she'd never forget.

"One down," Brendan said, taking a step forward to address his men. "Who knows how many left to go? Get some rest. We'll be working from sunset to sunrise until the last of these things are gone."

And with that, the group of men dissolved. It seemed the majority of the guards from the Keep would be staying at Thomas's inn — she saw them heading back that way, clapping each other one the shoulders in congratulations for a good night of hunting. Brendan was headed back to the Keep to keep the Laird and his people up to date about what was happening — he gave Connor and Karen a little wave as he headed for the stables to fetch his horse for the ride back. And then they were alone.

"Well, then," Connor said, a smile dancing across his face. "I suppose we'd best do as we're told and get some rest."

She followed him to his cottage, smiling to herself. Something about his expression suggested that while they might be headed for bed, sleep might be a while away just yet…

CHAPTER 51

I n the end, it was mid-morning before the two of them fell asleep, wrapped in each other's sweaty arms and utterly sated. She'd never had sex like this before in her life — not that she was especially experienced on that front, but the handful of sexual relationships she'd had included sex as a kind of obligation, something she felt more or less like she had to do to keep the peace. Not that she hated it — it was enjoyable enough, in its way — but she'd never understood the wild passion that some of her friends reported, that seemed to happen in books and movies about love and romance. The idea of being so infatuated with someone that your body physically ached for them... well, until she'd met Connor, she'd thought that was just a poetic exaggeration. Now, when she felt his hands on her body, his lips on hers, his hot breath against her throat, against her chest, tingling up and down her spine as he kissed and caressed every inch of her... well, she understood why people talked about passion and desire as though they were an all-consuming fire.

Fire was a good metaphor, actually. Her feelings for Connor had certainly flared to life like a struck match, building slowly over time as they'd fed on the kindling of his company. In his arms as they made love, she felt like a bonfire... but when they lay together afterwards, that was her favorite feeling, like a little campfire crackling in the centre of her chest. Like hearth and home, that fire, the embers warming her, the cheery flames keeping her spirits up even in the midst of everything that was going on. And as he gazed down at her, a soft look in those gray eyes of his, she felt utterly safe with him. She knew he felt something similar... knew that whatever this was between them, it was important to both of them.

It felt like all day that they slept, but it was really only a few hours. It was late afternoon when they got up, dressing slowly, ambling into the main room to put together a late lunch of bread and cheese.

She was no stranger to odd sleeping patterns, having worked just about every possible combination of shifts at hospitals in her time — medicine was a twenty-four hour profession, after all. And she was more than ready to be nocturnal for a few weeks if that was what it took to defeat these creatures one and for all, and to restore safety to the villagers.

So, the days wore on. She'd gotten into the habit of staying up all night with Connor. She'd join him on patrol on the quiet nights when the sky was clear… but when the west wind howled and the clouds scudded over the moon and stars, that's when she'd station herself at the inn. The first night of Sluagh attacks after their first successful kill made it clear the watchmen might need medical aid if they were to continue fighting — the creatures took to diving and slashing at anyone with a torch or a bow, confirming their suspicions that the creatures were not only intelligent… but deeply malevolent, too, and keenly interested in getting revenge for their fallen comrades.

But despite this, the bravery of the watch was prevailing. The Sluagh lost a few more of their numbers each night they attacked, and though they still hovered over the homes of those male villagers with the pox, they were much more reluctant to swoop low and try to drag anyone out of the windows. They seemed to sense that it was the Watch who were their enemy now, and dove and slashed at them, clearly trying to disrupt the village's protection. A few minor injuries eventuated that first week — most of them wounds from the claws of the Sluagh. Karen, ready and waiting at the inn with all the supplies she could muster, handled them with ease.

"Those creatures are filthy," she muttered to herself as she cleaned a wound for a young man who'd managed to slice a Sluagh's head clean off when it had dived on him, shrieking, after he'd shot an arrow at its companion. He was quite pleased with himself, though wincing at the deep gash the Sluagh had left in his shoulder — a wound that was full of festering matter that she couldn't identify but reasoned had come from the creature's claws. "Without treatment, this wound would fester and kill you," she told the young man, taking the smug look on his face down a notch or two.

Thankfully, with Thomas's help, she'd been able to produce some home-made saline solution with boiled water and salt, and it was easy enough to clean out the shallow wound thoroughly before bandaging it up and sending the man on his way.

"Will I be able to fire an arrow?"

"Not for a while," she said, frowning after him as he headed back to his quarters with his shoulders slumped. That was a good point. She was grateful there were no serious injuries yet — but any injury serious enough to put a watchman out of commission was a problem. What if they ran out of able-bodied men to defend against the Sluagh?

As the weeks wore on, the creatures grew bolder and bolder as time passed with no kills… for all the world as though they were growing hungrier and hungrier. What was it that they fed on? The bodies that had been recovered hadn't been eaten in any way — was it the life force that they drained, as Maggie had said? Thinking of it made Karen shudder, and she devoted herself anew to making sure that the injured men were keeping their wounds clean. She also visited with every reported cowpox patient to make sure they understood how important it was to keep their lesions covered to stop the disease spreading… and to double-check their window fastenings, as the disease made them a prime target for the Sluagh. She was fairly certain the spread was slowing, if not entirely stopped, when a week had passed with no new cases coming to her attention... but there were half a dozen young men with pox, and she was worried for their safety if the Sluagh were not stopped.

The nights were crazy, and she worried for Connor every minute she spent sitting in the inn, ready and waiting for anyone who might need medical attention. But when the dawn came and the watch were dismissed from their duties, he'd come up the street to collect her, that tired smile on his gorgeous face... and they'd head home together and fall into each other's arms as the sun climbed into the sky.

She knew she was taking comfort in the wild infatuation that marked the beginning of a new relationship, and that so was he... but despite knowing that she couldn't help but feel that there was something else here, something more to this relationship than just the physical. She knew it was still too early in their relationship to make any big decisions — especially with everything that was going on with the epidemic and with the Sluagh — but she couldn't help but think about what Father Caleb had said during her confession, about marriage. She'd never been the kind of woman who gave marriage much thought... but then again, she'd never been a doctor in medieval Scotland, either and that had been an easy enough change to make.

Something to be thought about later, she always told herself when she found those thoughts creeping into her mind... usually in the mornings, after she and Connor had made love, when they were drifting off to sleep in each other's arms. Plenty of time to figure out what this relationship was once they'd saved the village from the threat that still stalked it almost every other night.

And maybe, her treacherous mind would whisper before she could stop it... maybe even a wedding to plan.

CHAPTER 52

The next night the Sluagh came again. The now-familiar sound of their high, keening shrieks mingling with the west wind interrupted their dinner at sunset, and she shook her head, a little annoyed that they were back again. She'd been looking forward to simply patrolling with Connor tonight... the Sluagh's presence meant that she'd be holed up in the inn again, waiting for injured men to turn up. There'd been more and more injuries of late — it seemed that the Sluagh were getting more and more bold as time passed, and cleverer, too, picking on men when they'd run out of arrows, avoiding flying in a way that outlined them against the sky and made them easy targets for arrows. As a result, the cull had slowed a little, too — though they still had a total kill count of eleven. The men were resentful that they couldn't keep the bodies as trophies, but they dissolved each morning at dawn, even if kept out of the sunlight. No wonder there was no fossil record or other evidence of the existence of these creatures, Karen thought, if they disappeared without a trace when they died… she was beginning to see that science might have more than a few blind spots when it came to getting a full and accurate picture of the world.

But something was wrong. She'd only just settled in for the night at the inn, her supplies prepared and ready for the wounded — it was maybe a few hours after sunset when the familiar sound of the west wind battering at the inn's shutters began to fade away. Karen didn't notice what had happened at first — she'd grown so used to the west wind's howling, and to the noxious stench that rode on it when the Sluagh were out in force, that the absence of both went unnoticed aside from a general sense that something was missing. Then Thomas stuck his head out from the back room where he'd been washing bandages, a frown on his face.

"Did the wind just ease up, or am I losing my hearing?"

Frowning, Karen got up and headed for the front doors to investigate. She stepped out onto the veranda, staring up int the night sky with absolute shock. When she'd gone into the inn, the night had been cloudy and overcast, the distant howls of the Sluagh making it clear that they were afoot — but now, only hours later, she looked up to see a clear blanket of stars. It was a still night, too, with a barely a breeze rustling the branches of the trees, and she put her hands on her hips, nonplussed. The Sluagh were gone, it seemed. But where?

"Have they given up for the night?" Thomas was at her side, frowning up into the sky as well. "Not like them to turn in early." The creatures had hunted til dawn for the past several weeks… the only exception was that first night, when they'd taken the six men and disappeared, and the second night, when little Malcolm had been taken. But why had they disappeared tonight?

Feeling a low sense of dread in her gut and not knowing why, Karen turned and strode up the path toward the church, instinctively seeking out Brendan and Connor to see if they knew what was going on. It wasn't long before she ran into

Connor, who had a tight expression on his face and could barely offer her a smile when he saw her.

"What's going on? The Sluagh…"

"Not sure," he said, voice low. "But I have a bad feeling..."

They were close to Rosemary's house, she realized with a start — the Sluagh still spent a lot of their time circling this particular house. Connor wasn't sure whether it was because they remembered successfully capturing little Malcolm here and were hoping to find more easy prey in the same place, or because they were drawn to Rosemary's despair… either way, the guards tended to focus their attentions on this particular spot when it came to Sluagh hunting.

So, it surprised her a great deal when one of Rosemary's neighbor's doors opened a crack, and a pale, worried face peeked out into the night air, gesturing to them to approach.

An elderly woman who lived next door. Karen couldn't remember her name, but she'd checked a little sore on her arm for her, one that she was worried was an indication that she'd caught the pox — it hadn't been a cowpox lesion, in the end, but the woman had been very grateful for the reassurance. Her face now was anything but pleased — she looked like she was about to cry.

"It's Rosemary," she said as soon as they came close enough to the door. She was wearing a night-gown with a shawl wrapped around her shoulders and had clearly not been to bed yet. "A little while ago, I thought I heard her door slam, so I opened my window to check if the wind had pried it open. I saw her walking down the street like she was sleep-walking."

Karen's heart felt like it dropped straight into her boots. She could see panic coming to life on Connor's face, his gray eyes wide with shock, and he reached out for the elderly woman, his voice urgent. "Are you sure? Which way did she go?"

"Toward the Loch," the woman said, shaking her head. "I called after her, but she didn't look back — I didn't want to go out there in case those things came swooping down…"

"You did the right thing staying put," Karen told her firmly, and she nodded her gratitude for the reassurance. "We'll see if we can find her."

Then they were off, half-walking, half-running toward the shore of the Loch, striding out of town and down toward the beach. Connor called out to the nonplussed members of the Watch as he walked and many of them fell into step with them, clearly wanting to help with whatever was going on, feeling at a loss with the sudden, early retreat of the Sluagh. It wasn't long before Brendan was with them, too, Connor giving him a brief summary of what the old woman had told them had happened.

Karen could feel the dread prickling at her stomach as the guards peeled off in pairs and headed off around the lake, searching thoroughly in groups for any sign of Rosemary. Part of her knew what they were going to find, understood already, on some level, what had happened. Why had she done it? Why had she walked out into the night where monsters were stalking? Karen had a horrible feeling she knew exactly why. Some traumas were just too awful to recover from... and after all, didn't the Sluagh feed on despair?

She wasn't shocked when she heard shouts from two of the guards, wasn't surprised when they approached the huddled mass on the ground, lying just as though it was sleeping... though there was something not quite right about the angle of the limbs, about the heaviness of the sprawl. Karen dropped to her knees beside the woman, checking her over in the light of the torch, feeling an odd numbness spreading out from her chest as she remembered meeting Rosemary, remembered the grief and anger on the woman's face... remembered how alive she'd been. Now, she was nothing but a crumpled body on the sand... and the expression on her face was one of bitter resignation, far from the abject terror of the men who'd been the Sluagh's first victims. Karen passed her hand quickly over the woman's eyes, grateful that she'd been able to close them before rigor mortis set in.

"What did she think she was doing?" Connor breathed.

She looked up at him — he was kneeling beside her, a look of grief on his handsome face, tears standing in his eyes. He looked at her, and she realized that he knew as well as she did what they were looking at. Rosemary wasn't foolish enough to go walking on a night when the Sluagh were hunting. It may have been those creatures who'd snatched her up and drained her life... but the cause of death, if Karen had been filling out a certificate, would be suicide.

CHAPTER 53

They walked back to Connor's cottage in silence. Old Maggie had appeared not long after the body had been found, still and impassive in the cold night air — she'd accepted responsibility for the body and recruited two guards to help carry it away, toward her cottage, where she said she'd give the woman a proper burial.

"Shouldn't Father Caleb…?" Karen had asked, frowning, but Maggie's eyes had flashed, and Karen had felt Connor shake his head, just a little. But hadn't Rosemary been religious? Surely, she'd want the priest to take care of her burial…

"He won't take her," Maggie said, her voice gentler than Karen had expected, and she realized with a rush what the two of them meant. Suicide was a sin... of course. The injustice of that chafed at Karen as she watched Maggie and the guards carrying Rosemary's body away. Surely someone so utterly lost as Rosemary deserved God's love more than anyone... but at least Maggie was there to ensure she was given a proper burial, whatever her cause of death. It bothered her a lot, though, that the six rapists had been buried by the priest... even if their crimes hadn't been known then.

"I just can't help thinking about those men and what they did," she said, gritting her teeth, when Connor asked her why she looked so angry. "They're responsible for this, for all of this... and nobody knows it was them, that it was their fault. They got to be buried in the church yard with everyone else, too, and poor Rosemary who's only a victim of all this —"

"I know," Connor said softly, taking her into his arms and holding her close. She comforted herself with the smell of him, the warmth of his body, the sensation of his arms around her... but her mind wouldn't leave the topic alone. "It's unjust. But Maggie will take good care of her. She's a good woman... I've attended services she's held for the dead. Rosemary's soul is in good hands… if some-what unconventional ones."

"I wish I'd known she was…" Karen sighed. "Not that there was anything I could have done, but still. I wish I could have talked to her."

"So do I," Connor said bleakly. "She seemed just fine when I spoke to her last… honestly, I thought she was coming out of her grief a little. She was moving around, at least, which hadn't been the case…"

"That can happen," Karen said softly, remembering a psych rotation she'd done back at med school. "It's common, for suicides… once they've decided to go through with it, it feels as though a weight is lifted, and they can seem quite cheerful and carefree. It's one of the signs we're advised to watch for."

"Not much chance of anyone feeling carefree at the moment," Connor said with a sigh. The village was waking up as news spread of what had happened — dawn hadn't yet broken, but already the villagers were in the street, talking amongst each other in low voices. Karen lowered her eyes, feeling again like an interloper on their grief, and then looked up at Connor with a sudden determination burning in her chest.

"Enough of this," she said, keeping her voice low even as her temper blazed. "We have to go and talk to Mary. There has to be something she can do to stop this."

"I thought you didn't want —"

"I wanted to give her space to heal, true," Karen said, shaking her head. "But people are dying, Connor. How long will it be until one of those creatures takes a watchman up into the air and kills him? How much longer until someone leaves a window open and another child is taken? These creatures are wicked, and intelligent, and getting hungrier and hungrier. We need to be more proactive. We need to find out exactly what's going on here — and that means getting the full story from Mary." She shook her head. "I don't want to traumatize her, but we need to find out how exactly this curse works… and whether we can reverse it, somehow."

Connor nodded. "I'll come with you."

They agreed to head up to Mary's cottage later in the day — by that time, she hoped the news of Rosemary's death would have reached the girl, and maybe she'd be in a mood to share what she knew about the Sluagh in case doing so could help prevent any more deaths. Besides, it had been a while since Karen had checked in on the families up there, to make sure their houses were well barricaded.

In the end, they rode up just after midday, after a deep sleep during the morning hours had replenished some of their energies. Though the day was bright, the atmosphere in the village was still tense… she did see Father Caleb deep in conversation with some of the women who'd been Rosemary's closest friends, and it was clear that some kind of memorial service was being organized. That would have to do, she thought with a pang of sadness, offering up her own little prayer for Rosemary. Suicide or no, she deserved the same kind of remembrance as anyone else.

They knocked hard on the door, and it wasn't long before Cameron answered it, looking uncharacteristically sleepy and grumpy, as though they'd just gotten him out of bed. It was clear that he was still taking his duties seriously, however — the long iron knife that Connor had given him on their last visit was in his hand, and he relaxed his guard only a little bit when he recognized who was visiting.

"We need to speak to Mary, Cameron, is that alright?" Karen asked, trying to disguise her impatience. As sweet as it was that the little boy wanted to protect his big sister, it was getting a little inconvenient to have to play this game every time they wanted to talk to the girl. He hesitated, still looking bleary-eyed, and she frowned a little. This wasn't the sharp-eyed boy they'd met.

"What's wrong, little man?" That was Connor, dropping to one knee to speak to the child at his level. "Were you up late last night?"

"I was making sure the shadows didn't come and bother Mary," he said in a small voice, rubbing his face. "I don't want anyone upsetting her."

"That's good," Connor said with a smile. "We don't want that either. But we do need to talk to her, Cameron. Will you let us through?"

He hesitated … but Connor had managed to suggest somehow, with his body language and the slightly fixed quality of the smile on his face, that this wasn't a question that Cameron could say no to. Looking a little resentful, he stood aside, and Connor and Karen started up the stairs with the little boy trailing after them, still wielding the iron blade. It was good that he had it, Karen thought with a smile, remembering what Brendan had told her about the protective effects of iron. And he probably knew a lot more about how to use the thing than she did, too.

Mary was looking a lot better when they crept into her room. The curtains were still shut tight and the room was still very dark, but Karen could tell that the weeks of rest had helped a little with her lesions, and with the disease. Still, the gaze she turned to them was listless, and it was clear to Karen that she was still deep in the depression and probable post-traumatic stress that the rape had caused. How was she going to recover from this? It was a complex issue even in Karen's own time... and she was far from an expert in psychology or psychiatry. Even if she'd known where to start, there was no guarantee she'd be of any help to the girl...

But that wasn't why they were here, she reminded herself — helping Mary wasn't their goal here.

They were here to see if Mary could help them — and the rest of the village — in dealing with the Sluagh threat.

CHAPTER 54

But she didn't want to just go straight in with that question. She hesitated a little, exchanged a glance with Connor, aware they hadn't spoke of strategy here — then shrugged, deciding to just improvise.

"How are you feeling, Mary?"

The girl shrugged, swallowed hard. "A little better. My bruises are healed."

"That's good," Karen said softly. She moved a little closer to Mary, noticing with some relief that Connor chose to stay back by the door — probably safest, given what the girl had gone through at the hands of men. "I'm glad to hear that. How are your lesions?"

"Hate them," she said listlessly. "They're everywhere and they're never going to heal."

"That's not true," Cameron said stridently, surging forward. The little boy looked heartbroken that his sister was so upset, but he lifted his chin fiercely. "They're getting better. I've been helping put on salve from Old Maggie and they're going to heal right up and not even leave any scars, that's what Maggie told us, and she's magic so you know she's telling the truth."

"Tell you what, Cameron? Why don't you and I head downstairs and fetch the girls something to drink?" Connor didn't give Cameron a chance to argue — just headed downstairs with him in tow. Grateful to be alone with Mary, Karen pressed the advantage.

"What about your visitors, Mary?" Karen asked gently. "You know the ones I mean. Last time, you called them the angels. Have you seen them again?"

That got the girl's attention. Mary looked up sharply, a frightened, wary look on her face as she processed what had been asked. "No," she said, a little too quickly. "They're nothing to do with me."

"I have bad news, I'm afraid," Karen said softly, encouraged by the way Mary was at least looking at her and listening to what she had to say. "About the creatures. They're not angels, Mary. They're called the Sluagh, and they're extremely dangerous indeed. The men they killed that first night… they deserved it. You know I don't blame you at all for sending them after those men. But I'm afraid that something … something's happening. The Sluagh… they're not just hunting bad men. They're hunting anyone — man or boy — who has cowpox. You know that included little Malcolm. And the disease has spread… at least four more boys have it, all children. All like your little brother."

She was shaking her head, her face a mask of misery. "I don't — I can't —"

"It's not your fault, Mary. I believe that. But if we're going to stop this… if we're going to stop more innocent people dying…" She took a deep breath. "I need you to tell me the whole story, Mary. Can you do that?"

"I can't," she whispered, her face a mask of misery. "I can't… I can't —" A sob escaped her, and then she collapsed into tears, her frail shoulders shaking as she wailed loudly enough to echo through the house. Karen felt for her acutely, but frustration still twisted at her stomach… all she needed was information, information that might help save lives… How could she get through to her?

There was a sudden commotion on the stairs, the sound of pounding feet echoing through the wall, and then the door burst open and little Cameron was standing there, his face furious and his knife drawn. Connor was behind him, and the look on his face was incredibly grim — Karen looked at him, a little puzzled by how acutely dismayed he looked. Had he overheard Mary explaining that she couldn't tell them what had happened?

"Mary, don't cry," Cameron said miserably, moving to the girl's side and reaching out with one trembling hand to comfort her. As he did so, the long sleeve of the sweater he was wearing pulled back with the motion of his arm, and Karen gasped at what she saw there. For a moment, she hoped against hope that it was just a scrape or bruise — even an infected knife wound from his practice — but no, there was no mistaking it. There, on the underside of the little boy's arm, red and raw as anything, was a fresh cowpox pustule.

"Cameron," she gasped, reaching forward to take hold of his elbow. Realizing what had happened, his eyes went wide, and he yanked his arm away, tugging the sleeve down as quick as he could to hide the pustule… but it was too late. She'd seen more than enough… but Mary hadn't. The girl was looking at Karen, clearly a little concerned by her shock — but the expression on her face made it clear that her little brother had been hiding his condition. "You know what that is, don't you?"

"No," he said defiantly, clearly lying.

"Cameron?" Mary said in a small voice, her eyes moving to her brother. He looked delighted to hear her say his name — but then his face twisted. "What's wrong?"

"I — nothing. I just hurt my arm. I fell down. I cut it with the knife, I —"

"That's cowpox, Cameron," Connor said firmly from the doorway, shaking his head. "You know as well as we do, so why lie?"

"It's fine," he said miserably, reaching out to grab his sister's hand as her eyes filled with tears. "I'm alright, Mary, really, I don't even feel that sick —"

"No, no, no," Mary was whimpering, her face a mask of horror, and Karen shook her head, full of grief about the connection she must be making. Cameron, her beloved little brother, now fit the profile she'd given to the Sluagh — the victims she'd volunteered for the slaughter now numbered her little brother among them.

"You have to help us, Mary," Karen said softly. "We can stop them — we can keep you safe. Both of you. Everyone in the village. But we need you to tell us what's going on. For Cameron."

Mary gazed at her little brother for a long, long time. The little boy's eyes were full of tears — he'd sunk down onto her bed, all the fight in him gone, and as she stared at him, he lay down beside her, putting his head in her lap. "He's been so strong," Mary whispered, stroking his hair back from his face with a tender gesture. "He — he kept me alive. Never gave up on me…"

"So, help him. Help him, Mary. Help him by helping us."

"The herdsmen had been bothering me for weeks." Her eyes didn't shift, and her tone was flat and emotionless.

Karen could tell she was shutting herself down, trying not to feel anything so she could get through the story. Her heart leapt with hope and she leaned forward, wanting to take the girl's hand in hers, to help her be brave and get through her story — but Mary had her eyes fixed on Cameron's face, almost in a trance as she stroked his hair. Distancing herself from the story. Well, whatever she needed to do, Karen was happy to let her. She could see

Connor standing at the doorway, barely moving or breathing — she glanced at him and he moved carefully back, out of Mary's field of vision but still in the room.

Was this it? Were they finally about to learn how they could defeat the Sluagh?

CHAPTER 55

"I couldn't get them to leave me alone," Mary said, her voice barely a whisper. "I tried everything. First, I was nice to them, played along with their jokes. Then I was cold but polite, doing what I could to avoid them, never to be alone with any of them. First it was just staring. Then it was comments and jokes about me, about my body, about my…" She passed a shaking hand over her torso, a general gesture toward her breasts.

Karen fought the urge to scowl. The way men reacted to the perfectly natural development of breasts in young women as they went through puberty, even adult men… it was disgusting.

"I tried and tried to get away from them. Tried begging them to leave me alone. Even tried giving them what they wanted, playing along, flirting back. But none of it helped, none of it worked. I tried to talk to the farmers, talk to their parents, talk to the priest and the village leaders and everyone. All of them just laughed. They told me that that was what boys were like. That all the milkmaids were used to it, that one day a boy I liked would do the same things and I'd love it." Her whole body was shaking as she spoke.

Karen wished she could do something, anything, to ease the pain she saw on her face.

"Nobody believed me when I said I was scared they were going to hurt me. Everyone just told me I was overreacting. Then…"

"It's okay," Karen said softly as she hesitated. "It's okay, Mary. You're safe. Keep going when you can." She gave her a cup of water from the bedside table — the girl's hands shook as she took a sip from it.

"I was walking home across the hillside," she said softly. "It was dark. I'd been walking the long way every night for two weeks because they… they were always in town, they were always on the street where I walked, and I didn't want them to scream things at me… so I'd been walking across the pastures instead. And they… they saw me, I guess, or found out. They came after me. Danny was the one who grabbed me — grabbed me by the hand," she said, lifting her left hand. "Squeezed me. It hurt so badly — I could tell he'd burst one of my sores but when I tried to tell him he just put his hand over my mouth. Then —"

Her face twisted and Karen took a breath. "You don't have to go through it, love. I know what they did, you don't have to retell it if it hurts you."

"It was so dark when they stopped," she whispered. "I was lying in the grass — William threw his cloak on me and they all left. I was there for… I don't know how long. I don't remember getting home but when I woke up, I was here."

"Why didn't you tell anyone?" Karen said softly. But she already knew the answer.

"I knew they wouldn't believe me," Mary murmured, tears streaming down her face though she barely seemed aware of it. "Or they'd tell me it was my fault… that I'd been leading the men on, that I shouldn't have walked across the field, or that that was just what men do and I was just unlucky…"

"Those men were monsters," Connor broke in unexpectedly. He was clearly controlling his voice, his anger, but Karen could hear how his voice was shaking with the strain. "Their actions were their fault and their fault alone. You did nothing wrong. I'm utterly ashamed of them, Mary."

She gave no sign that she'd heard him — but her voice did sound a little stronger when she spoke again. "When Mam asked what had happened to give me so many bruises and spread the pox all over me, I said I'd fainted and fallen down the stairs. I thought I was safe… thought they were finally done with me. That they'd gotten what they'd wanted, and they'd finally leave me alone. Then… then they came here. Cameron tried to stop them coming up the stairs," she added, a soft smile crossing her face as she stroked the boy's hair.

He'd fallen asleep, Karen realized with a start. Maybe that was a good thing. It might break his little heart to know what had happened to his sister — he'd find a way to blame himself for not protecting her.

"What did they say?"

"They said they all had pox — that it was my fault, that I'd better do something about it. Threatened to kill me. It was only that they saw Da coming home that they left. I think one of them was watching the house," she added, frowning.

Karen remembered with an icy chill the day

she'd run into Danny outside of the cottage. If only she'd known then what she knew now… she'd have hauled him off to the village elders herself to answer for his awful crimes.

"I was so sad… so frightened they'd come back, that they'd hurt Cameron or our parents, I just…" She shivered. "I knew it was a sin when I thought of it but I…" She hesitated, then reached into the bedside table drawer and withdrew a small knife. "I didn't want to live," she said, tears rolling down her cheeks. "I wrote a letter to my family and everything, explaining and saying that I was sorry… I thought if I was dead, they might be safe, but I couldn't… I wasn't brave enough to —" Her shoulders were shaking as she dropped the knife back into the drawer and covered her face with her hands. Karen wanted to hold her but knew touching her was a bad idea. "That was when they came," she whispered. "The angels. They came to my window in the dark of the night when I was in my deepest despair, and they whispered that they could take me away, make me forget it all. I was tempted. For the longest time, I thought about going with them… about leaving all this behind for good. But it's a sin," she whispered. "I couldn't. I didn't want to go. So, I told them…" She shivered.

"I told them I wanted to live. They looked so angry. They told me they'd take me whether I wanted to go or not — unless I could offer them another life in my place." Her face was hard. "I told them I could offer them six."

Karen took a deep breath. "You named the herdsmen."

"It was all I could think of," she whispered. "The only way to keep my family safe. But I didn't know all of their names — only Danny, and William — and the creatures didn't understand when I tried to give them a description instead. So, I told them to look for any men with cowpox. I thought… I didn't know anyone else would get it other than milkmaids," she whispered. "I thought it was only if you touched a cow, or did what they did to me, I never thought…"

"I know, Mary," Karen said softly, wanting so badly to comfort her but having no idea what to say. "You did your best, I know."

"I don't want anyone else to die," she whispered, her face a mask of sorrow. "They come to me every night, now… they whisper to me, tell me that once they're finished with all the men with pox, they're going to come back for me unless I give them someone else…" Her face twisted. "I should let them. I should have let them take me in the first place."

"No," Karen said fiercely. "No way, Mary. You survived what those men did to you, I'll be damned if you're not going to survive this Sluagh thing as well. We're going to beat them, okay? If we have to kill every last one with arrows, we'll beat them. We'll keep you safe. You're going to live a long life, Mary, and one day you're going to be happy again. I promise you."

Mary gave her a half-smile. But Karen could tell that she wasn't convinced.

CHAPTER 56

Not long after telling her tale, Mary confessed that she was utterly exhausted, and politely asked them to leave both her and Cameron to rest. The little boy was still fast asleep, his iron knife gripped tightly in his fist. Connor and Karen agreed to go and headed out of the little cottage, through the kitchen and out into the front yard, where they stood blinking dazedly in the mid-afternoon sun. Somehow, it felt like it should have been later than this… it felt like they'd been with Mary for hours and hours, and the sunlight shining warmly down on them felt utterly out of place.

"They'll be back tonight, I'd warrant," Connor said finally, his voice rough, and she could tell that he was just changing the subject from what they'd just learned about Mary. She understood completely why he was doing that. She had no idea what to say about any of it — in a lot of ways she suspected she'd be processing it for a long while yet. What could they do for Mary, after such an unthinkably awful thing had happened to her? How could she provide post-traumatic counseling in medieval Scotland? The closest thing this place had to a therapist was Father Caleb... and he was far from the kind of person she could see helping a young girl with a problem like this...

Then again, who knew? Maybe she was underestimating the young priest. He had a youthful, slightly sallow look to him, but he'd more than proved that he'd earned his position. The villagers loved him... and Karen knew first-hand how difficult it really was to win the love and trust of these people. She made a resolution to talk to him about Mary once they'd gotten the epidemic and the Sluagh under control. Maybe he'd have some ideas for the best way to help the girl — ideas that didn't rely on a whole lot of infrastructure that just didn't exist in this time and place.

She and Connor rode down the road in thoughtful silence. By the time they reached town,

Brendan was already there — he and his men were in the habit of meeting earlier than sunset, just to make sure they were all on the same page regarding the night's activities. Connor slid off his horse and immediately headed over to the watch captain, gesturing for Karen to join him.

"Connor, Karen. How are you faring?"

"Well as can be expected," Connor said, glancing sidelong at Karen as he sighed. "We've been doing a little research into the Sluagh and we've learned a great deal today."

"Is that so?" Brendan looked at them both, his eyes sharp with interest. "Anything that can be of use to use? More effective weapons? Knowledge of their attack patterns?"

"It's got more to do with their origin here," he said with a quick shake of his head. "They're drawn to despair… we found the source of that despair, a young woman who was treated awfully by the first six men to die. It seems the creatures come to those in the depths of misery… and offer to carry them away to their deaths. If the victim refuses, the only way to dissuaded the creatures is to give them the name of another victim to kill — or a description. In short, these creatures are being sent after men with cowpox."

Brendan's eyes widened. "That would explain the patterns we've been seeing. But why did they go after Rosemary? She was neither a man nor did she have the pox…"

"It's one of two explanations," Connor said, shaking his head sadly. "Either they weren't hunting her, but they attacked her when she wandered down onto the beach in the open like that because they were ravenous and she was easy prey… or, and I suspect this one is more likely, her own despair grew to such a fever pitch that they were attracted to it as they were to the first young woman's. Either way… she's at peace now, and these monsters are still on the hunt."

Brendan looked at Karen, his expression set. "Karen — do you know how many people are currently afflicted with the pox?"

"Yes, I've been keeping careful records," she said, nodding. "There are about a dozen current cases, including four who match the description given to the Sluagh."

"Then we'll double the guard around those houses," Brendan said firmly, calling a couple of his men over to spread the word about the new tactics for that evening.

The men looked at Karen curiously, clearly not

sure what her role in all of this was, but they nodded as Brendan and Karen explained which houses would be in need of extra protection that evening. Connor cleared his throat.

"If it's all the same to you, Brendan, I'd appreciate being stationed at the young woman's house up on the hill. Her little brother is one of the potential victims, and I want to see if the creatures come to her. I've an idea or two about how to fight them."

"You go where you're most needed," Brendan said firmly. "I trust your judgment on this, Connor. You've been instrumental in handling this threat, and you have my gratitude and the Laird's."

With that, Brendan gave them both an appreciative nod, then turned and headed back to the gathering crowd of watchmen. Karen looked up at Connor and saw to her amusement and delight that there was a broad smile on his face — what Brendan had said had clearly brought him a lot of happiness. She squeezed his hand, feeling proud and fond of him, and he looked down at her with a brightness in his eyes she hadn't seen in a little while.

"Want to come with me to the blacksmith? I've an order to pick up before dark."

She hadn't been to the blacksmith's before.

There was a little forge in a side street, out in the open air though it had a roof erected over it to keep it from getting rained on. There were men busy at work there — a couple of younger lads who seemed to be apprenticed to the main blacksmith, a heavyset man with a hammer in his hand who seemed to recognize Connor instantly when he saw him. With a shout of greeting, he put his hammer down and headed over, wiping the sweat and soot from his forehead with one hand as he offered them both a toothy grin.

"Connor Grant, I've got your special order ready and waiting. Ma'am," he added, giving Karen a little nod, which she returned.

"How've you been here?" Connor asked, leaning on the counter as the smith rummaged in a chest that stood by the counter.

"Utterly frantic," he said with a chuckle, jerking his head in the direction of the young men behind him, one of whom had an armful of arrows he was carrying towards a crate full of them. "The Watch looks to be working on exhausting the whole region's supply of iron. I'm thrilled to do my part, though. Terrible business what happened to poor William's family. His wife, his little son… terrible."

What William had done had been equally terrible, Karen reflected, feeling an odd pang — she wanted everyone to know what monsters those six men had been, but it didn't seem the right time to unleash such news on the villagers... not with everything else going on. It wouldn't be helpful, and it might complicate the grieving process, too. So, she held her tongue... but she knew that sooner or later, the truth would need to come out.

The village couldn't keep holding those awful men up as martyrs.

CHAPTER 57

It wasn't long before the smith brought out a little bag that clinked when it swayed from his hand. Connor accepted it with a broad grin, and she peeked into it when he opened the neck of the bag. It was full of what looked like small, round iron pellets, each about the size of an acorn.

"That's a small fortune's worth of iron," the smith warned him. "I'll be checking on how many Sluagh you bring down with 'em, make sure the village's got its money's worth."

"I'll do my best," Connor assured him with a broad smile, weighing one of the little iron pellets in his hand. "This is fine work. Thank you."

"Any time, Connor Grant."

"We'll leave you to it."

The smith was already hard at work again as they left, and she smiled to herself at the sound of the hammer striking the forge. So that was what that sound was. She'd heard it dozens of times but always assumed it was just general village noisiness. So many things to discover in this place… she realized with a shock that she was really looking forward to exploring a little more once the crisis was over and they had more time to themselves. She'd walk every street of the village, learn her way around, maybe work on getting everyone's name memorized… and find a good spot for a medical practice…

But all that could wait. Right now, they had monsters to hunt. And Connor seemed to want to practice with his new toys before nightfall. They headed for the hillside where she'd found him practicing with his sling all those weeks ago — it felt like years since their relationship had really begun, and she smiled softly to herself at the memory of that night, at how shy she'd been. She sat on the hillside and watched him as he flung iron pellet after iron pellet at the dead tree thirty paces from his spot, hitting the bark again and again with a satisfying clunk. It was dark by the time he was satisfied with the bullets, and the two of them headed back into town, alert and waiting for the sky to come over cloudy and for the west wind to start howling.

In the end, it was two days before the Sluagh came again. Connor, Karen and half a dozen other members of the Watch had taken to guarding Mary's house, reasoning that the creatures may come there early — either to visit with Mary and try to entreat her to let them take her, or to capture Cameron, who now matched the description Mary had given the monsters. The last two nights had been still and quiet... but tonight, a wind was stirring, and Mary could smell the faintest hint of the foul scent of Sluagh on the air. Sure enough — that meant they were coming. Her heart pounded — she hadn't seen the monsters up close since the dead one she'd inspected, though there had been eleven taken down so far.

To her surprise, these ones circled down low around the house almost immediately, clearly not aware of the guard that was lurking in the bushes around the house. Connor held up his hand to stop a couple of them drawing their bows — his eyes were fixed intently on the crowd of creatures gathering around a window that Karen recognized as belonging to the little room Mary slept in. Sure enough — horror clutched at her heart as she saw the window sliding open, and Mary's pale face, drawn but set with determination, peeked out at the Sluagh.

"What's she saying?" Connor murmured, frowning.

For it was clear that Mary was speaking to the creatures in a low murmur, her eyes wide with the intensity of what she was saying — but neither of them could make out the words over the rustling and flapping of the wings of the Sluagh, or over the low keening of the wind in the rooftops. Then, as quickly as she'd opened the window, Mary slammed it shut… and a shriek went up among the Sluagh, who began to flap their wings hard, hovering outside the window.

But that wasn't all. Karen's heart sank as she glanced over her shoulder and saw more winging their way in to join their fellows. Within minutes, their numbers had doubled, then tripled — it looked like the whole swarm was gathered here, beating their wings hard as they hovered outside of Mary's house, wreathed in shadow and uttering ugly hissing sounds as they gazed into the window.

As Karen watched, two of them grew bold, flying straight at the window and battering at the sturdy frame with their wings. More swooped the window, and more — it became clear that they were determined to break it with their bodies if they could. And more still were coming to join them. Karen was confused — what about all the other potential victims? Why were these creatures all amassing here, outside of Mary's window?

They heard an ominous creak as the window began to give way under the onslaught, and it seemed that that was enough for Connor. He roared an instruction to the men and leapt out of the cover of the bushes, whirling his sling around his head and releasing it with deadly accuracy. A single iron bullet went flying and struck a Sluagh squarely in the ribcage — and Karen's eyes widened as she saw the little pellet melt and tear through the monster's body like a knife ripping through paper. Screaming and flapping its wings fruitlessly, the Sluagh crashed to the ground outside the house — and the rest of the men surged forward, loosing hails of arrows from their bows and shouting in triumph as Sluagh after Sluagh fell from the sky.

The wave was merciless and destructive. At least fifteen of the creatures fell, maybe twenty — it grew hard to keep track. Why were they all gathered so close together, she wondered, torn between being confused at the creatures' behavior and thrilled that so many were falling. Why had they all grouped up in one place? It wasn't long before the remainder of the still-airborne Sluagh turned tail and fled, winging their way off into the cloudy night sky as the west wind howled… and the men sent up a raucous cheer of triumph. That had to be about half the flock that had fallen to the arrows… including several that had been destroyed by Connor's sling, she noticed with a smile of pride for her bold lover and his keen aim.

"What were they doing here?" Connor wondered aloud as the men counted the bodies, eager to have a number to put to their victory. The rest of the watch were heading up the road from town, clearly nonplussed, and the story was beginning to spread of the great slaughter here at Mary's cottage. It seemed that the initial flock had spread itself between several locations, including the houses of the young men and boys with the pox. But at a certain point, they'd all turned and begun winging their way toward Mary's cottage, up here on the hill. But why?

Karen slipped away from the crowd, suspicion

growing. She crept through the downstairs door to Mary's house and tiptoed up the stairs. Sure enough, the girl was still wide awake, peering out through the window at the mound of Sluagh corpses below. Her expression was blank, but she offered something that resembled a smile when she turned to see Karen.

"The men did well," she said softly. "Do you think they'll be able to kill all of them?"

"I hope so," Karen said. "What did you tell them, out there?"

"What?" But Mary's expression was evasive.

Karen knew that look. "Mary, we all saw you speaking to them… and not long after, the whole flock descended on your cottage. What did you tell them?"

"Nothing," Mary said again… but Karen narrowed her eyes and folded her arms, an old trick of her mother's. Mary exhaled. "Fine. I told them to stop hunting men with pox, alright? I told them to come after me and me alone… if they could get me."

Karen's eyes widened. She'd amended the instruction… and the creatures had obeyed. "Mary…"

"That way, everyone's safe," Mary said firmly. "Everyone who wants to live will live."

"But what about —" She took a deep breath when Mary fixed her baleful gaze on her. What could she say to that?

How could she comfort a girl who was determined to die?

CHAPTER 58

The Sluagh started coming every night, after that, the west wind howling whenever the sun began to set. The Watch was first exhilarated at having more opportunities to hunt the creature, and that first night Mary's cottage was utterly surrounded by eager men with bows and arrows. But it seemed that the Sluagh had changed tactics... the ones that remained were much cannier than the ones that had been slaughtered the night before, and arrow after arrow flew without finding any target but shadow and air. The mocking laughter of the creatures made the men angry, reckless, and several injuries were sustained by guards breaking rank and getting dived on by an agile Sluagh he didn't see coming. Karen was back on medical duty, patching up the wounds that were dealt, frowning at every low curse from a soldier whose shot went wide.

"I just don't know what to do," Karen confessed to Connor a few days later as they lay together in the afterglow of a rather pleasant afternoon of love-making. Physical contact was of great reassurance and comfort to them both, and sex was as good a way as any of dealing with some of the stress of their situation… but it was never long until the worries started creeping back.

Connor heaved a sigh, squeezing her tight to his side, not even needing to ask what she was talking about at this point — they were both equally preoccupied.

"I mean, what can I tell her? Set the monsters on your little brother again?"

Word had spread through the village that the Sluagh were focusing on Mary's cottage now. Nobody was quite sure why — Connor and Karen were keeping the full story to themselves for now, so the prevailing theory was that the monsters had gotten a taste for young children with the pox, and as such were stalking Cameron. Whether or not the little boy himself knew the full story was anyone's guess — gripped by the cowpox, he was spending most of his time either feverish or fast asleep, and was hardly in a fit state to be told that he was being stalked by the airborne monsters that were at his sister's beck and call.

"I don't like that we didn't see them fly off again last night," Connor muttered, frowning. It had been three nights since that first night defending Mary's cottage, and morale was low. The creatures were so hard to kill that they'd only brought three down since that triumphant first night, and at least twenty remained, maybe more. At this rate it would be weeks until the things were all dead — and who knew what could happen in that time? There had already been so many near misses… it was only a matter of time before a Sluagh grabbed a tired or unwary guard and carried him away. They were getting hungry again after feeding on Rosemary…

"Where do you think they went?" she asked, frowning a little. Usually the Sluagh disappeared into the sky just before dawn, but last night they'd stayed out surprisingly late for them — before disappearing rather abruptly, and without their usual ascent into the sky, though shadow had obscured their passage and she hadn't been able to see where they'd gone. "The sunlight kills them — they'd not be in the forest or something, surely."

"I have my suspicions that they're lingering in the root cellar under the cottage," Connor said with a shake of his head. "That means they'll be out the minute night falls."

"We'll get them," she reassured him, pressing her head affectionately against his shoulder. "Whatever it takes. And maybe in the meantime I can figure out something to tell Mary to do … some way of fixing this. I don't want them taking her."

Sure enough, when they headed up the hill later that afternoon, the rest of the watchmen had assembled early, too. A skeleton crew was left guarding the rest of the village, with Brendan concerned that the Sluagh might take the concentration of guards at Mary's cottage as an opportunity to prey on the rest of the village while it was undefended. But it seemed the creatures were very good at following orders, because none of them had been so much as spotted outside of the vicinity of Mary's cottage.

As they waited, Karen frowned, blinking a little as she looked at the field adjacent to the cottage as the last of the sunlight faded from the sky. There was a strange, shadowy quality to the light there, as though it wasn't quite reaching the ground… and she cried out in shock as she realized what was happening. A cellar door was being lifted, slowly but surely, and Sluagh were creeping out of it, their horrible black eyes fixed on the unwary guards with their backs to the cellar.

Thankfully, the warning helped spare most of them. The guards spun, shouting in fear and alarm, and were able to draw their swords — but to Karen's horror, not before a Sluagh had struck, and struck successfully. It dug its hideous talons deep into his shoulders even as he flailed at it with his iron sword — but the weapon dropped from his fingers as with a few powerful beats of its horrible leathery wings, the Sluagh bore him aloft. Karen screamed, powerless to do anything as she watched the guard's feet rise higher and higher above the ground, kicking and flailing as he went. The other guards were shouting too, falling over themselves to ready arrows as the gloomy night closed in. Shot after shot went wide… it was clear they were all too worried about hitting their friend to shoot the Sluagh, and their aim wasn't helped by the fierce west wind that buffeted the arrows out of the way as though under the control of the monsters. Then the clouds covered the man, and he was gone. And just like the night that Rosemary had died, so too did the Sluagh disappear along with the west wind, leaving the guards shellshocked and lost under the twilight sky.

"No," Connor said, dropping his shoulders as he stared into the clouds that had covered his comrade.

Karen was horrorstruck — all she could do was take his hand in hers and squeeze it. He'd shot bullet after bullet at the creature, but all of them had missed — they were agile, these remaining Sluagh, and very clever.

The rest of the night passed miserably. The guards all trekked down to the hillside where the first group of bodies had been found, a grim search party that knew exactly what it would find. Sure enough, the young guard's twisted body wasn't far from where they'd found Danny. His face was twisted in horrible fear and Connor hastened to close his eyes for him, which went some way to making his face seem a little more peaceful. The guards stood in somber silence for a long time under the dark, cloudless night sky, and Karen felt like an interloper again, an intruder on their grief. She hadn't known the dead man… didn't even know his name. And now he was gone… a victim of the Sluagh.

"It seems they're not restricted to the named victim," Connor said heavily, later that night, when the body had been carried to Father Caleb and the guards had been dismissed for the night.

Most of them had gone to the inn for a drink and a kind of unofficial wake for the dead guard — Thomas had been more than willing to open the doors up, given the circumstance — but Connor had come home with Karne after making a polite appearance. Without speaking, they'd climbed into bed together — Karen could tell that he needed the comfort of her touch now more than ever.

"That killing was done out of spite."

"Retaliation," she said softly, thinking of how angry the creatures had been that first night when so many of their fellows had fallen. "Vengeance for how many have been killed."

"I was right," he added, frowning. "They're hiding in that root cellar. Gives me an idea."

But before she could ask him to elaborate, he was kissing her, hard and urgent… and she was more than willing to stop the conversation and let their bodies do the talking for the next little while, at least.

CHAPTER 59

They slept late the next day. There was a somber atmosphere in the village when they finally got up and headed to Thomas's inn for a late lunch. The innkeeper was yawning when he served them, and when questioned admitted that many of the guards had stayed at the inn until dawn, talking and reminiscing about their fallen comrade. It had been as good a memorial as any, and though the man's funeral was planned for later in the week, it seemed like the guards had already done what they needed to do to bid farewell to their friend.

Once they were done with lunch, Connor disappeared into the streets of the town, returning with several heavy flasks and a glint in his eye. When he shook the flasks, they sloshed — and he explained he intended to use oil and fire to burn the Sluagh out of their little hidey hole in the root cellar. They headed up well before nightfall with the rest of the guards, all of whom had heard about the plan and were keen to see if it would work on the Sluagh. Karen had insisted he wait until the guards were there to help with the attempt — she was worried that if anything went wrong, the creatures might attack Connor, and she couldn't handle losing him. Not now. She couldn't stop imagining what would happen if they carried him away the way they'd carried that guard into the night...

She stayed clear of the cellar door, not wanting to get in the way. She peered up at the cottage — Mary's face was visible in the glass window, impassive and pale, though she could make out streaks on her cheeks that suggested she'd been crying. Her heart ached for the poor girl. She'd tried to visit with her a few times, to lift her spirits and help her to try to find a way forward... but it seemed she was set on a horrible death, sooner rather than later. As the men set their fire, she headed into the house, determined to speak to Mary.

Cameron was there, fast asleep in Mary's bed — she had a suspicion that the girl wasn't sleeping much when she looked at the shadows under her eyes and the pallor of her skin. She turned from the window, clearly surprised to see Karen there.

"Hullo, Mary. How are you feeling?"

"Terrible," the girl said simply, with a matter-of-fact shrug of her shoulders that made Karen's heart ache. "That's three deaths on my conscience, now. How many more will they kill before they finally take me?"

"None, if I have my way," Karen said fiercely. "Don't you go disappearing into despair again, Mary. Who's going to keep Cameron safe if you're gone? Do you really think those creatures will stop once they've killed you? They'll stop for the night, sure," she said with a roll of her eyes. "But they'll be back again the next night, and the next… and this time they won't have you to exercise any control whatsoever over them. They'll be free to hunt and kill anybody. We need you, Mary. We need the control you have over them."

Mary turned back to the window abruptly, and though Karen could see her shoulders shaking with sobs, her voice was clear when she spoke. "What are they doing down there?"

"They're setting a fire in the root cellar," she said, moving over to the window to peer out there.

"Trying to drive the creatures out… or burn them."

"They've been whispering to me from down there," Mary said softly. "Whispering all through the day and night. I can't sleep."

"What do they say?" Karen asked softly. Was it true that the creatures were talking to her? Or was it just another part of the girl's trauma? Hard to say — Mary only shook her head at the question, but the look of horror on her face said all it needed to say. "Mary — you mustn't listen to them. There's a path out of this misery, I promise you."

But she didn't seem convinced. And Karen bit her lip, for a moment even more worried about Mary than she was about the guards out there about to do battle with the Sluagh. Something told her that Mary's suicidal depression wouldn't just magically lift if the monsters were defeated. It ran deeper than that… not that they were helping with it, of course.

A ragged cheer went up outside, and Mary and Karen saw flames licking out of the open cellar door. The two of them shivered as an unearthly shriek went up and shadows seemed to flicker and burn in the twilight… but then the men fell back, raising their swords in alarm, as a couple of shadow-shrouded shapes went flitting up into the sky, hissing with alarm. They circled the house, and Mary's face twisted.

"They sit up on the roof at night," she whispered. "They talk to me…"

"How many were there?" Karen demanded. "How many did they burn?" But Mary was lost — she was sitting in a chair by the window, clearly lost in her own grief and sadness, and Karen sighed before heading down the staircase. She knew when she wasn't being listened to. Maybe some time alone would help Mary think through what she was going to do when all of this was over.

Connor looked exultant, his face marked with soot and a broad grin dancing in his eyes. She smiled a little to see him — it was hard not to feel cheered by that smile — and he scooped her into his arms, swinging her about before setting her down with a laugh. "We got nearly all of them, Karen! Heard them shrieking and burning down there, then went down to check on them — empty. Those two are the only ones left," he added, nodding at the two they could see perched on the rooftop. Mary's face at the window… and was she imagining it, but was shadow creeping down from the Sluagh, seeping through the window, touching her face?

"They have to die tonight," Karen breathed, realizing it as she spoke. "Mary's not strong enough to last another night with them dripping their poison in her ears—"

"What do you mean?"

"The Sluagh are drawn by despair, right? They feed on it — it sustains them," she said, her eyes fixed on those shadowy figures in the gathering night. "But they don't just feed on it, Connor. They're not hunters… they're farmers. They drive people into despair. Sure, they pick on people who have plenty of despair to begin with… but they make it worse. That's how they got Rosemary. And Mary… she's not far off either. She won't stop talking about how her death is the only thing that will stop them… but her death would only free them."

Connor was staring at her, nodding as she explained her theory, clearly in agreement that it made sense. He hesitated, biting his lip. "About that. I have an idea that might — that will probably kill both of the remaining ones, here and now, tonight. But… you're not going to like it."

She stared up at him, nonplussed. "What do you mean?"

"I mean…" He hesitated. Then he told her.

And when he'd finished speaking, she felt like her heart was going to break. "You're not serious."

"It's our best chance, Karen. To end this now — to finish them off before they can drive Mary to despair or take another of my men."

"You'll die," she said, shaking her head blindly as the fear that she'd been keeping at bay so successfully came raging through her. "They'll kill you, Connor, you can't be serious about risking something so dangerous —"

"I have to," he said stubbornly, and she felt real anger flare to life in her. "For the village, Karen. I know it's dangerous, but… I'd give my life if it meant keeping these people safe. I owe them that."

"What about me?" she said, teeth gritted. "What do you owe me?"

"Karen — " He looked anguished.

She realized how torn he was — that she was asking him to choose between her and his duty, the thing he loved, the work that was his life. Could she really do that? Could she be the person who asked the man she loved to walk away from his duty? What would she say if he asked her to stop her work — to stop risking her own health to care for her patients? Didn't she take risks every day? Hadn't her own job's dangers been what brought her here?

"Please," he said softly, moving close to her. "You have to understand."

She took a deep, shuddering breath. "I understand," she said through gritted teeth, feeling the effort of speaking like a physical weight. "You... you have to do this. I get it. I do stupid, dangerous, idiotic things for my stupid, dangerous, idiotic job too." His eyes filled with hope. "But if you die, Connor Grant, in the pursuit of this damn fool objective, I'll personally bring you back just so I can kill you myself."

She hadn't realized they were being overheard until a roar of laughter distracted her — she realized with a shock of embarrassment that the guards were standing around them, listening intently to her little speech. Well, let them. With a flare of odd courage, she realized she didn't care if they overheard her — didn't care if they knew how she felt about this man. Impulsively, she took a step forward, grabbing Connor's hands in hers. "I love you, Connor Grant," she said fiercely, and the look of utter shock — and transcendent joy — on his face made her heart swell two sizes in her chest.

"I love you too," he half-whispered, and the men around them roared their approval again.

And that joy burned like a flame in her chest as they set about the plan he'd come up with. It was close to midnight by the time everything was arranged. Connor, standing in the middle of the cottage's front yard. The men gathered around him with their bows taut, ready, and waiting to intervene if something went wrong. And Karen, peering down at the scene with her hand clenched around the iron knife in her pocket — peering through Mary's window. The girl gave her a worried look — and she nodded, giving Connor the signal as Mary stepped forward and slammed the window open.

There was a shriek — and the Sluagh were there, wings beating, unholy eyes gleaming in the night. Mary lifted her chin, warding them off with a fistful of iron bullets from Connor's sling. "Hear me! I offer you a life in place of mine! I offer you Connor Grant!"

The response was instantaneous. The Sluagh spun and dove toward Connor with another of those unearthly howls, the west wind flapping around them. But Connor was ready and waiting. As the two swooped on him, he brought his hand up and sent a knife flying — and it hit home, tearing through the throat of the first Sluagh and leaving it fluttering weakly on the earth as it died. She clenched her fist in triumph, hearing the men roar — but then there was a horrible beating of wings and she almost screamed as she saw the Sluagh carrying Connor aloft, its talons dug into his shoulders. He was fighting to reach it with the dagger in his hand, but the blade glanced off its talons and he couldn't quite get it higher. The creature rose, and rose, the men on the ground yelling their fury but unable to fire for fear of hitting Connor and dooming him... he was almost level with the cottage window now…

Then Mary straightened her back, and with a furious shout that contained more force than Karen though the girl had in her, she hurled the fistful of pellets in her right hand toward the creature. It shrieked as the iron touched it, hissing and bubbling at its flesh — and Connor took the opportunity to twist his body upwards in a Herculean effort that gave him just enough altitude to drive the blade into the Sluagh's heart.

The monster fell to earth, its wings flapping weakly, Connor now clutching its wrists to slow his descent just enough to allow him to land safely. Then Karen was running down the stairs to him, her heart pounding as the adrenaline screamed through her, relief almost choking her as she hurled herself into his arms.

"Are you okay? Did it hurt you?" she stammered, pulling back, but he only smiled down at her.

"Nothing but bruises. It didn't even pierce the armor." A smug glint in his eyes. "I told you it would work."

And at that, she was so exasperated that all she could do was kiss him.

CHAPTER 60

The Sluagh were gone. And to Karen's great relief, with them it seemed the worst of Mary's near-catatonic despair. She still had a lot to work through, of course... and it didn't help matters that word managed to spread through the village, in the days that followed that last battle, that Mary had been somehow connected to the monsters that had stalked them and claimed so many innocent lives.

It took Karen a little while to find out how word had spread, but she got to the bottom of it eventually. It seemed that one of the rapists had confessed his crimes to his mother, who'd been horrified by the revelation... and soon after, utterly grief stricken by the death of her son and the five other men the Sluagh had taken that first night. But as time had gone on, and the Sluagh had continued to stalk Mary's cottage, her suspicions had grown that her son's death had something to do with Mary.

Officially, the Watch denied all connection between Mary and the Sluagh, insisting that the creatures had only gathered there because they'd wanted to kill Cameron. But the rumors spread regardless, and it wasn't long before Mary was getting the kinds of looks that Karen remembered getting back when the whole village suspected her of being a witch.

Worrying about Mary cast something of a shadow over her courtship with Connor. Knowing the monsters were banished and they were safe in their bed again was one thing... but the damage had not yet been mended. The epidemic proceeded apace, with several new patients diagnosed before the spread had finally been seen to have stopped, and Karen was run off her feet over the next few weeks bringing food and supplies to the sick patients to ensure that they stayed in isolation. Still, they spent plenty of time together... especially that first night, when she'd dragged him home after his triumphant battle with the last Sluagh to bathe his wounds for him.

There, by the firelight, they'd revisited the topic they'd discussed before the last Sluagh had been killed. He'd asked her if she'd meant what she'd said... and she'd dropped her eyes for a moment, focusing on cleaning the dirt from a graze he'd sustained when the creature had dropped him.

"Karen?"

"I meant every word," she said simply. "I love you, Connor. More than I've loved anyone."

"I love you too," he said softly, a broad smile on his face. But he'd hesitated, too. "Are you... are you going to stay?"

She stared at him. "Stay?"

"You have such a brave, exciting life back home. Given the chance, you'd leave this place and return to it... wouldn't you?"

"Of course not," she said, shocked — and as she spoke, she realized it was true. "I — Connor, I'm happy here. I'm incredibly happy. I can do my work, and I can help people... and I can be with you. Why would I ever want to leave? I'm yours," she said, her eyes full of love for him. "I'm staying as long as you'll have me."

"Forever, then," he'd said, pulling her into his arms, heedless of the half-bandaged wounds he was interfering with. "Forever, for a start."

And so, the time had passed, as time did. She'd said she'd wanted to wait until the epidemic was over and done with before they exchanged their vows... but in the end, the pair of them had been far too impatient, and they'd been married a month before the epidemic could be said to have officially ended, with the final patient declared lesion-free. The herds were clear, the village was hale and healthy again, and Connor was at her side, her best friend, her partner, her husband... but there was one shadow that lingered.

Mary.

It was early one evening that she was roused from some reading by a knocking at the door. Bleary-eyed, she wrapped herself in a cloak to chase away the chill before going to get it. There, on the doorstep, stood Mary, dressed for travel, a fine cloak around her shoulders and a clear, cool look in her blue eyes. A look that spoke of clarity, as well as grief. The look of a young woman who had made up her mind. It broke Karen's heart to see how old the sixteen-year-old looked... but she was glad, too, to see that the lesions were all healed, and that the lingering marks left by her attackers had finally healed, too. The rest of the damage... well, that remained to be seen.

"Karen," Mary said with a smile, and the two embraced. "I wanted to say goodbye."

"Goodbye?" Karen said, dumbstruck. "You're leaving? I didn't — nobody told me —"

"Nobody knows," Mary said softly. "Father Caleb thought it was best to keep things quiet. I'm not exactly the most popular woman in the village."

Karen sighed. "They're just superstitious, Mary. Those rumors —"

"It's starting to reflect poorly on Cameron," she said simply. "I don't want his life ruined by this as well as mine."

"Where are you going?" There was a black horse tethered by the gate that Karen didn't recognize, and Mary glanced over her shoulder with a smile.

"A convent," she said softly, reaching up to touch the crucifix that hung around her neck. "Finding my faith is the best thing that's come out of this. The best place for me is in His service. I know that as clear as I've ever known anything."

Karen hesitated. She knew the girl had been spending a lot of time with Father Caleb, praying, healing… but this still came as a surprise. But as she looked into her clear eyes, saw the look of peace there, she knew instinctively that it was the right decision… and all she could do was smile. "I'm so glad you've found the right path, Mary. But I'll miss you. Will you visit?"

The girl smiled. "I'll try," she said softly — but she didn't seem certain.

"Well, I'll certainly visit you."

"I don't think I ever said thank you," Mary said softly. "For everything you did for me. I was … I was in a dark place, Karen, and you were a ray of light that helped me find my way out. The Lord brought me the rest of the way, but… well, if it hadn't been for you and Connor…" She reached out to touch her hands, just gently. "I so badly wanted to be at your wedding, but I didn't want to cause a scene. I wish the two of you every happiness."

"You too, Mary," Karen said softly, smiling at her. "God be with you," she said, a memory of her half-forgotten Catholic upbringing stirring.

A real smile crossed Mary's face then — possibly the most beautiful thing Karen had ever seen. "And also with you," she said softly. And with that, she was gone.

Karen stood in the doorway to the cottage for a long time, listening to the hoofbeats echoing down the quiet streets.

It wasn't long before Connor came out to join her, half-dressed in armor — he had an overnight shift tonight. Watch duties didn't cease just because there was no active supernatural threat — but it had been quiet, lately, and he often complained about how boring the night shifts were. Thinking back to the perilous few weeks they'd been stalked by the Sluagh, Karen decided that she was pretty happy to take a boring night or two.

She explained where Mary had gone, and he seemed a little surprised too — but happy for her finding a path that suited her. "That would explain why Cameron's been learning to tend the herds," he said thoughtfully. "I thought that one would end up on the Watch, but I think he'll be a cowherder instead."

"He wants to care for things, not fight to protect them," she said with a smile. "Just like his sister."

He kissed her goodbye, a long, lingering kiss that made her think very seriously about trying to convince him to stay with her a while longer instead of going to work... but she settled for a promise that he'd well and truly wake her when he returned in the wee hours of the morning. Smiling to herself, she headed inside... but a shiver ran down her spine as she heard the eerie howling of the wind, crossed to shut the rattling western windows of the little cottage. Frowning to herself, she headed straight for bed, pulling the covers tight and close around her.

Try as she might, it was hard to get to sleep with that west wind howling… and she hoped Connor would be home soon.

IF YOU LIKED THIS STORY, THEN DEFINITELY MAKE sure to sign up to get notified for what happens next with the next book in the series! Click here to sign up!

In the mean time, make sure to check out my other series that I think you will love, starting with Highlander Found, which is book 1 in the Highlander In Time series! Click here to get it!

PREVIEW OF
HIGHLANDER FOUND

lick here to get Highlander Found!

At midnight, Audrina James finally laid her head down, gratefully onto her pillow. It had been another grueling day in Trauma One, it was always the worst when the nursing staff and doctors of the trauma ward lost a child. Audrina looked at the ceiling where she had taped pictures of stars, lush green fields, exotic ancient castles and the forests of her ancestral homeland, vowing to herself that she would visit Claran Castle in Scotland someday. Audrina had put the pictures up so that she could clear her mind of the grue-some scenes that she faced in the E.R. day after day, night after night. They'd worked hard to save the boy from the ravages of a car crash, but Donald Nightingale, of sunny northern California, flatlined at eleven-thirty, after half a day's worth of surgeries, blood transfusions and plasma bags. Audrina didn't cry much anymore after working in the trauma center. But there were a few patients who tugged at her heartstrings. Donald would be one of them.

"Look at the pictures. Look at the pictures," Audrina chanted to herself. She used them as a platform to spring her mind into more pleasant thoughts before she drifted off to sleep. Audrina had been fascinated with the stories and lore of her ancestry when her grandfather used to sit her on his knee and recount tales of his youth, roaming the Highlands of Scotland. That was before a potato famine reached his homeland and forced his family to immigrate to the United States. Audrina would spend hours, daydreaming as she roamed the redwoods behind the house, pretending the tall trees were the ancient forests of Scotland. She knew now that Scotland was much greener, and the forests were made of tall oaks, and rowan trees, beech and pine and ash. But she had promised herself she would visit and discover it for herself someday.

That was all a couple of decades ago, when

Audrina had been just seven. After high school, she had gone on to nursing school, and now was faced with the ever-increasing violence of the San Francisco Community Hospital that came through the doors. The timing had just never felt right. There was always one more case to oversee, or one more patient to look after and successfully care for until they walked out the door of their own volition, and not in a body bag or stretcher.

Audrina certainly had the money saved for the trip, but she always felt there was something holding her back. Some small fear she had that there was something Grandfather neglected to tell her about the ancient folklore. Audrina never quite made the jump to buy the plane ticket or book the hotels. She'd never really been sure why, but as she laid there, thinking about all of the never did's that young Donald was never going to experience, she thought, *"Why am I holding back? I have no solid reason, no proof that there is anything in Scotland I should be afraid of."*

"I'm going to request the time off tomorrow and start booking tickets after my trip to the museum," she vowed out loud.

There was no one to hear her proclamation, she realized. There wasn't anyone in her life that she could tell really. *"I guess that makes it kind of sad, maybe even a little pathetic. Sure, I have my co-workers, but they would all say, "Finally, you are taking a vacation," when I tell them,"* Audrina thought.

Audrina had become a trauma nurse after Mom had suffered the same fate as little Donald. She winced as the memories of that day entered her mind. It had been much like Donald's parents rushing into the hospital. The only difference between her grandfather being informed, and Mrs. Nightingale's heart-wrenching screams, had been significantly different, but as equally as devastating. That's when Grandfather had taken her in. She didn't know who her dad was, and it never occurred to her to go looking for him. She knew that she was loved when Grandfather took her, a scared little girl, home that night. He had cared for her and she didn't need anyone else. Anyone, that was, except her mom, but she wasn't coming back. When Grandfather had passed away she was twenty-one, she was left with no one. She hadn't even bothered getting a pet. Audrina was never home because she worked so much. She'd always felt like it was her duty to save people because, well, she couldn't save her mom back then.

Audrina tried to roll over onto her side. She was

disgusted with herself that she was caught up in her own head and wallowing in self-pity. Her vow was just that and she was sticking to it. She realized, as she flipped back onto her back, that she had never been able to fall asleep unless she was looking up at her pictures. Grandfather had printed them for her the week that Mom had passed. He wanted her to have something to think about, other than the sadness of losing her mom.

As Audrina's eyes began to flutter closed, and she emptied her mind save for thoughts of faraway lands and lost familial ties, something, perhaps the moonlight, sparkled in the pictures above her. A small light that glowed in the tower of the castle, appeared to be brighter in the picture. But she squinted at it, and then chalked it up to fatigue and weary eyes. Her lashes batted against her cheeks one last time, and she fell into a deep, sound sleep.

CANDLES SURROUNDED HER IN A CIRCLE, haloing the circular room with an ethereal glow. Long thin tapers of white sheep's fat burned low and lit the gloom of the dark

tower. She'd been locked in there for so long, she had lost track of time.

There was a straw mattress, in a splintered bed of Ashwood. The thin blanket cast across it, was worn and frayed at the edges. A small wooden chair, equally as uncomfortable, sat at the base of the bed. It wobbled on three legs, having relinquished one of the legs long ago, for the usage of a handle for a torch. The torch, had long ago burnt to ash, and was scattered and lost amongst the dust and dirt that caked the cold stone floor. She rocked back on her heels and murmured a soft prayer to the Gods, the Spirits, anyone who would listen. The tower was a prison, a tortuous place that seeped into the soul like the smoky blackness of a demon, coming from the bowels of hell to inhabit and ingest the goodness of the person's humanity.

There were bones in the ashes and they cried out to her. Begging her to release them of their captivity. She couldn't help them that night. They would remain tethered there until the angels came for them on the day of reckoning. Thunder clapped outside the castle and lit up the tiny room in an intense light that threw the stark furnishings of the room into harsh contrast. The candles flickered, and she feared they would blow out. Cotswold Castle had many frivolities, protection from the elements in the prison tower, was not one of them.

Rain lashed against the stone tower and sprayed into the room in droves of unending dampness. It rained often in Scotland. She hadn't been dry since she was thrown into that room. The water collected in puddles at the base of the windows. She sat in the middle of the room in an attempt to keep herself and her activities dry.

She knelt over a carnelian kilt pin. It glowed in the candlelight like fire. She reached out her hand and touched it as she murmured. The contact sent a spiral of heat through her fingertips, and she jerked her hand back. How could the stone set in silver be warm to the touch? There was no fire there. The brooch had not been warmed against constant contact with her skin, as she had been shivering since she arrived there. The cold was such that it seeped not only into her bones, but into her very soul.

There was no possible way the stone could be warm.

Her eyes fixated on the glowing center of the gem as she continued to murmur, "Bone of my bone, flesh of my flesh, through spans of time, I cannot rest. Seek thee my kin, and pardon my sin, that I may reincarnate, and new life begin. And with this pin I shall be returned to my love, cast through the ages, by touch of mine blood, and light from sun up above."

The kilt pin glowed ever-brighter in a hue of burnt orange that lit up not only the room, but blazed like the dawning of the early morning's sun, sending spirals of light from the tower window. She heard shouts from below and quickly loosened the stone nearest the door, about halfway up the wall. She hid the pin behind the stone, where someone had hollowed out the stone behind that, and replace the stone so that it looked seamless. She prayed that someone would find it someday, and that she might rise up, released from the ashes of the debris of bodies from that hellish place. She heard footsteps on the stairs and boots clunked up the stone steps. She hurriedly pushed the stone back in place and managed to take one step back, as the door was thrown open and she screamed in terror as..."

❧

AUDRINA WOKE, SITTING BOLT UPRIGHT IN BED.

"What the hell?" she muttered as she glanced up at the pictures. *"What the heck was that?"* she wondered to herself as she let her tired body fall back against the pillows. She stared at her pictures and then pushed herself back up to a sitting position. She used her hands and pushed to stand up, so that her upturned face was almost nose to nose with the picture of the castle. Audrina stared at the tiny light in the tower. It had faded over the years, but she could have sworn last night it glowed brightly. So brightly it almost lit up the room.

And then...and then, that dream. What a strange dream. Who was that woman in the dream? What happened to her? She must have died there. Audrina could feel the drive of her trauma nurse training kick in. She had to save her. *But how? That's silly. The woman...me...that was centuries ago when she cast the spell. And what kind of a spell was that anyway?* Audrina's mind began to fog over, the dream becoming misty around the edges, as reality and the present day slowly seeped back into her mind. She looked around the modern-day bedroom and laughed at the absurdity of her mind's vehemence that the dream was somehow a reality way back when.

She climbed off the bed and hit the shower, enjoying the feel of the warm jets hitting her body as the ache from the previous day's strenuous shift was washed away. She combed out her dark red hair and swiftly braided it down her back as she stared into her own brown eyes in the reflection of the foggy mirror. She wiped away the condensation and flashes entered her mind. The reflection of a woman in the puddles on the floor as the lightening lit up the room. *Did she have brown eyes like my own?* Audrina wondered. She shrugged and finished her braid and then donned her typical casual wear of jeans, an oversized tee-shirt and a ball cap. The ensemble fit well on her athletic frame, and it was just what she needed to walk down to San Francisco's Museum of Natural History. Audrina enjoyed the casual wear on a rare day off, and she was equally as pleased that the museum was hosting an exhibit on loan from Scotland. She figured she could kill two birds with one stone. She could get her walk in and surround herself in ancient artifacts that made her yearn for a time and place that she had not yet discovered. She pulled her ballcap low over her eyes as she walked out the front door, not minding in the least that she had been accused on more than one occasion of being a tomboy.

CHAPTER 2

When Audrina reached the museum, she purchased her ticket and queued to get in line to be let into the exhibits. She was about ten minutes early and so she began to read the pamphlet that was handed out at the ticket booth. She had been to the museum so many times, she was only interested in the exhibit on loan from the Scottish Museum of Ancient History, but she figured she might peruse a few more on her way out. She read about the various artifacts that were on display, quite impressed with the vast array of items that have been amassed.

As she flipped the cover open, she paused, staring down at the pamphlet stupidly and didn't really register what she was seeing and reading on the pamphlet. As she stared down at the glossy photo, the memory of the dream from last night was a bit hazy, but there was no mistaking the kilt pin from the dream. The one that the woman, that she, had cursed. Or maybe the woman in the dream, she, had placed a spell on it. But there it was, shining back up at her from the brochure. Audrina blinked rapidly in the sun, thinking that maybe she was mistaken, and this was another pin that was excavated from some site in Scotland, and it just looked similar. But as she continued to read, the weighted feeling in her stomach became heavier and heavier.

"The Cotswold Pin, a rare and expensive carnelian-gem set pin, was discovered last year in the ruins of Cotswold Castle's eastern most tower. Archeologists and Historians know very little about the pin, except that it was discovered hidden behind a lose stone near the doorway to the tower, where a mason was reinforcing the towers infrastructure. Cotswold Castle is host of a long and bloody history in the Scottish culture and it is well known that Lord Cotswold, imprisoned many native Scotsmen, in his long and cruel English reign over the Scottish people. It is speculated that the pin was hidden by one of the prisoners. Most likely in the event of their impending death and the desire for such a rare

gem to not fall into the hands of the English. It is known that Lord Cotswold's reign was filled with such terrors and atrocities against the Scottish people, such as imprisonment, torture, and rape. He often invoked the First Rights, also known as Prima, against many young Scottish Brides. It was well known that many of the ones he impregnated he had accused of, tried, and found guilty of witchcraft and subsequently sentenced to death. It is no wonder that whoever was bequeathed such a rare treasure as this gem-inlayed kilt pin, would have wanted it hidden from such an atrocious and vindictive lord and ruler."

Audrina's hands trembled, and the pamphlet shook as she read and re-read the description under the brooch. *"How can this possibly be? How is it that I dreamt of this very kilt pin, only last night? I have no memory of such a pin, even from the countless hours spent with Grandfather pouring over history and ancestry books,"* she wondered.

She only realized that the line had started to move, and people were entering the museum, when someone shouted, "Are you going to stand there all day?"

She jumped and shouted, "Sorry!" over her shoulder as she hastened to the door.

She followed the map of the museum to the new acquisitions and the new exhibit that was on display and it took her a full ten minutes to push through the throngs of people who were gathered around the ancient claymores and thread-bare tartans. She looked for a case, a glass case, figuring, if the museum was going to display rare and beautiful jewelry and gems, they would have it resting on a bed of velvet and enclosed in a high-security, alarm activated case such as the ones she had seen countless other relics, and objet d'art displayed in before.

She found the very case she was looking for and made a beeline for it. She waited at the back of the line and tapped her foot restlessly, as she waited for the older couple who were fawning over the brooches and tartans and listing off their family tree and origins, dating themselves back to the days of yore and their own ancestors. Just when her patience couldn't possibly take any more waiting, the line moved ahead, and she was able to press in, face to face with the kilt pin.

Audrina found it extraordinary that, even after centuries sitting behind a stone, even though it was unexposed to the elements, it was still in pristine condition, as if it had never survived centuries of time passing by. She was sure that it was probably dusty when the mason found it, possibly even the gem was scratched or worn and thus had to be restored, but the pin was pristine.

The burnt orange gem sat at the apex of a silver hill. The silver had been bent and molded onto a swirling pattern to resemble the crest of the hill, so the gem was the representation of the sun. From what Audrina knew of Celtic mythology, the sun symbol was more widely used in the sun cross symbols, which were indicative of Christianity's introduction to the Celtic peoples. But this sun was a literal representation of the sun, suggesting that whoever designed and forged the pin, was still a practicing pagan, possibly giving the pin druidic or witchcraft origins. On the outset of the circular pin, the silver swirled into a Celtic knot which was wavy around the edges, like a river. Audrina knew this because as Grandfather and she had investigated the Claran, or MacClaran name, it was discovered that the Claran's were one of the older tribes of Scotland, but those particular tribes were ancient, nomadic druids who traveled the waters from the Isle of Eire, also known as Ireland. The modern day Claran's were to be found inhabiting the areas on the River Clare and the name Claran literally meant, "One who lives near the River Clare." So, Audrina knew her ancestors had been an ancient people of magics and mystery, and the warring tribes had caused them to take root in Scotland as one of the founding tribes, and they had taken their name and origins with them. The evidence was right there in the pin that resembled the pagan magics and the river beds from whence her people came. The tribes, like the rivers on the pin, were split between Ireland and Scotland.

Audrina felt her excitement at having found such a connection to her ancestors, begin to grow. She stared with her face almost pressed to the glass, willing the pin to do something, anything to give her a sign that she belonged there, with it. She felt like, somewhere deep in her soul, that the pin belonged to her, but she knew this was silly, because it belonged to the museum in Scotland. It didn't change the connection she imagined she could feel through the glass.

As she stood there, she again realized the grumblings of the crowd around her as she had allowed herself to be lost in her thoughts. She was about to exit the line and circle back around, when the crowd was jostled and parted by the streak of a black clothed and masked figure, who shoved them aside. When the intruder got to Audrina, he shoved her so hard, she knocked into the glass and it smashed as the sirens from the museum began to wail. Audrina cut the back of her hand on the glass as she tried to stop her fall, but with the rest of the crowd, she tumbled to the floor. Audrina looked up, just in time to see the masked figure reach into the case and grab something. A flash of orange and silver registered in her mind, and she clawed her way back up and ran after the thief, as he dashed outside the museum with what she could only proclaim as "her" kilt pin.

Audrina chased after him as the wail of sirens from the museum's security, and the automatically notified police screeched in her ear. As athletic as she was, it didn't take her long to catch up to the thief, and she tackled him, expertly maneuvering him into a judo hold from her years of training with Mr. Tanaka at his Japanese dojo. Audrina had needed an outlet for her rage and frustration for losing everyone she had ever loved. And she had miraculously stumbled upon it in the classes offered at the dojo and Mr. Tanaka's ever-patient and serene temperament.

The thief was quickly apprehended at Audrina's capable hands, just as the police showed up and began to cross the sunny court-yard.

"Hey lady, are you nuts?" one of the officer

called. "You don't chase after a criminal! What were you thinking!" he shouted.

Audrina didn't answer him, but reached out her shaking hand toward the pin that had fallen to the ground in the take-down of the thief, and as her bloodied fingers from the cut on the glass closed around the pin, the sun shone brightly through a cloud cover, landing directly on the pin, the blood and her hand, and then suddenly, there was a black and gray mist, and Audrina was falling, falling, falling.

Click here to keep reading Highlander Found!

ABOUT REBECCA PRESTON

Rebecca lives in New York City with her dog. She loves sweet love stories with great characters. She loves traveling the world and experiencing new cities and cultures. Jane Austen is her favorite author.

Sign up below!
eepurl.com/c-chk9

ALSO BY REBECCA PRESTON

Highlander Forever Series
Rescued By The Highlander - Book 1
Stranded By The Highlander - Book 2
Swept By The Highlander - Book 3
Distracted By The Highlander - Book 4
Needed By The Highlander - Book 5
Troubled By The Highlander - Book 6

Highlander Of Time Series
Highlander Found - Book 1
Highlander Warrior - Book 2
Highlander Protected - Book 3
Highlander Smitten - Book 4
Highlander Fallen - Book 5
Highlander Cursed - Book 6

Highlander Avenged - Book 7

Jane Austen Fan Fiction
Arranged To Darcy
A White Darcy Christmas
A Convenient Darcy Marriage
Married To Darcy
Elizabeth And Darcy
Saving Mr. Darcy
Mr. Darcy Forgotten
Mr. Darcy's Pride